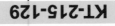

Head Start

Head Start

JUDITH CUTLER

Allison & Busby Limited
12 Fitzroy Mews
London W1T 6DW
allisonandbusby.com

First published in Great Britain by Allison & Busby in 2016.

A CIP catalogue record for this book is available from
the British Library.

First Edition

ISBN 978-0-7490-2070-5

Typeset in 11/16 pt Sabon by
Allison & Busby Ltd.

The paper used for this Allison & Busby publication
has been produced from trees that have been legally sourced
from well-managed and credibly certified forests.

Printed and bound by
CPI Group (UK) Ltd, Croydon, CR0 4YY

*For Adrian Griffiths and Jamie Gisby who transformed
the useless bag of pain at the end of my right arm
into a functioning hand*

CHAPTER ONE

We might have been reprising my interview, with the solemn faces topping sober clothes. The governors sat in a rough semicircle facing me across several classroom tables pushed together to make one formidable barricade. Richard Morris flicked a friendly wink in my direction but within a nanosecond his expression was as hostile as most of the others'. Only the vicar, a grey man in his late fifties or early sixties called Mark Stephens, seemed disinterested – and, as the meeting progressed, actually uninterested.

As chair, Brian Dawes began the interrogation. He leant heavily forward, supporting his massive neck and shoulders on thick arms. A bull, ready to charge. But his question was neutral enough. 'How have you found your first week, Miss Cowan?

How indeed?

I am monarch of all I survey.

But I am not a castaway, alone on a desert island – though like Alexander Selkirk I chose to be alone. I haven't got trees and bays to worry about, but I do want to look into every nook and cranny, so that I can place everything on my mental map. And I can do it in private, at the end of my very first day. Staff and pupils have gone home. The cleaner doesn't arrive till six-thirty tomorrow. The place is mine.

When I first went to school, thirty-odd years ago, the very sight of the head teacher had me scrabbling for the most obscure corner. I didn't want even her shadow to touch me. Then she and her iron grey hair and sensible shoes disappeared – I don't think I'd grasped the concept of retirement – to be replaced by a man who was probably in his forties. Was his name Phillotson? Although he smiled a great deal, soon vague advice to avoid him seeped round the school. No one would, perhaps could, explain why to a naïve little coward like me. Funnily enough it was the feistiest boys and girls who seemed to be most wary of him. None of them wanted to run his errands, and none wished to be sent to him for some petty classroom crime. I still didn't know, never having been anything other than a well-behaved nonentity, why one week the knots of mothers who always gathered at the playground gate huddled more closely than usual, shutting their mouths tightly when their children appeared, grabbing them and dragging them away.

Mr Phillotson didn't come in one day. Or the next. But for days, perhaps for weeks, women with stern but kind faces would sit in his office and ask teachers to let one child at a time to come and talk to them. They were told not to tell the rest of us what had been happening. But we soon knew that Mr Phillotson had interfered with several girls and two or three boys – though I had no idea what 'interfered' meant. Thereafter we had two more women head teachers, one of whom made everything from spelling bees to changing for PE competitive, while another banned races in case someone came last.

By senior school, I was getting a bit savvier. I knew which teachers you could enjoyably cheek unpunished, and which you had to respect. By the time I went to university I realised it was those you respected who got the best results.

So here I was, on my first day in my own school, a head teacher myself. I wasn't as young as some of the new breed of superheads, but I was still a couple of years short of forty, with a variety of non-teaching jobs behind me, as well as plenty of classroom experience. I refused to feel daunted, though the head had retired at the end of the summer term and not been replaced immediately. The deputy head was on long-term sick leave, apparently because of stress: was this surprising, if she'd been expected to cover the head's admin role as well as her own? There was so much to get to grips with I was glad that the supply teacher who'd covered my predecessor's classes all last term would be continuing till the end of the week in order to teach mine. Time enough to worry about marking and preparation when I'd covered all the other bases, of which there were many, since the school and its hundred and twenty pupils had been without a leader for so long.

The school?

My school.

A typically fierce grey stone Victorian building, it originally had separate entrances for boys and girls, though both were now blocked and a unisex one opened up. The windows were so high that no child could possibly see out of them and the even higher ceilings sucked up any warmth. It had had a sixties extension tacked on, not entirely sympathetically. Actually, not at all sympathetically. But it held the vital assembly hall, which doubled as a gym, and also the kitchen, itself recently extended and refurbished to provide the children with a cooked lunchtime meal, a pair of his and hers loos with just two cubicles in each, and two stockrooms. The car park was on the far side. The old and new parts were connected by a glassed-in corridor, the roof of which was leaking after a day of heavy rain. Judging by the stains on the floor, this was nothing new.

At least it was in a pretty setting, on the edge of the picture postcard village of Wrayford, not far from Canterbury. Many state schools struggle for even playground space; here the pupils enjoyed not just a playground but a playing field big enough to hold a football or cricket pitch with a running track round the perimeter. Currently it had neither, but in time I would make sure it had both. There was certainly equipment for any number of sports, stowed carelessly in as big a stockroom as I've ever seen – but see into it was all I could do. One false move would bring down on my head a cascade of boxes and bags and posts and nets and goodness knows what else. The stockroom next to it was equally chaotic; it seemed to be dedicated to old chairs, scenery of long-gone plays, and two or three rails of what looked like rags. And yet more boxes. In the old days a head teacher would have been able to summon a live-in caretaker to deal with it all. Now I was glad to be offered the former caretaker's house just across the playground at a rent I could manage – there were no affordable houses for sale in this village or any of its neighbours. It was hardly a bargain: built in the fifties, it had metal window frames and a sad air of having been built on the cheap.

The mess was something I'd deal with another day. I still had boxes of my own to deal with, in the house across the playground. Home. It didn't feel like it yet, of course, since I'd only arrived in Wrayford on Friday afternoon.

Yes, it was time to switch off the hall lights, locking up behind me, and to head back to my office for my coat.

What should I have for supper? No takeaways this far into the sticks, of course. There was a pub at the far end of the village, which I had yet to try; for what seemed like for ever, I'd felt uneasy eating alone in public. Vulnerable. The plus side, I suppose, was that now I could make a meal out of whatever I happened to have to hand – a sort of personal MasterChef, I guess.

So my mind was drifting along the lines of pasta, bacon, courgettes and capers – in other words, I wasn't doing what I constantly told my pupils and even colleagues they should always do. I wasn't concentrating, as turning the catch behind me, I moved into the glass corridor.

I wasn't alone.

I had been. I had locked and double-checked every outer door, and even connecting doors, as I moved along. I know I had. How long was it since I had not taken such an obvious precaution?

I was concentrating now. With every fibre.

The January dusk had deepened into darkness. My bravado in taking this tour had backfired, to say the least. As I froze, the merciless overhead strip lights exposed me like an actor centre stage through all those big windows to anyone outside. I couldn't see my audience of one. All I could see was palely distorted versions of my own face. Earlier in the day it had worn a confident smile, to match the sharp new hairdo and even sharper new suit – though perhaps in such a backwater the shoes I'd chosen had been a tottery mistake.

Now instead of effortlessly taking charge, I needed to defend myself! A weapon? Where in a modern school would you find anything that if dropped, shaken or even flourished might constitute a danger to a child, let alone a marauding adult? Should I hurl tiny indoor shoes at an assailant? Brandish a forgotten Fireman Sam lunchbox?

Tickled by the absurdity, I was ready to laugh away my terror when I heard a clatter, then a slam. So my intuition was right. When hadn't it been?

The noises had come from the extension. To investigate I must go back through the hall, and into the utility corridor with the stockrooms. Or I could leave the building now.

The question was answered for me. There was another slam – from the hall this time. A window I had latched myself swung back and forth. I peered out. Someone in jeans and overlarge hoodie hurtled towards the playing field. Male? Female? Within seconds the figure had been absorbed by the darkness. Gone.

Despite the pounding in my ears, the sweat-slippery palms, I checked the rest of the building. Nothing. Except that the stockrooms, which I had left locked, were now unlocked. As far as I could tell nothing had been disturbed, let alone taken – not so much as an underinflated football.

An old-fashioned caretaker could have changed the locks in minutes. But education cuts meant the species was pretty well extinct. A locksmith? On my budget? At least I could take care of it myself – goodness knows I'd had enough practice fitting new locks over recent years.

What I'd not had practice in was wandering round unlit villages. I was a city woman, never realising that street lights were a luxury I'd have to manage without. It was fine for stargazers, this lack of what I'm sure they'd call light pollution; for someone who shuddered at every movement in the shadows, it was a trial. I'd thought of going to the pub, had I? No, there'd be no evening walks for me till I'd got hold of a hefty torch, a hand-held alarm and anything legal by way of a deterrent spray. Even crossing the fifty yards of playground tarmac was enough to have me gasping for breath, clutching my bag and laptop to my chest as if they were a shield. I might have had the foresight to stick my key in my pocket to save the endless search in the depths of my bag, but my hand was shaking too hard for me to slot it in first time. This was like the bad old days, the ones I thought I'd put behind me for ever.

And this house didn't have a panic room.

The ugly curtains I'd not had time to replace firmly drawn across locked windows, I sat down at the kitchen table to review my situation. Come now, I'd done enough breathing and relaxation exercises to be able to deal with this. *Breathe out. Remember that every time you breathe out you relax* . . .

I might repeat the soothing mantra myself, but it took longer to work than the persuasive professional voice at the top of my playlist.

Still wearing my coat, I reached for my iPhone. But instead

13

of conjuring up a recording, my fingers found their way, all by themselves, it seemed, to the phone pad screen. All through the Simon business, the protracted, unnecessary Simon business, when I'd been a battered spouse trying to elude his increasingly brazen attempts to beat every injunction going and to kill me, Pat Webber had been my tower of strength. Originally my police liaison officer, Pat had become a friend, though very much within professional limits. A half-friend, to be honest, since I knew a great deal about much of his professional side, and very little of his personal life, while he knew more than most about my marital problems, and no more than he needed to about the jobs I'd taken in a vain attempt to shake off Simon.

Would he mind a call now? Would he even sound pleased to hear me? Even when things were darkest, he almost managed to persuade me that working to protect me was an honour and a privilege.

He answered first ring. 'Hi, there, Avo!'

That's right, Avo. Not Ava. Short for Avocado. Many people wouldn't want that as a nickname: I liked it. My leathery carapace stopped people seeing the soft, bruised flesh inside. And at the heart was a stone that would refuse to break down in a compost heap but sprout nicely if encouraged. Yes, I was proud to be an avocado.

'How's things in Worzel Gummidge Land?' he demanded.

I could always be honest with Pat. 'They'd be better with a panic room.'

'I'm sure they would. But the guy's locked up, Jane, for the best part of the rest of his life. Key's lost, if not thrown away. Isn't it?' His Wolverhampton vowels were wonderfully unexcited.

'I know. My head knows. But the bit of my body that squirts adrenalin by the bucket-load doesn't. Not when I'm locked in an empty building with an intruder.' I told him my tale of woe. 'And there are no street lights in the village,' I added, probably sounding like Eeyore.

'And no rural police within twenty miles, I daresay. Well, school security is the local council's responsibility, so long as it's the children's safety you're worried about.'

'Not any more. Everything comes out of our budget.'

'In that case, you need to fund a few intruder lights at the very least. As for your house, can you get your landlord to improve your home security?'

'It's run by some agency. Even if the owner eventually agrees it'll take for ever.' My voice rose in a lamentable wail.

His came flat and sensible. 'I'm sure you could "lose" your keys and have to fit new locks. If you had internal shutters fitted, you'd have to take them down at the end of the tenancy and make good any damage, but I can't imagine anyone arguing if they knew your recent history.'

'They know very little. Not even the governors know everything.'

'You've got used to the new name?'

'And the new nose and hair. I've changed everything about my appearance, even wearing some stupid killer heels to alter the way I walk. Simon's in the nick, but I bet he's got friends who aren't.'

'Hmm. I suppose by the nature of things solicitors know all sorts of low lifes.'

'It's a shame I'm so ambitious.'

'Why? What's ambition got to do with the price of coal?' he demanded.

15

'It's easier to be anonymous in a backstage job. Ordinary classroom teacher. But no, I have to stick my head above the parapet.'

'It's not exactly Eton you're running,' he pointed out dryly.

'It'd be a first for womankind if I was. Enough about me.' It was, without a doubt. 'How's your marathon training going? Have the blisters healed yet?'

As if fired by Pat's can-do approach to running, his brand-new hobby, I set out with newly straightened shoulders for the nearest late-opening big DIY store, just off Canterbury's tortuous ring road: it was better to buy locks now than to sit around belly-aching, to use Pat's phrase, about the bad ones. Good ones for the stockrooms – check. And very good ones for the house – check. And fish and chips – not very good – from an edge-of-town chippie. As for my boxes, they'd have to wait till another night – there weren't all that many, of course, because most of my personal stuff, anything to identify me with my past, was safely in store in a city two hundred unlikely miles away.

My carpentry tools, though somewhere in my house, were at the bottom of one of them. So waiting till another night was no longer an option.

CHAPTER TWO

It might have taken me longer than I liked to fit the new stockroom locks, but before Val, the cleaner, arrived I had finished them, and, as if I were somehow guilty, disposed of the evidence. I had also printed off a short note to all the staff asking them to remove anything they valued from the stockrooms, the keys for which were in the office. I left a copy on each teacher's desk, with a few duplicates pinned on the noticeboard.

Next into the building was not a teacher, but a kind-faced woman in her fifties: Melanie Pugh, the yellowed and peeling label on whose door said she was the school secretary. But with her knowledge of everything from first aid to the politics of the chair of the governors she could have run the school rather better than I could. Her bright blue eyes shone with alertness.

She greeted me with a smile and a glance, which might equally have been admiring or forbearing, at my shoes. All the photos of my predecessor, Mrs Gough, had shown her in footwear so sensible it might have been prescribed for a Saga walking holiday. How this affected Melanie's appraisal of me I couldn't yet tell. I suspected, however, that her opinion would count for a good deal.

My handing over the new keys with a request that she keep track of whoever borrowed them and insisted on their return raised an eyebrow.

'Ofsted. Security,' I lied. I could see myself making Ofsted the scapegoat for every change I wanted to make, just as people used Health and Safety as an excuse to deny people innocent pleasures.

She took the keys, noticing that I'd labelled them A and B, rather than anything more specific. 'This is all very cloak-and-dagger,' she rightly observed.

'We had an intruder last night.'

'Here? My God!'

'I didn't see him or her properly. Not well enough to identify them. I dare say it was only a youngster seeing if he could nick a football.'

'Even so! It must have scared you to death!'

'Nearly. Anyway, I thought we should tighten things up a bit. In my old place we had a lot of trouble with ex-pupils, one of whom attempted arson – we ended up with security lights and CCTV cameras recording everything going on inside and outside. But in a nice little village like this?'

Her face closed. 'It's not always perfect.' She busied herself with a loose-leaf folder. 'A is which door?'

'The sports rubbish.'

'So B is the other rubbish. Fire hazards the pair of them, if you ask me.' Her look was challenging. 'Ofsted or no Ofsted.'

'No Ofsted,' I admitted.

My reward was a complicitous grin. 'Mrs Gough used that excuse once when she banned mobile phones. Kids, not staff. She said they were an invention of the devil. She wasn't the type to be . . . rigorous . . . but she was absolutely firm about that one. And she made us promise to continue with the ban when she left.'

'I'll make sure I do too. Meanwhile, getting everyone to help tidy them up is towards the top of my To-Do list. Actually, I've been trying to work out the best time for a staff meeting,' I said, registering that her cupboard contained both a kettle and a toaster. Breakfast was a long time ago. 'But the staff are so busy with after-school activities, not to mention deputising for the lunchtime supervisors, who seem to be perennially sick, I've no idea what would be the best time to schedule it.'

'Early morning's no good,' Melanie said, standing and easing her back with an audible crunch. She allowed herself to wince, her almost unlined face suddenly middle-aged. 'Both Tom and Liz have to do the school run for their own families.'

'I should imagine they have to collect them too – right? Or can they be popped in their own after-school clubs as a one-off?'

Her silence told me there was a problem. She didn't need to spell it out, anyway. It was Tom Mason. A tall, broad-shouldered man in his thirties, he'd completely shaved what was obviously a balding head and looked as if he should have a commanding presence in the classroom. He'd wanted my job – and why not? One of his children was in the preschool group, which acted as a feeder to the reception class; two much older ones went to the comp in the nearest town. His wife was a practice nurse in the local surgery. He hadn't been very gracious in defeat. Yesterday, each time we met in a corridor, he nearly but not quite jostled. He looked as if he might be a fully signed up member of the Awkward Squad.

'When did Mrs Gough hold her staff meetings?'

'Fridays, three-thirty till five. So everyone will be bracing themselves for one at the end of the week.'

'My goodness! Did anyone ever turn up? Quite. Well, let's try Mondays, three-thirty till four-thirty, with a timed agenda.'

'Monday is Chess Club.' She pulled a face.

'Actually, every day has an after-school club, doesn't it?' Unlike in many schools, catering for early-starting and late-working parents, this one could only deal with children till four-thirty. 'How many children actually attend, as a matter of interest? We need to choose a day that will minimise parent complaints.'

'Monday, Chess; Tuesday, Ball Skills, very popular, except that Helen's still on crutches, remember, after her skiing accident; Wednesday, Music and Movement – the girls like that, but there are no boys at all; Thursday, about twenty go to Choir, which segues into Drama when there's a play in rehearsal.'

'Like now.' Someone had already started painting a backdrop for the temporary stage. 'So Thursday's sacrosanct. And every child needs more running around and letting off steam than they get in the average school week . . . Tell you what, I'll take over ball skills myself until Helen's recovered.'

'I'll let everyone know it's running again from next

20

week.' She made a note. Looking up with a sardonic grin, she added, 'Every pushy parent will be frog-marching their kid into it now.'

'Did I ever say I objected to frog-marching? That leaves Monday, but chess is so good for the kids' brains. If they play, that is,' I added, in the face of Melanie's pointed silence.

'You'd have to ask Tom.'

I wouldn't swear aloud on school premises. But I could expel my breath very expressively. 'I'd rather ask you.'

Melanie looked around conspiratorially, then formed her hands into a pretty round zero.

'So he gets the brownie points for being a good little volunteer and does his marking and lesson prep at the same time. Hmmm. OK, we'll go for a short meeting this coming Friday, and make Monday the official day in future. Do you usually deal with notices of meetings and agendas?'

She looked puzzled. 'Mrs Gough believed in word of mouth.'

'Ofsted are sticklers for the written word. Think of their last report.' Our mutual grin acknowledged my earlier fib. 'So every last sneeze will have to be minuted. Problem?'

'Actually, I never had to stay. Not unless anything directly involved me. It was a bit of a perk, you see.'

'A well-deserved perk. We'll have to find you another one: in fact coming in at this hour you've already earned two at least. Hey, I should have asked if a late finish on Monday is all right for you.'

'Better than Friday. But I'll be here this week if you need me.'

'No way. I've been known to take the odd set of minutes myself,' I said.

But Melanie was looking very embarrassed, trying not to look at her watch. 'I'm sorry – I know the children haven't even arrived yet, but today I really need to get away for an hour. I've got to take my father to the doctor. It's urgent or—'

'Fine. Absolutely no problem.'

'I'll be back as soon as I can. And I'll make up the time.'

The hands of her old-fashioned wall clock told me it was not yet eight. 'You've already made it up. Off you go. Actually, I'll take your place for a bit – it could be quite an education.'

My own office door had a big brass plate screwed onto it: HEADMISTRESS. Much as I'd like to replace it with one saying HEAD TEACHER, I could imagine the ramifications of getting a different sized plate and rubbing down and repainting the door. No, I'd have to put up with it for a while. I was housed in an imposing, high-ceilinged and very cold room with, if I stood, a superb view of the old, unused bike sheds at the back of the building. Melanie's, however, was right at the front, a plus in itself, and very much warmer, the radiator twice the size of mine in a room half the size. That was a real bonus. So was the much lower window. If I adjusted the vertical blinds a little, I could see the road outside without moving from Melanie's desk. So I was treated to an unparalleled parade of expensive cars, mostly 4x4s, all of which decanted children right by the gate. To do so just there, of course, meant the driver stopping on the yellow zigzag lines you see outside every school. They're there for a reason. Child safety. Here any children arriving on foot had to weave their way between these monsters, some so high off the ground that I doubted if the drivers could even see people less than a metre tall. I'd have liked to go out and smash windscreens and kick in lights. Instead I made plans:

Cones.
The police.
Myself as temporary crossing warden? It might lack
dignity but could be very effective.
A walking bus: it would take time to sell the idea
but would tick a lot of boxes, including health.

Staring out of the window, I bit the end of my pen: any or all of these would raise my wretched profile.

But that was nothing compared with the children's safety. Heavens! Wasn't that a governor, no less, a guy who'd quizzed me on the interview panel, dropping off what must be the granddaughter he'd spoken of with such pride? Tomorrow I'd be unofficial Lollipop Lady come what may. Tomorrow? At the end of school today!

I was still at Melanie's desk, typing a notice of meeting and asking for agenda items for Friday's meeting, when a tall woman materialised in front of me. She had a shock of greying red hair, as if that Victorian artist's model Lizzie Siddall had lived into her late sixties, and looked bemused at my obvious shock.

'I was completely engrossed,' I explained. 'I never noticed you come in.'

She pointed at a side door, which I had last registered as

being bolted on this side. 'Melanie always leaves this open on Tuesdays. So I can sign in our team.'

'Team?' I repeated stupidly: I had a weird vision of elderly footballers taking on five-year-olds. Trying to get a firmer grip, I added more coolly, 'I understood that everyone who wanted to come into school had to be buzzed in through the main door. I'm Jane Cowan, by the way.' I stood, extending my right hand.

Although she shook it, it was her turn to look puzzled. 'You're never Mrs Gough's replacement? Goodness me! Just sitting here? I thought you must be standing in for poor Melanie.'

'Maybe I can be both a replacement and a stand-in?' I found the visitors' signing-in book and some plastic IDs under the in tray.

'Oh, we never use those. In any case, you wouldn't see them under our costumes. I just tell Melanie how many of us there are, sign the book and that's it.'

And, as I recalled, it was one of the procedures that offended the inspectors. But I wasn't about to throw my weight around just now; there were some battles I had to win myself, some I'd get Melanie to fight for me – like this one.

I read, upside down, what she had written. *Tamsin Powell and the OTB team (11)*.

'OTB?'

'Yes. Open the Book.'

'Ah. Bible stories.' Yes, I'd heard of that initiative.

'That's right. Old and New Testament. I've an idea Mrs Gough only invited us in to fill the odd half-hour a week, but she discovered that the kids enjoy watching us perform almost as much as we enjoy acting. Though acting might be too strong a term.' She added anxiously, 'We're totally non-denominational – not at all preachy.'

'Don't worry – I've heard very good things from my colleagues of other Open the Book groups. Now, you mentioned costumes?' I had a nasty feeling about the stockroom's new locks.

'We try to look a bit Biblical. But you'll see in a few minutes, won't you? When you attend assembly.'

'Of course I meant to – but Melanie's been called away urgently, and someone has to hold the fort. I'm trying to find someone else to take over even now.'

'Good. Because the other thing I came for was to complain that someone's locked up our things.'

I handed over key B with a request that she make a point of returning it. But she was already halfway through the door and probably didn't hear me.

Leaving control of the office to a student teacher, a slender girl with bubbly blonde curls called Fearn, broke every rule in my book, let alone Ofsted's, but that was the only option. Firstly I needed to make my peace with the team, who were decked out in those rags – they turned out to be home-made unisex tunics for disciples and villagers alike; red-and-white-check tea towels round their heads were held in place by what looked like twisted tights. Secondly, of course, I had to be present when guests gave up their time to educate the kids with stories they'd probably never hear otherwise. If I was disconcerted by seeing Tamsin as Jesus, I wouldn't show it.

One man, small, wiry, and in his late seventies, read

the story with a decidedly Yorkshire accent. Similarly aged actors, books in hand, read the dialogue – but that would be to underestimate their fervour and commitment. Some people only had miming roles. But all acted their hearts out. Homespun it undoubtedly was, and probably not to the sophisticated tastes of city-dwelling inspectors, but every pair of eyes was glued to the players. Even the teachers were absorbed. Heavens, I was! The woman of Samaria had only done bad things, the embarrassing words *sin* and *adultery* soiling no one's lips, but she sported lovely scarlet nails and a matching silk head covering as a possible hint. They concluded with a simple moral and an uncontroversial prayer. Everything was fine. Except that when, having sincerely thanked the group, I reminded Tamsin about returning the key when they'd stowed their gear, she looked at me as if I had two heads.

'But we always have one. How else can we get everything we need?'

'Melanie will kill me if it's not back in its place when she gets back,' I lied cheerfully but apparently convincingly. 'In fact, there's a new system I should have explained earlier. We lend you the key every time you sign in – you sign for the key too – and then you return it when you sign out.' Clearly that concept was alien to her. But I was after a bigger fish: 'Which reminds me, you never told me how you got into the building this morning.'

'Through the kitchen, of course. To save using the entryphone and disturbing poor Melanie.'

Elf and Safety! Food hygiene regulations! I had to stop this – but how could I without offending them?

'In any case, Dougie – he was the narrator today – has a door key. He could let us directly into the hall.'

Or anywhere else.

He was a man who radiated honesty. But I'd have to get that key back. Or find a locksmith – our poor budget! – to change those locks a good deal sooner than later.

'So Dougie is the team leader? I thought it was you.'

'We're all equal. He just gets here earlier than most of us. I suppose Belinda is the leader because she directs all our performances. She used to be on the stage, you know, but is happy to step out of the limelight and let us lesser mortals have a go. She writes plays for village hall fundraising evenings – so talented. Do you act, Jane?'

Only every hour of every day. 'Not really. Time, of course.' I spread my hands. 'It's been lovely to meet such a generous and talented group, Tamsin, and thank you again. Now, I've left a student teacher in charge of the office, and I'd better take over before she panics.'

'Young Fearn? You'll be fine with her. She's got a good head on her shoulders. Elaine's niece, you see. One of the gossiping women by the well,' she added by way of explanation.

The moment she'd gone I popped into the kitchen. The cook in charge, a tiny woman called Adele – 'the kids call me Addle!' – seemed quite pleased her lovely clean floors were no longer going to be walked over by all and sundry. She was more than happy to keep the outer door locked. So I had one ally.

It was a good job Melanie kept a kettle. I was in need of a very strong coffee.

* * *

27

So was Melanie by the look of it, arriving just as I switched the kettle on. She produced crumpets, kept with individual butter pats, from a tin next to the toaster.

She threw off her coat, dumped her bag and settled at her desk in one not entirely fluid movement. 'Oh, Jane, you are a star: just what I needed. But you're the boss: I should have made it for you.' She eased off her boots, replacing them with neat, wholesome loafers. 'You have children and look after them and they leave home and you heave a sigh of relief, to be honest. And then you find you're supposed to do childcare for them, which would be lovely except your parents are turning into children and you have to look after them too!' The angry buzzing of the entryphone interrupted her. 'Heavens, don't be so impatient! OK, OK!' She pressed a button, without checking who the visitor might be.

'Fred the Fiddle,' she explained tersely. Was she psychic? 'He'll need a hand.'

I was nearer the door than she. I opened it to receive a violin case and something that might have been a junior cello.

'Some bloody idiot locked the back door,' our visitor said. In his forties, with his hangdog face and heavy posture, he might have doubled for Eeyore. 'Whoever it was should try carrying this lot from halfway down the street. More outside,' he said, ducking back to retrieve another couple of instrument cases – flute? Clarinet? Surely the poor man didn't have to carry all those around with him?

'The same idiot who locked your music stands in the stockroom, I daresay,' I said, passing him the coffee I'd made for myself.

'No. I bring my own. They're in this bag.' He dropped it, the contents clattering appropriately.

'You mean the school doesn't supply them?'

'Used to, but they disappeared.'

No comment. 'Instruments? You bring them in each week? Shouldn't the children have them full-time so that they can practise at home?'

'You think they'd bother?'

'There's no point in learning if they don't, surely! Half an hour a week? You don't get to be Nicola Benedetti like that. Nor even play well enough to get any simple pleasure.'

He put down the mug and pointed. 'See that – it's a pig flying across the road. Time you got real, sweetheart.'

My put-down expression had been perfected over many years. It worked now. He gobbled like a turkey.

'To think I was on your side till ten seconds ago.' I looked him up and down. 'But I'd better not hold your petty misogyny against you. If you think the kids need their own instruments, I'll move heaven and earth to get them. Now, the Ofsted inspectors say anyone entering the building needs to sign in, yes, each and every time. And has to wear ID. So that's the way it's going to be. But at least next time you come, you'll know there's one thing you don't have to carry – music stands.'

I didn't warm to the man. But at least he'd provided me with the excuse I needed to mobilise the staff to sort out those stockrooms.

Or, given that someone wanted something badly enough to flee as soon as I turned up, wouldn't I prefer to do it myself?

* * *

I'd prepared and personally signed notes for every parent and carer reminding them that parking directly outside the school was illegal. However, as thickening sleet slashed across the village, it struck me that handing them out in person was pretty quixotic – particularly as in this weather I might well have done as they did. At least the governor, Richard Morris, parked fifty metres away when he saw what I was up to, and, to do him justice, came and helped me – after all, as he pointed out, he could address people by name. Since he was six foot tall and broad with it, to say nothing of tending the gardens of half the villagers, people neither answered back nor balled the notes into the overflowing gutters. Not that they did with the ones I handed out, after they'd seen me shove the sopping wet paper back though the open car window of the first mother to try it.

'If only we could create a dropping-off zone,' I said, as Richard gathered up Rosie, his granddaughter, who'd been playing imaginary hopscotch in the windblown playground. Why no one had painted real hopscotch there permanently I didn't know. 'A place where cars could pull off the road . . . If we could move the staff car park somewhere nearer the school, and—'

He raised a hand. 'You're talking folding money there, Jane. Not a chance in the current climate. Look, that's almost the last car. Rosie's frozen, aren't you, sweetheart? Best get you back home for a hot drink.' He tipped his cap to me, and headed off, another gargantuan vehicle narrowly missing him as it pulled out without so much as a helpful signal.

* * *

Having spent so much time doing peripheral things, I knew I'd have to stay late to deal with proper head teacher work too routine to recount – though I did have one minor triumph with a local firm promising to fit security lights within five working days.

That done, it was time for my prowl round to see that all was well. I took a roll of black sacks with me and key A. And my mobile, of course.

At least the vile weather meant that no one had left any windows open, and this time I was fairly certain that I was the only one on the premises. Heartened, I opened the sports stockroom, taking in battered tennis racquets, a cricket bat minus a chunk of its toe, and several random socks and boots. The most obvious detritus was a pile of stinking muddy, mildewed football shirts, in a variety of colours, none of them school regulation; they were mostly Premier League strips at least two seasons old so I felt no compunction in stowing them in one of the black sacks. Outside the village hall was a charity collection point for fabric and rags. This would be my first bulging donation. Should I continue with the clear-out? No, not until someone – me? – had put a new light bulb in the empty socket in the centre of the room. Fishing in the shallows lit by the corridor lights was one thing; plunging into possibly shark-filled waters in semi-darkness was another.

Shouldering the sack, unlocking and relocking doors on my return to my office, this time I kept eyes and ears open. And my nose shut. The bundle stank so much it couldn't spend the night anywhere near civilisation, or whatever in a school might pass for it. Grabbing my bag and case in my spare hand, I let myself out of the main door and headed out into the night. I hadn't bargained on its snowing as hard as it had been raining earlier, or I might have abandoned the stuff on my back. But I wasn't, as Pat had reminded me, one to give up easily, so I trudged precariously on. I felt and possibly looked like a female Santa. It was only about fifty yards to the village hall, wasn't it?

The distance was just long enough to attract the attention of someone who crept up behind me and snatched not my Radley bag, nor my laptop case but – just as I was popping it into the hopper – the sack of clothes.

CHAPTER THREE

Snow. High heels. Giving chase was impossible. I told myself I was lucky that the thief had only stolen rubbish that wouldn't fit anyone bigger than a slender ten-year-old. I still had my computer and my bag. But I was angry and uneasy in equal measures. Snow was falling very thickly now, covering his tracks. His. Yes, I was pretty sure that the figure disappearing into the whiteness was male.

As I teetered back to the caretaker's house – *my* house! – I was too busy staying upright to think. Once locked inside, however, I reviewed my options. Actually, I didn't have that many. I hadn't got round to stocking the fridge or the freezer with provisions for a country winter, and if I wanted to eat breakfast I'd have to save the bacon and heel of bread. I could risk a drive to the nearest supermarket, though I had little faith in the provision of grit and salt for roads out here. Or I could plod out to the pub. Perhaps if I took a book I'd not look as forlorn as solo diners usually do. But if I read, I'd not have my radar alert for Simon's unpleasant associates. If any, of course.

Furious with myself for even imagining such an unlikely scenario crammed with unbelievable coincidences, I dug out a rucksack, my walking boots, stable but incredibly heavy after the high heels, and my alpine poles. Waterproof trousers to go with the heavyweight cagoule? A head torch? Sure, I'd look ridiculous. But who would care? Who would laugh at me in this white, unlit place?

My yeti outfit hung up on a hook in the porch, I joined the three other occupants of The Jolly Cricketers' bar. They huddled round the open fire, backs to the room. I preferred the less romantic radiator, which warmed my back fitfully as I took up my usual position facing the room, with a keen eye on the door. My glass of Cabernet Sauvignon was acceptable; I'd had far worse chilli con carne. No one talked very much, either to their colleagues by the fire or to the landlady, a round-faced woman in her early sixties with hair cut so well I'd ask for the name of her hairdresser when I got to know her. To be honest, although she seemed pleasant enough, she didn't go out of her way to encourage conversation. We exchanged a few sentences about the weather, that was all. One of the other customers called her Diane when he demanded another pint.

I waited till I was ready to pay; as evening's entertainment went, this hadn't been great, so I might as well get something out of it.

'A really funny thing happened to me on the way here tonight,' I said.

'We'll have to rename it The Forum, won't we?' she responded, straight-faced.

'We could. But no togas were involved.' I gave the briefest of explanations.

Result. 'Someone steals your rubbish before you can bin it? What on earth were you throwing out? Christian Dior? How weird,' she acknowledged, as I shook my head.

'Just old stuff,' I assured her, 'that didn't fit me.'

'That's all right, then.' She turned away.

Her lack of curiosity baffled me. Weren't bar staff supposed to thrive on absorbing and disseminating apparently useless bits of information? She'd made no attempt to find out who I was, or why I'd turned out on a night like this. Perhaps she knew – perhaps she was Tom's auntie, and already primed to loathe me.

As I withdrew to the porch and my Arctic garb, she adjourned to the window. What she'd no doubt like was the men leaving too, so that she could call time on the whole uninspiring evening.

I set off purposefully, grateful for the poles – by now I couldn't tell the pavement from the road. Sometimes I was helped by the light from people's living room windows, their lives framed for an instant as I passed. How strange to let the world into your home, like a mini reality show. Had no one told them that drawing curtains kept the warmth in? But really I envied them. I would never dare leave mine open. Probably never would. Putting my head down, I walked all the faster. I had a job waiting for me: to check the forecast and to decide if I should try to keep the school open.

The best thing about snow is that anyone or anything crossing it leaves tracks. A couple of years back Simon had been either too arrogant or too stupid to realise this, and had succeeded in proving to the satisfaction of the police and then the court that despite all the warnings and banning orders, he had been not only in the neighbourhood of my house but actually peering through the triple-locked windows.

I made myself pull back the curtain a crack to see how much snow had fallen overnight: about a foot. The V of light from my window showed that my overnight visitor had been of the four-legged variety, though in my townie ignorance I couldn't identify it. A cat? Too sensible, surely, to leave a nice warm hearth. Would a dog be allowed to roam alone? Surely not. In a county renowned for its sheep. A fox, then, even though it wasn't cunning enough to disguise its prowling. Why had it headed to the school? At least I could safely assume that it didn't have free access to the place and would want to rummage in the stockrooms. The kitchen bins would be its target.

My own breakfast quickly out of the way, like the fox I trekked across the playground. I didn't wear quite all last night's cold-weather gear but I carried the rest with me: if I had enough staff to keep the school open, any child turning up would have the time of its life. We could look at snow crystals, calculate the weight of snowmen, work out why snow slides became slippery and then, with red fingers and noses, adjourn inside and write about it.

As I let myself into the school a giant tractor appeared, snow-ploughing its way through the village. I gave what I hoped was a neighbourly and approving wave, but perhaps the driver was perched too high to respond.

Top of my inbox was an email directive from Brian

36

Dawes, the chair of the governors, to try to keep the school open. In fact it was nothing to do with him. Such decisions are the head's only, and a major, major headache. Whatever decision – close or stay open – is the wrong one for someone. I'd have liked to talk to the union rep, but to my shame I didn't know who that was – or even if there was one. So rather lamely I replied to Dawes that I would do my best, and got on with contacting as many parents as I could with the good news, adding a request for the children to bring waterproof clothing and wellies. The teachers got the same upbeat message, which perhaps not all would welcome. One job I'd endured had been so bad I'd actually sat and cried when I learnt I was supposed to be at work.

Here I had more to do than mope. I had a school to run and a message about road safety to hammer home. Cones. Snow cones. Painted bright poster-paint yellow. Yes!

But motorists did have some rights. Soon large notices appeared at intervals along the playground fence. DO NOT THROW SNOWBALLS OUT OF THE PLAYGROUND. I also produced some arrows pointing to THE SLEDGE PARK, in other words, the bike shed.

To my surprise Melanie looked less than impressed by my efforts, but had no chance to say anything, as the phone started ringing the moment she arrived. I made her coffee and returned to my office to deal with emails. All nice, safe routine emails. So why was I so uneasy?

About half the children had arrived by registration, most of them on foot or towed by their parents on sledges. More trickled in over the next half-hour. Of the staff, Tom was very late, and only Fearn, the student who hadn't yet learnt about teaching's Dunkirk spirit, was absent altogether. Soon kids and adults alike caught the spirit of the day, the only downside being an outbreak of welly-wanging amongst the oldest boys, already on the verge of puberty and inclined for a moment to challenge my stern demand for better behaviour. Some of the youngest were so tired by lunchtime that we set aside the hall as a dormitory; the rest had to go to their classrooms and do all the sums and writing and artwork I'd asked the staff to plan on the hoof. At the end of the day I maintained a silent presence in the cloakroom area, and not a single welly went anywhere except on the appropriate foot.

Once the music and movement club was over, I decided not to stay on at school – I could always return in the evening – but to risk a quick foray for food. Sadly, the village shop had closed a year ago and still stood empty and unused, so I headed out for the nearest supermarket to stock up. Not surprisingly I wasn't the only one: I saw several of my pupils as I trundled the trolley around. Most waved. A couple of parents stopped in midstream to congratulate me on the day's fun. Several, to judge by the mountains in their trolleys, anticipating a siege, didn't: was I being paranoid to sense a letter of complaint in the air? But I got round without any interruptions, and smiled happily at the checkout lad as I decanted all my goodies. I'd enjoy methodically filling the completely empty freezer, and pondering what to treat myself to when I'd finished.

But those simple pleasures would have to wait. I got home to find that someone had been busy. Someone had garlanded my house with the rubbish that had been stolen last night.

I wanted to scream and drag everything off. But that

would be to destroy evidence. In a forced state of calm, I did indeed put away my shopping. Only then, with a hot mug of tea in my hand, did I call the police. Not 999: even I could reason that this sort of attack didn't for other people rate as an emergency. 101. The non-urgent number. It took five minutes for my call to be picked up. I gave a succinct account to a pair of apparently disbelieving ears.

The woman taking the call gave a little squeak. 'What a cheek, stealing from a charity.'

There didn't seem any point in explaining again. But I did say, 'You don't think it's a bit weird to hang what they stole all over my house?'

'How did they make them stay there?'

Good point, even if she seemed to be missing the main one. Why hadn't I thought of that? Because I'd panicked and not thought things through. I'd check as soon as the call was over. 'I didn't want to disturb a possible crime scene,' I said glibly.

'I'll make a note. But it's a nasty night – I can't promise to send an officer round anytime soon.'

'Can I take everything down? Put it in the charity bin?' I know what I'd have said to such a stupid question.

'Well, you don't want to leave it for everyone to have a laugh at, do you?'

No. I didn't. Not the headmistress part of me, anyway. But as someone who'd been on the receiving end of crime for a long time, I knew the value of putting everything on record. So, once again swathing myself as if for a polar expedition, I took as many photos as I could: thank goodness for a clever camera that didn't object to the dark. Now what?

Another black sack. Another harvest of unwanted clothes, though at least their unauthorised airing had diminished the stench a little. They were now wringing wet, however, and the mould and mildew already lurking would love the new improved environment. If I did consign it all to the charity bin, assuming no interruptions this time, some poor worker would eventually have to open the bag to see what recyclable treasure lurked within and find some vile mycelium that would scare even Doctor Who. It was too late and too cold to hang around pondering. Was it desperation or simply common sense that propelled me to the sledge park, aka the cycle shed? I tied the bag to a strut, with luck out of anyone's reach. Perhaps inspiration would strike me over one of those tempting ready meals lurking in the fridge. Or more likely in a glass of Shiraz.

'Picking up first ring? Sounds a bit desperate, Avo.'

'Possibly. Even someone trying to sell me PPI compensation would have a human voice, wouldn't they?'

Pat snorted. 'I'd have thought after a day surrounded by screaming kids and yapping parents silence would be – in the old cliché – golden.'

'There's a difference between country silence and city silence,' I said. 'In Leeds or Reading I could just nip out and be anonymous. Here – well, I'd leave deep tracks for a start. We've got a foot of snow, and my central heating doesn't seem to be coping. I was just thinking of going across to the school and working there for a bit.'

'But?' Pat always knew when a *but* was involved.

'But then I'd have to turn out of school warmth and come back to my lack of it.'

'And?'

'Those tracks. People would know my house was empty.'

'And?'

Damn the man. 'And they'd be able to have another go at decorating my house.' I explained. The kind donations had simply been soaked and frozen into place, as I discovered when I opened an upper window and tugged.

'But that begs the question of how they got put there in first place. Any signs of a ladder?'

'Not necessary. There's a nice strong trellis that would cope with a child's weight, at least. And a stem of wisteria as thick as my arm shooting out from it – the whole tree has been carefully trained, I should think. It must smell lovely in early summer,' I added to fill the silence of his thinking.

'Weird. Dead weird. And are the shirts in the charity collection now? No? Good. Let me have a think about this, Avo. Remember the drill, now: all curtains drawn, lights on—'

'—in every room,' I continued for him. But he was right to remind me. It was what I should have done before I headed for the supermarket. And I should have left a radio on.

We nattered for a bit about nothing much and then hung up.

It was then that the depth of the silence hit me. And the cold. Why wasn't there a quiet hum from the boiler? And why were the radiators cooling quite palpably? The heating was supposed to stay on till ten. The timer had worked before. Why not now? You might have power cuts to knock out electricity, but you can't have gas cuts; and then, slapping my forehead in frustration, I remembered.

Unbelievably, in the twenty-first century, the village had no mains gas. Apparently it was too far – four short miles! – from civilisation in the form of a town. That's why there were green tanks by every house – by the school, indeed. They held oil or LPG. The school used oil. I assumed this house did too: in fact the woman who had given me the keys assured me the letting agency had organised a delivery for me before I moved in. The school was nice and warm. Why wasn't I?

Because someone had emptied my oil tank, that was why. It was time to phone my friend on the 101 number again.

I should have been reassured when she told me it was one of the most common forms of rural crime, and that half a dozen other people in the area had been robbed in the last week. She even managed to give me a crime number, so I could claim on my insurance. But tonight I didn't want to be part of a crime wave, even a little one. I wanted to be warm. And safe. And not to have to huddle over an inadequate and probably hazardous electric fire, which had come with the house, knowing that the snow had started to fall again.

CHAPTER FOUR

A simple precaution like leaving a radio on to deter intruders wouldn't work during the daytime, of course: everyone who knew who I was knew where I'd be – even the oil delivery firm, which I called the moment their switchboard eventually opened.

Not that the oil company could promise a same-day delivery, the bored-sounding woman at the other end of the phone told me, since obviously this was the sort of weather when everyone wanted a top-up. Furthermore, since the village wasn't scheduled for another visit for a while, I'd have to pay a special call-out fee. She took my credit card details straightaway – I gathered it wasn't unknown for customers to agree a delivery with one firm only to change their mind and switch to a rival supplier. I wasn't surprised. But in any case, I didn't have time to trawl through the phone book for alternatives – the first teachers were already arriving, stamping the snow off their boots and talking about hot chocolate. I would join them – the bite I'd snatched in the cold hole of my kitchen was a long time ago. In fact, I'd share with them the croissants I'd bought last night. I nipped out to fetch them. It would be highly indecorous to stomp across the pristine playground kicking snow for the simple pleasure of it, but one of my therapists had insisted that simple pleasures were good for you.

It then dawned on me that at least the fresh fall of snow would expose the footsteps of anyone stepping over my fence. Step was the word – it was a perfunctory affair, comprising lengths of two by two set edgewise on stubby little posts with v-shaped notches to accommodate them and narrow bands of zinc or something to hold them in place. It was too low for a child to creep under it, but a five-year-old could just about jump over it, especially if someone held their hand. So it marked a boundary, but no more. Yesterday the children had ranged over it unchecked, but now the pristine novelty of the main snowfall had worn off I would declare it out of bounds – though I suspected the prohibition would be honoured more in the breach than the observance.

That had been the fate of my snow 'No Parking' cones, now no more than unlovely smears – the same colour, now, as the stains of animal urine against the school gates.

My colleagues seemed a mite uneasy in my company when I joined them in their minute staffroom, but accepted my largesse with abandon. They seemed to be waiting for me to start the conversation. I suppose I might have started by asking where Tom was: if Liz, who also had to take her children elsewhere could be in, why couldn't he? But I'd wait till I could corner him alone.

What I did say was that they all deserved a breakfast

Buck's Fizz, with more champagne than was normal, for all they had done yesterday. Helen grinned: chocolate was warmer, she said. 'In any case, I don't really deserve anything: all I did was act as Base Camp yesterday. It was everyone else who ran round.'

I turned an enquiring eye in her direction. 'And you'd have been really safe in the playground on your crutches, wouldn't you? I honestly wouldn't have been surprised if you'd called to say you didn't dare try to get in. And you managed again this morning, too. Well done.' I turned to the others. 'In fact, well done, everyone. We'll celebrate by having the most perfunctory staff meeting possible tomorrow. I daresay that Melanie has already circulated a notice of meeting? One of the items on the agenda was going to be changing the usual staff meeting day from Friday to Monday to give you a better start to the weekend: would that suit everyone? No home or family commitments on Mondays? Excellent. And just to warn you – I like short, swift meetings. So I expect any reports to be circulated beforehand – email, so that Melanie can simply download them as appendices to the minutes. Short reports. In English, not jargon. Now, there are four croissants still begging to be eaten: I promise you the calories don't count as much in weather like this.'

If I was surprised by the muted responses to anything I said, and a decided avoidance of eye contact, I didn't have time to ask any questions now, though there would be a few delicate enquiries when I could speak to individuals. And no doubt Melanie could enlighten me when the morning rush was over. As it was, it was action stations for us all: the first bell was sounding, so the children should be lining up ready to march into school, and we should be lined up inside to greet them. There would be more outdoor jollity later, but not until we'd decided when.

'Why not just make a longer lunch break?' Liz asked. 'It'd be a good way of motivating. No progress with maths, no fun later.'

'Or even the second half of the afternoon, so they could go straight home and their mums and dads would have to deal with the soggy clothes?' Tom chipped in, appearing at the half-open door.

'But that would look like extra playtime, not a learning experience,' Liz objected.

'God, get her and her jargon!'

'Liz has a point, Tom. What I want you to do is choose yourselves if and when you go out, making sure they have appropriate tasks and time afterwards to complete them. Let me know so I can come out with you – not in any way to supervise you but to be there in case of an accident. OK, people – time to let them in.'

I watched from the sidelines. In the children trooped. Class by class. Not tidily and not quietly.

On the other hand there was no running. And definitely no welly-wanging.

But there was staring.

So far in my brief time in the school no one child had stood out in any way. There were short children and tall ones, some thin, but more fat, almost entirely white, with one little boy of Indian origin whose parents were optometrists, and one stunning Malaysian girl, whose mother, according to Melanie, worked in a local care home. They all had abilities I wanted to nurture and difficulties I wanted to help them

overcome. But not one of them was like this child. She had
long, dark auburn hair, with the pallor that often goes with
it. But her pallor was extreme: she might have been wearing a
white mask. With eyebrows and lashes invisible, the illusion
was even more marked. Her round eyes were as black as
buttons. Her mouth, already pursed as an old woman's, was
minute. The only large feature was a desperately prominent
nose. I wanted to feel sorry for her; instead I was repelled.
As she made her way to the cloakroom she stared. As she
yanked off her wellies, she stared. As she hung up her coat
and stowed her gloves neatly in the pockets, she stared.

It wasn't until she trotted off to her class that she spoke.
'Your heels are much too high,' she said, closing the door
behind her.

'Prudence,' said Melanie when I mentioned the incident.
'Prudence Digby. Not Special Needs, not at all, but – just
like that. She . . . she's not popular.'

I wasn't surprised, if that was her usual demeanour.
'With the kids or with the staff?'

Melanie shrugged expressively. Her back crunched
again. 'Rumour has it that with her propensity for
eavesdropping – some people even call it spying – she's in
training for MI5. I've got her sick note here: apparently
she's had the D and V bug going the rounds.'

'I thought I hadn't seen her before.'

'I suspect you'll see her again. Quite often.' But the
phone rang before she could say more.

They were all good teachers, no doubt about that. They'd
all devised suitable tasks, some more inventive than others,

but everyone, from Tina, a wisp of a girl who had her group doing snow sculptures, to Liz, working out the best weight for a throwable snowball, had come up with something of which Ofsted would approve. Even Tom was working with a will, organising a competition to devise the best snowshoes and skis, to which I contributed my mite in the form of those very elderly tennis racquets I'd found in the sports stockroom: I didn't mind investigating that in broad daylight, and certainly hadn't uncovered anything to cause any alarm but, thanks to Simon, I still wasn't sure about doing it on my own at night.

None of the racquets had strings intact; most were, in my view, too heavy for the average primary school child's wrist. I would sacrifice the lot. They became templates for some shoe designs, while other children tied them over their wellies as they were. At the end of the period, Tom started a race for his group to give the new designs a proper testing. I stood at the finishing line, applauding.

As they trooped in, I fell into step with Tom. 'That was a cracking lesson – well done!'

'Just so long as you're not expecting me to teach tennis in the summer.' There wasn't a glimmer of a smile.

'If I do, it'll be with more appropriate racquets.'

'You've no idea how long it took me to get those – I raided every charity shop in a twenty-mile radius.'

'And paid for them yourself, I gather? There was nothing left in the budget?'

'Diddly-squat.'

I picked up his tone: it would have been hard not to. 'And tennis matters enough for you to go to all that trouble and expense? You play?'

'Wrist injury. Like Laura Robson's. Ended everything.'
He made a vicious slicing gesture, presumably with his
non-playing hand.

'I'm so sorry. But tennis's loss is teaching's gain. It's a great
shame an Ofsted inspector didn't happen to be passing,' I
added, when he didn't respond to my genuine compliment.
Or did he find my comments merely ingratiating? Come to
think of it, perhaps they were. I'd spent so much of my life
being ingratiating to Simon to try to defer the next assault
it had become horribly like second nature. 'Now, in future,
I'm going to hold my staff meetings on Monday afternoons
after school; I'll let you know well in advance so you can
let all the Chess Club kids know.'

'Why?' he demanded, like a child being told vegetables
were good for him.

'Because every teacher I know is so knackered by Friday
afternoon that he or she deserves to go home at a civilised
hour. Even – perhaps especially – if you all spend most of
your weekends working. OK?' I fell out of step with him
lest he modify his demeanour from grudging to downright
rude.

Stepping from behind a waste bin, Prudence materialised
at my side. 'It's quite obvious that he doesn't like you, Miss
Cowan. And equally obvious that you don't like him.'

As I opened my mouth to rebuke her for such
inappropriate comments, however beautifully they might
be expressed, someone just behind her fell over and needed
instant repairs and comfort. But I would be keeping my eye
on Prudence.

Still awaiting an oil delivery, I returned to my office
to continue working after a hasty supper. Though I was

tempted to watch series episodes I'd missed on my computer, I resolved to master yet more documents. Emails first, of course. The first pinging its way into my inbox was from the Chair of Governors, no less. It was a request to make myself available for a meeting of the board of governors at nine on Saturday morning – so many governors now worked that this was felt to be the most convenient time. An agenda would follow shortly. I might smile ruefully at the notion that having governors who had to work for their living instead of swanning round like Lord or Lady Bountiful with endless leisure was somehow newfangled, but I also seethed. An agenda needed preparation from all concerned, especially the newcomer – me. At least I had prepared and circulated the agenda for Friday's staff meeting, attaching, thanks to Melanie, minutes of the last one, chaired by the now sick deputy head. They didn't seem to have discussed much: I wouldn't have held a meeting with so little to worry about.

What I did have to worry about was Saturday's encounter with the governors: how on earth could I acquit myself with any honour if I had no idea what facts I needed to know? I had a nasty feeling, as I picked my way back to the cold of my house, that they were going to be more interested in what I didn't know; and, of course, what I hadn't done.

CHAPTER FIVE

The joy of meetings is vastly overrated, with the charm of analysing statistical returns a particularly dispiriting part. But it was Friday afternoon and the promised staff meeting, so it had to be done: absences of both staff and pupils; scores in classroom assignments leading in time to SATS and league tables; any concerns about individual children. Riveting stuff. I'd added a quick appraisal of the snow-days' activities.

Naturally I wanted to raise the subject of Prudence: there was nothing in any of her records to suggest behavioural issues, let alone anything like autism. On the contrary, she was always described as a model pupil.

'God knows why! She's not model at all, unless she's a model Machiavelli, complete with a copy of *The Prince* in her bag,' Tom said. 'Trouble, pure and simple. The trouble is she's so bright that she can twist words and situations, to her own ends.'

Liz nodded. 'She was the one who kept trying to bring her mobile in, despite Mrs Gough's diktat. She said that the rule violated her human rights. Human rights! She involved one or two of the others too. But Mrs Gough stuck to her guns.'

'Wasn't there quite a row with the parents last term?' Helen asked. 'We had to point out that just because Mrs Gough had left no one had changed the rule.'

Liz said, 'Long story. It seems—'

'That the clock is ticking,' Tom said baldly.

'But what you have to say may well be important,' I said, trying to override him, though I couldn't have made the point more succinctly myself. 'Liz, perhaps you could brief me next week? Any other pupils I need to know about? Not because their behaviour needs to be recorded, but just because you might be uneasy?'

Liz and Helen exchanged a look. 'A couple of reception kids are soiling or wetting themselves – they don't seem to like using the loos.'

'Boys' or girls' loos?'

'Both. Not the main ones, just the ones near the stockrooms. They're useful for kids using the breakfast club, which these children go to.'

'But they don't have problems when they get to their classroom and can use the ones serving the rest of the school? Odd.' I made a note. 'Has anyone talked to them? To their parents?'

Helen said, 'I know their parents quite well: I'll try to catch them on Monday – the snow's made it all a bit chaotic, hasn't it?'

Which got us neatly into the last item. I thought we'd have a nice mutual congratulation session. Wrong. A lot of parents were unhappy, according to Tom – who else?

'On what grounds?' I asked.

'Oh, you know the sort of thing.'

'I've never run a snow day at this school so I don't. Did you have time to circulate a list of criticisms, Tom? No? Did anyone else have negative feedback?' I looked around. 'Helen, you were *hors de combat* while it was all going on and therefore neutral – could you spend ten minutes, fifteen absolute max, gathering everyone's comments and email them to us all? If I get the mini-report by eight on Tuesday morning I can put guidelines together for our next Arctic adventure.' I looked ostentatiously at my watch. 'We all have homes to go to.' Except me. 'As you know, I'd like to move these meetings to another time. Is three-thirty on Mondays a good time for everyone? Excellent. Not next Monday, obviously: we've covered everything and you need to make proper arrangements. And remember, you email any document or reports to Melanie and indeed the rest of us so that we waste the minimum of time. Now, just one more thing. The stockrooms the other side of the hall. They're both chaotic, dangerous even. There's been no response at all to the note I sent you all earlier.' I looked each in the eye, receiving blushes and mumbles in response. 'I've been trying to empty them on my own, but it's like a flea biting an elephant. If you think there's anything worth saving there, we'll have to sort it out. If you don't, I'll get in a contractor to clear the lot.'

Tina, who had been almost anonymous all week, raised a hand as if she was one of the children she managed so beautifully. 'If people put stuff in there, they must have thought it was worth keeping, mustn't they?'

'Like those tennis racquets,' Tom observed to the room at large.

'In that case, in the absence of volunteers, we'll have to have a working party to deal with it. Tom, would you consult everyone and decide the best time to do it? Soon, of course. Very soon. Thanks, everyone: go safely and have a good weekend.'

You'd have thought after all these years I wouldn't mind going home to an empty and unwelcoming house, but I still did. Especially when I was cold and wet, having measured my length as I left the school. The steps, which I had personally cleared and salted, were a sheet of ice. It looked as if someone had poured a bucket of water over them. At least my bag and laptop were undamaged, and all I sustained were bruises. But the ice was something I must certainly deal with before the governors' meeting – two at least were elderly women, and might have wrists and ankles weakened by osteoporosis. A fall like mine would do them no good at all.

At least I'd soon be warm. I'd seen the oil tanker delivering to other houses in the village, even though I'd not had time to have the pleasure of watching it fill my tank.

If I'd had all the time in the world I'd not have seen it fill my tank. My tank was echoingly empty. Perhaps the tanker was still around the village somewhere? To my embarrassment, I pulled my coat tighter and started running round the village streets. At least everyone was tucked into their cosy living rooms and couldn't see me. As it happened, I did come across the lorry, just about to pull on to the main road out of the village and, more or less daring the driver to run me over, I flagged him down.

'The Old School House?' The driver, a balding man in his fifties, spoke with a slight but perceptible Black Country accent, very like Pat's, and strangely reassuring. The label stitched to his overall bore the name of Terry.

'No.' If only I could afford that! 'No, the old caretaker's house. The tank's absolutely empty.'

He pulled over and got down from his cab, clutching an old-fashioned clipboard, and then, less confidently, pulled out a mobile phone and scrolled down with an uncertain thumb. 'Yes. You were on the list. But the Old School House woman said she needed a top up and she knew you'd be all right because you'd had a delivery only last week.'

'I might have done. But someone stole the lot, as I told your switchboard colleague. I was supposed to be an emergency – she even charged me for the privilege of a special delivery. I've had no heat for three days.' I'm fairly sure my voice quavered, as if I was one of my own pupils.

'Haven't you, my wench? Look, I've only got a few litres, and that'll barely see you through the weekend. But I'll put you top of my list for Monday, and bugger your paying extra. I'll see you up there, eh?'

I scurried, still with scant regard for dignity, in his wake.

While Terry pumped the last of his load into my tank, and sank a mug of coffee we fast became friends: it turned out that though he now lived down South, he'd been born within earshot of Molineux, the Wolverhampton Wanderers' ground: he had a ticket for every home game. But his passion was cricket, and his son was going to have a trial for Worcestershire.

'Worcester's one of my favourite grounds,' I said. 'Lovely family atmosphere.'

'You're right there. Perfect setting. 'cept when it floods, of course. I reckon you'll like the St Lawrence ground and all, over in Canterbury. Nice friendly little ground, too. Now, my wench, you saw how easy it was for me to open your tank. You need a proper lock, and I hear these days you have to get them online – B&Q and such used to do them, but not any longer. So you take yourself in and switch on your computer right now,' he said, as fresh snow zipped across the playground. 'I'll bring the docket and the mug back in half a mo.'

It was the work of very few minutes to order what looked like serious security, not just for my house but for the school's tank too. Then it struck me that there was no sign of the docket or the mug. Or Terry. The tanker was still there, however, the hose still snaking across the tarmac. Terry wasn't in his cab: I actually scaled the heights to look for him. Eventually I caught sight of a shard – half a mug handle. The man himself was sprawled on the icy ground, a slight trickle of blood in the snow.

I knew about putting people in recovery position and keeping them warm, so I knelt beside him, ready to roll him over. But he was already opening his eyes and cussing freely under his breath. 'Must have slipped,' he said, with an extra adverb or two. 'Though I was ever so careful. Not so much as a skid all day. But you know what they say: "Did you fall or were you pushed?"'

I supported him as he struggled to his feet.

He dusted himself off slowly. 'It was almost as if – no, I must have dreamt it. Anyway, no harm done.'

'I reckon I should call the paramedics. Or take you to

A&E. At least,' I persisted, 'you'd better come in and have a sit down.'

He shook his head. 'Thanks, my wench, but I wasn't so much knocked out as winded. Bloody hell, it's cold out here. You get yourself in. I'll be on my way before the snow really gets going.'

'Shouldn't I call the police?'

'And say what? Some old geezer fell over? How interested d'you reckon they'd be, my wench?'

I stuck to my guns. 'Look, you thought you'd been pushed. Didn't you?'

'Even if I was, it'd only be one of your little devils acting up. No harm done. Come on, don't look like that. Least said, soonest mended.'

'OK. But let me get you to A&E. To make sure you're safe to drive. Heavens, you're in charge of a big truck, there.'

'You're right. I am. And how would it look parked there all night? Look, it was my hands took the worst, and they were inside my gloves. And my knees, just a bit, but I've had worse on the football pitch. So I'm off – right?'

Still anxious, I walked with him to the cab.

'And I'll be here about 6.30 on Monday.'

'I'll have a bacon sarnie waiting for you.'

'You're on – it's a deal.'

Dithering, I waved him off. Should I call the police? If I did I might get him into trouble. And he'd deny anything anyway. Bugger big tough Black Country men!

Although I dared now take the worst of the chill off the house, it was still too cold to concentrate. Tough. I needed to be at the top of my game for the governors' meeting, especially as there was still no sign of an agenda. So I set off for Melanie's office. The first thing I did was to record Terry's fall in the accident book, although it was technically in my mini-garden.

Now, where should I start? They already knew from my interview how I proposed to turn the school around. If any had cared to look, they'd have seen me out and about mixing with staff and children, and would have deduced from the light burning in my office that I was scarcely slacking, either early in the morning or late into the evening. What teacher does take life easy? Overwork is part of your DNA.

If I'd not omitted to do something, had I actually done something wrong? I could see that shoving the soggy flyer through someone's car window might not have been tactful, but if I hadn't I'd have reported her for dropping litter. Parents are supposed to be protective of their children, but in general teachers feel the same, unless they are one of the small evil and corrupt minority or have had their lives made intolerable by one of their pupils. I would swim through piranhas to rescue one of my charges, without having to be reminded that I was *in loco parentis* and honour-bound to put them first.

Trying to dispose of the football gear had been sensible but not tactful. However, decorating my house with it had scarcely been an appropriate response, so I must have touched a nerve somewhere. I could only brace myself for the moment when whoever had done it discovered where I had put the shirts subsequently. They'd not had their eyes on me that time, evidently. Though they could watch me now, couldn't they? Spotlit. Melanie hadn't closed the blinds fully, and neither, of course, had I.

Suddenly I didn't want to be here any longer. But I wouldn't leave via the obvious route, the main door. I'd sneak out through one of the others, as if I was somehow guilty. With luck the house would be warm.

Possibly it was. But I wasn't about to find out.

As I walked – slid – the short distance, someone gave chase, shouting and screaming. I wasn't about to turn and introduce myself, but I was outrun and thrown to the ground. Within seconds my arms were pinioned behind my back, and I felt the snap of handcuffs.

Handcuffs?

By now I was screaming too, despite the weight of knees on my back. Then, I was being hauled to my feet and shaken as a rabbit might be by a fox. 'Just move. And for God's sake stop that noise. You don't want to disturb the whole village.'

That's exactly what I wanted to do. To get everyone out here. To rescue me.

Then I registered the blue flashing light.

CHAPTER SIX

'You have to admit that it's a natural assumption,' the older officer, PC Lloyd Davies, according to his ID, declared, as he sat, arms folded, in my office chair, making me sit uneasily on the upright chair opposite, a visitor in my own office. At least they'd removed the handcuffs. 'Why should anyone be working in a school at this time of night?'

It sounded as though his woman colleague, PC Penny Taylor, had completed her inspection of the place and was making her way back here.

'Because that's what head teachers do,' I said. 'Teachers work long hours. Heads often have to work even longer ones. Especially if the school's not done terribly well under the head who retired at the end of the summer. In fact, I've worked late every evening. Why choose now to arrest me?'

'Correction: you've not been arrested, Miss. Miss . . . ?'

'*Ms* Cowan. No, of course not. I'm merely helping you with your enquiries, aren't I?' I turned to the young woman, who looked thoroughly embarrassed. 'Everything where it's supposed to be? Or do you need to check my house to see if I've hidden fifty pairs of children's trainers under the bed?'

Davies shifted in my chair.

'While you're here,' I said, suddenly realising that a calm conversation might be useful, 'may I ask for your help? The truth is that after what happened to me the other night when someone knew I was out, I'm not sure what to expect now.' I produced my phone and showed them the photos of the football shirts decking my house.

Davies sounded outraged. 'Why the devil should anyone do that?'

'Search me. But it felt like something of a threat since I'd been trying to shove them into the fabric collection box by the village hall,' I explained. 'When I found them spread over my house, I actually called 101, but as the woman taking the call pointed out it was a foul evening, and I couldn't really expect an immediate response. The shirts are now in a black sack over in the cycle shed,' I added.

Taylor looked at me with narrowed eyes. 'You've obviously made some enemies in the village. Any idea how?'

'I'd been here just five days when the shirts appeared.' I spread my hands helplessly. 'Apart from some stupid motorists who parked on the yellow lines outside, the only person who may have a grudge against me is someone I chased off the premises on Monday after school. Whoever it was had got into the stockrooms at the far end. I couldn't see if it was a man or a woman. Whoever it was would be hard put to find anything worth nicking in the stockrooms.' I found I could manage a dry chuckle. 'Do you want to see?'

They took the peace offering in the spirit it was meant, pulling faces when they saw the mega-mess.

'I've already changed these locks,' I said, 'and a locksmith's coming on Monday to replace the outer ones – there are far too many key-holders for my peace of mind.'

'No burglar alarms?'

'No, nor security cameras either. All those computers are lying around saying, "I'm here – come and steal me!"'

In response to a call to Taylor's mobile, they prepared to leave. But Taylor stopped. 'You mentioned a favour?'

'I did indeed. But if that shout's urgent— I've a friend in West Midlands Police,' I explained as her eyebrows shot up at the lingo.

'Not so urgent we don't want to know what the favour is,' she insisted.

'I'm just worried what I might find back at the house this time,' I confessed. 'I just feel paranoid after the shirts and after having all my oil nicked.' Now wasn't the time to go into my entire recent history.

'We'll go and check it over.' Turning from me she mouthed something at Davies, who raised an eyebrow but didn't argue.

While they gave the house the search of its life, even venturing to peer into the loft, on their instructions I checked the rooms they'd declared clear for anything unusual. I thought I'd left the phone handset in its dock, but perhaps I was mistaken. And what was that yellow fluff on the stairs?

'No sign of anyone,' Davies reported, 'or that anyone's been in and left. Just one word, though – your insulation's very poor, and there's no lagging at all on the pipes. There's some hard frost in the offing – you may want to do something about that.'

Frowning, I showed him the fluff. 'What do you make of this?'

Taylor looked over his shoulder. 'Looks like some sort of stuffing.'

Another call interrupted whatever else she'd been going to say. With an apologetic shrug, she said, 'This one's urgent.'

Davies dawdled. 'That loft: if you don't get any joy from your landlord, I'll talk to my nephew. He's just starting off. He won't overcharge you and if he tries to he'll answer to me.' Davies grinned, but his face was serious as he handed me his business card. 'Anything else goes wrong, don't bother with 101. Call me direct – OK? Now, lock yourself in.'

I didn't argue. On impulse, I popped the bit of yellow fluff into a food bag, and stowed it in my briefcase. I'd lock it in my office tomorrow morning.

My call to Pat went straight to voicemail. I didn't leave a message. What could I have said? I want to give up? I don't have anyone to talk to? I don't have anyone to turn to? He'd heard enough of that sort of comment over the years. This time I might have added another moan: I shouldn't have taken on this job. It's too much for me and I don't have enough support. Ninety-nine per cent of head teachers probably felt the same at this time on a Friday night, and none of them would be making panicky phone calls. I should be ashamed of myself.

So I was lonely and in a strange place? Of course I was lonely in a strange place. Except I would, come to think of it, have expected a bit of affability in the pub – even if it was just a ploy to get me to spend more money. I might have expected a neighbour to call round – except, of course, that this house didn't have any immediate neighbours, with the playing field at the back, the playground at the front and the school itself across the playground. As for the occupiers of the Old School House, they might know enough about me to know that I'd had a delivery of oil, but not enough to pop round with the offer of a drink.

Other lonely people had a cat or a dog, but after Simon's way of dealing with anything I loved I didn't dare repeat the experience. It was ironic that it had been the RSPCA that had been the first organisation to take him to court. But I mustn't think about Mutt or Daz – short of course for Dastardly.

I reached for the wine. And put it back. It was time for one last push at the preparations for tomorrow's meeting and then a prolonged session with the relaxation exercises.

CHAPTER SEVEN

We might have been reprising my interview, with the solemn faces topping sober clothes. The governors sat in a rough semicircle facing me across several classroom tables pushed together to make one formidable barricade. Richard Morris flicked a friendly wink in my direction but within a nanosecond his expression was as hostile as most of the others'. Only the vicar, a grey man in his late fifties or early sixties called Mark Stephens, seemed disinterested – and, as the meeting progressed, actually uninterested.

As chair, Brian Dawes began the interrogation. He leant heavily forward, supporting his massive neck and shoulders on thick arms. A bull, ready to charge. But his question was neutral enough. 'How have you found your first week, Miss Cowan?' Yes, a slight emphasis on 'Miss', as opposed to 'Ms'.

It was one of the questions I had expected, and tried to prepare for. But the more I'd thought about it, between the hours of one and five this morning, the less I could work out the right answer.

'My priority,' I parried, 'was to address the areas the Ofsted inspectors found particularly in need of urgent improvement. For that reason I've been grateful for the week's grace before I begin teaching.' I smiled at a smartly turned out woman in her fifties, Mrs Walker, who I gathered had pretty well bulldozed her colleagues into accepting her suggestion. I touched my fingers one by one: 'Security. It seems that quite a number of people have unauthorised access to the premises for a variety of excellent reasons, but for the sake of the children's safety I am sure we agree that this cannot continue. One route, the kitchen, is a food preparation area – the last place where people should wander round without regard to hygiene. Another is the hall. I'd hate to offend or inconvenience the many kind people to whom we owe so much, but Ofsted was adamant that there should be a proper system for signing in and out, with ID labels to be worn at all times. There is a set for teachers, another for peripatetic teachers, one for visitors, such as the Open the Book team, one for governors,' I said with a nod and a smile, 'and so on. There's also one for parents. Melanie will begin operating the system at 8.30 on Monday morning. I've drafted an explanatory leaflet to be handed out to everyone involved.'

'All this sounds very expensive.'

'It may do, Mr Dawes, but how much less expensive than facing legal action if property were stolen or, far worse, a child were attacked or abducted.'

Dawes's shoulders shook with feigned laughter. 'Perhaps you do not realise, Miss Cowan, that you are running a country school, not an establishment in the middle of a lawless city.'

I would have liked to retaliate, laugh for laugh, but I kept my eyes innocent and my tone neutral. 'I chased an intruder from the building on my very first evening; the oil from my tank was stolen earlier this week. The village is idyllic but not the Garden of Eden.'

'Your oil was stolen!' Obscurely it was somehow my fault? 'You must take measures to enhance your tank's security.'

It was better to be assertive than angry: my tank was, after all, the letting agent's responsibility. 'And the school tank's security – it's as elementary as that on mine. With many more individuals affected if the boilers can't work. Security lights will benefit both the tank and the rest of the school – as Ofsted recommended. They'll be fitted on Monday. And new locks.'

'Who will have keys?' Dawes demanded.

Not many people, that was for sure. 'One for you, as chair. One for me, another for the secretary and a fourth for the cleaner. I shall have to ask you to sign for it when you collect it – that's the security company's policy, not mine. And I have to keep any spares in a locked safe in my office.'

'So when will you go the whole hog and have a burglar alarm fitted?' someone drawled, his public school accent grating. This was one of the parent governors – was his name Toby? Toby Wells? Physically he was slight and unimpressive, but perhaps his delicate appearance belied his personality.

I treated the question as if it had been serious, not sarcastic. 'As soon as I can work out if the budget will run to it. Ofsted were appalled that there was no protection for

67

the hundreds of pounds' worth of computers and sound equipment. This is one time when I agree absolutely with them. I've never worked in another school, urban or rural, that didn't have alarms. In fact, I'd go further, and add CCTV.'

Dawes jumped in again. 'So you'd say that overall you're keener on safety and security than on the actual education of our children. Even though your vigilance – your vigilantism – has been excessive.'

Ah, ha! Parking! 'Mr Dawes, have you ever seen the effect a fatal traffic accident outside their school has on children's ability to learn? When one of their classmates was run over before their very eyes? Why, Mr Morris and his granddaughter had a lucky escape earlier this week.' Slowly, reluctantly Richard nodded as I held his eye. 'Which is why I've already asked Highways to repaint the yellow zigzag lines, which were very badly faded, as part of their duty of care. Next week, police community support officers should be in attendance at the start and end of the school day.'

'You've been very busy.' It didn't sound like praise.

'You appointed me to implement all Ofsted's many recommendations. But I'd say I'm less than halfway down the first page so far.'

'You must have burnt the midnight oil to achieve all this,' Mrs Walker said approvingly. She looked around almost challengingly.

'But it was not Miss Cowan's oil that she was burning,' said a kind-faced, white-haired woman whose name completely eluded me. 'It was the school's. The lights have been on all hours – before six in the morning, well after eight some nights. Why has Miss Cowan not been working in her own home?'

Mrs Walker smiled again. 'I think she just told us that she's had no central heating oil.'

'In other words, she's found it more convenient to use our oil and our electricity.' Clearly her face belied her personality. At last her name came to me. Mrs Tibbs, that's right.

Was this what this meeting was all about? 'Yes,' I agreed, 'and your computer and printer, not to mention accessing the paper files now kept under lock and key in my office. I'd be working there now were it not for this meeting.'

'Mrs Gough never felt she had to play the martyr, that's all I can say.'

So I was playing the martyr, was I? Surely someone would pick her up on that?

'That's true. And she was a fine woman: with us for fifteen years.'

'Yes,' someone agreed, 'if she'd been here a few years longer she'd almost have been one of us.'

Almost. I froze inside.

'Can you explain why you hung washing all over your house the other evening?' asked Mrs Tibbs

'Washing?' repeated Dawes, in hostile disbelief. Others seemed to snigger at the thought.

'It all looked rather jolly, actually,' I said. 'What did we have? Arsenal, two. Chelsea, one. Two different Manchester United strips. Manchester City. Let's not forget Liverpool. Wasn't there a Lionel Messi shirt, too? And a Ronaldo. If you want to check, they're all in a black sack hanging in the cycle shed.' I'd been too flippant; even Mrs Walker was frowning. 'I'm afraid I have no explanation,' I added much more soberly. 'But I have some background information for you. As part of my effort to clear one of the dangerously overfull stockrooms, I came upon about a dozen football shirts, all filthy, many mildewed, most torn. So I tried to dispose of them in the village hall charity bin for rags.' I gave a brief explanation of what happened next. There was very little reaction. 'Perhaps in my desire to rid the school of a health hazard I was overhasty. I should have written to all parents asking them to claim them.'

'You say they're in the cycle shed? Why on earth—?' This from my ally, Richard, almost squeaking in disbelief.

'Because whoever stuck them to the window sills and walls soaked them first so they could freeze in place. So when I removed them, they were wet as well as smelly. And I didn't want to try putting them in the charity bin until they were dry or they'd have ruined anything else in it. Why don't I show you,' I added, 'the state of those stockrooms? Lost in the depths of one of them are some music stands I promised the peripatetic string teacher I'd find for him – and he comes in on Tuesday, so I don't have much time. I've asked Tom Mason to get together a working party to deal with the sports stockroom – tapping into his sports expertise.' My smile was horribly ingratiating. I changed it immediately to one of sympathy. 'What a tragedy for the man that he had to give up his tennis career.'

'Oh, he's been spinning you that yarn, has he?' Brian Dawes did not sound sympathetic.

'He's a very good teacher,' I said, perversely springing to his defence. 'The task he set his class during the snow activities was both testing and fun.'

'Ah. The snow.' Two very meaningful syllables, oozing judgement. 'At least you stayed open.'

'Of course. Even without your advice I'd have tried to, Mr Dawes. Helen is doing a review of our activities to be circulated to us all on Tuesday. Would you like to be copied in?' It was clear I meant everyone in the room. There was a general nodding of heads.

'Very well. I understand your preoccupation with dealing with physical problems. But it is surely time now to address yourself to what you are paid to do. Teaching.'

Wrong: I had been appointed to manage the school, with just a few hours in the classroom. But just for now I'd keep mum in the face of what was surely a rhetorical question.

'A school rises or falls by its results. Mrs Gough was a very reliable teacher. And, of course, her class has only been taught by some supply woman for a whole term. We need improved SATs grades, Miss Cowan, and better eleven-plus passes. Forget spring-cleaning. The three Rs. That's what you should be addressing.'

I thought of Mr Gradgrind and his Facts. I was to be his Mr M'Choakumchild, was I? Who Bitzer, who Sissy Jupe? I was tempted to counter by reminding him that *people mutht be amuthed*, but thought better of it. What I did say, cautiously but firmly, was, 'One of my objectives in the classroom and in the wider school is to reduce gender bias. During one of the snow exercises, a girl showed real engineering skill, only for the boys to belittle what she'd done – because she was just a girl. One fairy step, to my mind, is to avoid labelling people with their marital status. As you know, I have been married, but no longer am. So I prefer the title Ms, please, when you speak to me face to

71

face or refer to me in front of the children. I'm sure you will understand.' I looked each in the eye. Firmly. Not pleading.

The murmurs sounded affirmative but embarrassed. Buoyed, I took the initiative. 'Are there any other matters you wished to raise? In that case, may I simply assure you that every aspect of school life will continue to receive all my attention.'

Mrs Walked smiled. 'We're not paying for your soul, Ms Cowan. You're entitled to your own life too.'

'Time for that when everything's running as we all want it,' I said. 'Though I do admit there's work to be done in the house.'

'Oil apart, how are you settling in . . . ?'

Just as I thought the meeting was dwindling to a close, Dawes took a text and, raising his eyebrows, turned to me again. Or was it turned on me? 'You were arrested last night. Police officers dragged you from the school! What the hell was that about? Believe me, this school doesn't need that sort of publicity.'

What little worm had turned on me now?

'You've been misinformed,' I said coolly. 'Someone thought that the lights burning in the school indicated that there must have been a break-in. The police came in response to their call, and established that I was there entirely legitimately.' I was tempted to throw the stolen electricity into the mix, but refrained. 'When they heard about the shirt business, they were so anxious about my safety they kindly escorted me to my house.'

He muttered something under his breath. Perhaps he had overplayed his hand; perhaps, on the other hand, judging by the expressions on some faces, he hadn't.

When there was no more baiting to be done he declared the meeting closed. The governors drifted away, without any inspection of the stockrooms or anything else for that matter. Mark Stephens, the exhausted-looking vicar, lingered: 'I don't suppose that you're a churchgoer, Ms Cowan? Sadly very few of the parents are.' He trailed after the others, as if he'd answered his own question.

What had they all got out of the meeting? Dawes had done what I should imagine was his daily dose of bullying; Felicity Walker had been supportive; Toby, though far from friendly, had appeared to accept my explanation of the shirt incident; I feared Mrs Tibbs and I might never exchange Christmas cards; Richard – how far could I rely on him? What about the vicar, who, apart from his brief attempt at conversation, had been entirely silent and disengaged for the whole session?

There was still a great deal of the morning left. I was far too well dressed to indulge in so-called spring-cleaning. But I had promised Fred that he would have music stands. I had better head home and change. First, however, I called the letting agent about the state of the loft insulation. He sounded genuinely surprised, so surprised he agreed to pay for any work PC Davies's nephew had to do.

Even as I put key B in the lock, I acknowledged that the governors had, of course, been right – it was no part of my job description, extensive though it was, to clean out other people's stockroom mess. Not that the Open the Book teams dressing-up clothes were mess. Not now I realised what they were. Perhaps the rather flimsy scenery was theirs too – I pulled out a night sky with a giant star, a roll of sturdy brown paper that I recognised as the woman of Samaria's well and a wooden cross that Jesus, whatever the gender of the actor, would have found a burden. There was also a paper carrier bag containing some enormously heavy nails and a crown of thorns.

I found myself putting these to one side with a respect bordering on reverence.

Next was a box crammed with old paperback textbooks. There was evidence of mice. I'd have to get some traps or poison. Anything I got would have to be absolutely childproof of course, or there'd rightly be a scandal of gargantuan proportions. Perhaps a proper pest control team would be safer – but would the budget run to that? Meanwhile, as soon as I had reached the gaggle of music stands, lurking like lopsided cranes behind another box of books, I would give up for the day. There! They were as hard to disentangle as a handful of wire coat hangers at the back of a wardrobe, and my struggle threatened to bring down other bulging boxes, stacked six high, on my head. At last I had retrieved all but one stand; I would abandon that to its fate. Putting back the OTB items as far out of rodent reach as possible, I regarded the two boxes of books with distaste. They were far too heavy for me to carry, and if I tried to drag them across the playground to the recycling bin, almost certainly the old cardboard would disintegrate. I could see a whole set of separate treks to the recycling bin coming up. First, though, I'd clean up the music stands – I could scrub them in one of the loos next to the stockroom. Out of long habit, I chose the girls', of course. How could it possibly have scared a child so much she'd rather wet her pants? There were only two cubicles, the loos the right size for a reception class child. Outside was a tiny sink and full-size hand-dryer. Everything was clean enough, though my efforts in the sink got water all over the floor, so I swabbed up the worst of the water with loo paper, and then resorted to the hand-dryer to deal with the puddles. It was extremely loud. Scarily loud? Perhaps the unhappy children preferred the paper towels in the other loos.

Now what?

Those boxes of books.

What I really needed was a wheelbarrow, wasn't it? Or better still a chain of little humans one morning, passing two books at a time till all were safely stowed away.

Which sounded disconcertingly like a line from a long-forgotten harvest hymn. Perhaps I ought to show my face in church tomorrow. From a distance it looked very impressive in a four-square solid way, with a stubby crenellated tower – Saxon or Norman, perhaps.

Meanwhile, I locked the books away.

CHAPTER EIGHT

'Church? Of course you've got to go to church,' Pat declared, his accent stronger than ever over the phone. 'This is a village you're living in, woman. A village with villagers. And villagers have expectations. Like it or not, you're heading one of the main institutions – the church, the pub and the school. And if you don't like it, you must just lump it. That's the way it is. What time's the service?'

'No idea.'

'Have they got a website? No? Parish mag? No, you wouldn't have one of them. They'll have a noticeboard. It's a nice crisp afternoon: take yourself for a walk up there. Then you'll have an appetite for your supper. I bet you've not even tried out the cooker!'

'Not yet. How's your running in this weather?'

'Treadmill at the gym, of course. Mile on bloody mile. Maybe I'm really a sprint man . . .'

Actually, it was good to be out and about, though the steep lane to the church, some two hundred yards from the main village, presented a bit of a challenge, even with my poles and heavy boots. I wondered how many of the people who'd confronted me this morning would be able to manage it. As Pat had predicted, there was a noticeboard, still with a drift of snow in the lower corners, and condensation obscuring the notices behind the heavy wood and glass doors. As far as I could work out, tomorrow's service was at eight in the morning, which would effectively scupper my one lie-in of the week. Still, as Pat would no doubt observe, needs must.

What Pat would have said when turning on two red rings on the hob blacked out the whole house I wasn't sure. In any case, I said enough on my own account. But this must be something for the letting agent to fix. I'd invite him to pay for the extra padlocks for the oil tanks too, but something told me I might end up forking out for them. Meanwhile, as I sorted out the fuse board, I resigned myself to microwaving yet another prepared meal.

The lane to the church was like a skating rink next morning – with the scary bonus of a gradient, of course. There was no sign of any other pedestrians making their unsteady way up, nor even of any of the 4x4s that crowded School Road that might have tackled it. Yet, when I reached the gate, clutching at it like an inexperienced swimmer grabbing the rail at the deep end, there was a light on, though the snow was quite virginal on what I assumed was the path. There was, however, a mosaic of footprints by the porch. People had obviously found an alternative route.

Not many people. The vicar, Mark Stephens, was there, of course, wearing a dramatic but sensible clerical black cloak to cover all his other garments. Three other people, two men and a woman, none of whom I'd ever met and all in their sixties or seventies, were also swathed to the eyebrows, with a tiny paraffin heater giving off rather more fumes than heat. The service was Holy Communion, using the old Prayer Book words, which I liked – though since I'd never been christened, let alone confirmed, I couldn't join the others at the altar rail.

Mark declared that as the boiler was still not working he would spare us a sermon, and since there were no hymns either, we were soon released.

It turned out that the boiler was so old a vital part was proving almost impossible to replace. Before I knew it, words were coming out of my mouth. 'Until the weather improves, wouldn't it be possible to hold services in the village hall?'

The men exchanged glances. Mark said, 'There's a block booking for every Sunday morning. Happy Clappers.' He sounded like an ecclesiastical Eeyore.

'Ah.' It didn't sound as if a bit of ecumenical cross fertilisation was likely. 'What about the school hall, then? I'm sure there's some sort of rental rate I've not yet discovered, but I'm sure it won't be high. You're a governor, Mark – would you know?'

He blinked. Had I committed *lèse majesté* by using his first name? There was what you might call a resounding silence all round in fact. Clearly I hadn't yet got the measure of Wrayford life.

I changed the subject quite violently. 'Do I gather that

you didn't have to walk up the lane? If there's another route, I'd be really grateful if you could tell me.'

'It's across a farmyard. And the dog needs to know you.' Mark shook out his cloak to reveal a triangular tear, not very well mended.

'Ah. So in weather like this . . .'

'The farmer didn't have time to clear the lane this time.'

'For a pedestrian track it's only a matter of spreading that sand and salt,' I said, pointing to a yellow plastic council hopper. 'I suppose the church doesn't run to a spade and a wheelbarrow?'

'Don? This is Don Talbot, the churchwarden,' Mark added quickly. 'And this is Giles Membury.'

The name might have come from Hardy, mightn't it? Giles shook my hand, as did Don, though with less enthusiasm, I thought.

'And this is Meg, who is our rock.'

Meg was Mrs Tibbs's age, with an equally round smiling face. But her smile deepened as she shook my hand. 'Are you thinking what I'm thinking, Jane? A bit of do-it-yourself snow clearing?'

I thought quickly – none of them might be as fit as they looked and I didn't want a cardiac arrest laid at my door. 'Only a tiny path – not enough for a car.'

Suddenly I was what I liked most – part of a willing group. It turned out that Giles had recently had a triple by-pass and was excused duties, and Mark had to go and take another service, but together the three of us put to shame, as Meg put it, the young men of the village. 'Not that they have time to do all that much, I suppose – they work such long hours and spend their weekends ferrying their children to this, that and the other. That's why we've no football or cricket teams any more, I suppose. And I fear that if you want any volunteers for school activities you'll get not parents but grandparents helping you. Heigh-ho – we've done our bit, anyway,' she added with pride, surveying a slightly wavering but well-sanded pathway down the hill.

Don trundled the wheelbarrow back up the hill to stow it wherever it lived, but only after Meg had made him promise to drop into her cottage for a cup of coffee. Tucking her arm in mine, she made it clear that I was going too. Who was I to argue? Though I might have queried the term *cottage*: her home was three or four times the size of mine, set in what I could only describe as grounds. There was a well-maintained thatched roof, a front patio swept clean so that it was easier to reach a battery of bird feeders and a front door with two locks. It was guarded by a serious-looking burglar alarm, which she killed while I eased off my boots.

Still giggling after our haphazard descent – the path had been wide enough for just one, remember – she took me into her mega-kitchen and set me to slice bread for toast.

'Home-made,' she conceded when I asked, 'but in that.' She patted a bread-maker. 'What sort of coffee do you prefer?' She patted another machine. 'I love gadgets,' she confided, unnecessarily. As she loaded a tray with what I suspected was Wedgwood china, she said casually, 'I should imagine that you've not had much time to learn about your new neighbours. And the school governors, of course.'

'Any information is always useful,' I said neutrally.

'Potential allies, potential enemies,' she pursued. 'A young woman on her own in a new job – I've been in that position and I did not enjoy it.'

'The villagers seem tight-knit,' I ventured. I needed facts and I needed them before Don arrived – unless he was a man given to useful gossip too.

'I'd not trust young Toby Wells as far as you can throw him. A man may smile and smile and be a villain. And of course there's his auntie.' She continued before I could ask about the aunt. 'Brian Dawes – now, he's old money, but he's acquired plenty of new – appears to be an old-school gentleman but I've never trusted men of his age with no apparent significant other. That's the term, isn't it? And he does so throw his weight around. Don – oh, and here he comes, as if on cue – Don's a nice man but he's pro-establishment, if you see what I mean.'

I caught her eye, making a zipping motion across my mouth.

'Absolutely. You must have smelt the toast, Don,' she declared as she flung open the front door. 'Leave your boots by Jane's. Excellent. They were saying on the radio this morning that this cold snap is likely to go on for days. Longer, maybe. Something to do with pressure over France.'

'Bloody France! Bloody Euro-weather!' Don snorted. It wasn't clear if he was joking.

Pro-establishment Don might even have been one of Dawes's chums, of course, which kept me, however much I despised myself, very much on the demure side of polite. I hardly ventured an opinion of my own without examining it three times before it left my mouth. If I was in any doubt,

I'd flicker an SOS in Meg's direction; she responded by prefacing all sorts of banal remarks with the words, 'I'm sure Jane agrees with me that . . .'

I probably gained more brownie points that way than by my hour's road clearing.

The trouble with having been sociable was that I didn't want to closet myself alone in the school again – or even in the house, doing more unpacking. Even a supermarket run would be more fun than that. Over in Sainsbury's swarms of middle-class locusts were stripping swathes of shelves: presumably the forecast wasn't great. I managed to grab bread, milk and bacon (for Terry's sarnie), and fought my way through to some fresh fruit and vegetables. I didn't need much, of course, but it felt as if I was establishing a precedent for singletons who needed to obtain rations too. I drifted to the drinks section – heavens, in a moment that would run dry – and to the kitchen section, pleasantly deserted. I didn't really need anything, but comfort-bought a couple of new pans, adding a jolly mug for good measure. And then I found a new lipstick, which I didn't need. And some shower gel. Anything. But not a newspaper. I wouldn't have time to read it. I had to work, didn't I?

And, whether in my office or in my house, alone.

I'd barely finished unloading the car when a courier's van pulled up behind it: the oil tank locks for my tank and the school's. The driver, a slip of a girl from Eastern Europe, could hardly wait for my signature – casting her eyes skyward, she said she smelt snow in the air, and we English were useless at dealing with it. I wouldn't have argued even if she'd given me time. She was back in her van and pulling away dangerously fast before I'd even shut the front door.

I just had time to fix the lock and, by now using a torch, to check the gauge – with luck I had enough to keep warm for the rest of the day – before the first flakes stung my cheeks. I had just one more thing to do. The recycling bins were emptied on Mondays, and I had those boxes of books to get rid of. I got a dozen armfuls in before the blizzard descended in earnest. The rest would have to wait.

In fact, though the storm was intense it was short, with barely four inches falling: surely Terry would manage to get through tomorrow. Please! And, yes, a tanker rumbled up soon after six the following morning. But it wasn't Terry for whom I opened the tank, but another man, shorter, stockier and older. Welsh. I might have been delighted to see the fuel, but my stomach clenched with anxiety.

'Is Terry all right? He had a bit of a fall here on Friday,' I added.

'No idea. This is my round this week anyway.'

'Really? Because I expected to cook him a bacon sandwich. To which you're welcome, of course,' I added hastily. 'The grill's on, if you've got time.'

'I've got my breakfast bars, thanks all the same.'

As I made the tea he asked for, I fretted. 'Were you scheduled for this area anyway?'

'Had a call on Saturday morning. That's how it works. Weather like this it's harder for drivers to get to the depot in the first place, but more people need their delivery. Terry's probably working nearer nearer the depot today. Good tea.'

And he was off to the next customer. Without incident.

Except to me. It was my turn to go base over apex. But, as I scrabbled to my feet, I could see no footprints except my own and the Welshman's. And miraculously the mug was intact.

Perhaps it was a good omen. To celebrate I ate Terry's sarnie.

CHAPTER NINE

So, as I made myself coffee in Melanie's office, it really looked as if everything might be going well: warmth at home; PC Davies's nephew scheduled to give me and the letting agency an estimate for insulation and lagging; warmth in the school; a police community support officer on duty outside, dealing firmly with the irate parents. There were no fights or falls in the playground. Everything was hunky-dory, in fact. As soon as assembly was over, I could retire to my office and prepare for this afternoon's teaching. Some teachers I knew liked to read through the files of their pupils to get a handle on them before they actually entered the classroom. I preferred to keep an open mind, unwilling to write someone off because a previous teacher had some prejudice. On the other hand, I'd certainly pore over them after school, to confirm doubts or suspicions I had.

To my chagrin, I found I was still prejudiced against Prudence, who sat and watched me unblinking throughout assembly, fiddling all the time with her hair. I could warn her that in future she must sit still, and make sure that she did, but I couldn't convert those endlessly long and apparently boneless arms and fingers into the average chubby limb. She reminded me horribly of Gollum and his Precious. I was totally ashamed of myself, knowing that I simply must not pick on her. Ever. For anything.

So rather than raise an accusing eyebrow in her direction, I ended the session with a flat instruction to the whole school to remember their manners. Once they were seated in front of me, they should cross their legs tidily and lay their hands in their laps. In class they would stand when any teacher, including myself, entered the room. They would behave like that for every visitor too, and always give way in corridors and hold doors open for adults. Long hair was to be tied back for safety's sake. I had plenty of rubber bands for any girl – or boy – bothered by their long tresses. Cue for laughter, of course, at one or two lads whose parents apparently liked their offspring to look like Little Lord Fauntleroy. While on the subject of manners, it was not only rude to run in the corridors, but actually dangerous. Did they understand?

Prudence's hand shot up. 'What would be the case if someone were chasing you?'

She must be the only child in the school to use that construction. 'If no one runs, no one can be chasing anyone.'

'But what if it's someone bad from whom it's necessary to escape?'

'I think you'll find that since we're changing all the locks – there's a workman coming this morning – you'll be quite safe from bad people chasing you. If it's another pupil, you find a teacher and ask for help.'

Prudence's hand shot up again. 'But that's telling tales,

Miss.' It was almost as if she had made a conscious decision to revert to language appropriate to her age.

'You all know that you are supposed to call me Ms Cowan, so I suggest that is what you do, Prudence. And if someone is behaving dangerously, it's not telling tales, but reporting their dangerous behaviour. Do you understand?' Stern-faced, I looked at each child in turn. 'There's something else you must understand too. Mrs Gough forbade you to bring mobile phones of any sort to school. That ban still stands. If anyone does bring one, I shall confiscate it and only return it to your parents on the understanding that it never comes into school again. Is that absolutely clear? Good. Stand up, Elm Class, and dismiss – which is not a cue to start talking, Robert!'

To my ears I had sounded tetchy, especially after the Prudence moment, but the kids reacted with sober silence and a decent approximation of a march. Tomorrow I'd make sure that they had music to march to. Meanwhile, still vaguely unsettled, I made my first call of the official school day, as opposed to all those I made before nine, to the oil company.

Whoever was at the other end of the line was more malleable than Prudence. Possibly my preamble softened her up – the speed of service when the firm realised my problem, Terry's kindness in squeezing the last drop of oil from the tanker when another customer had effectively hijacked the delivery meant for me, and the wonderful prompt delivery this morning. Having got her basking in a lovely warm glow of praise, I came in with my problem – anxiety about Terry after his fall. I knew as well as she did that a less helpful person would hide behind the Data Protection Act, but she sensed, I think, that my concern was genuine.

'He did call in Saturday saying he was all shaken up after a fall. But he's working today all right. Making a delivery near Sevenoaks, by the look of it.'

'I do hope he didn't lose any wages.'

'No. Just turned down a bit of overtime. Said something about watching Wolves on TV.'

'Phew!'

And more than phew. I was busy opening myself up to litigation if I was in any way to blame – though perhaps ice might be considered an act of God. But he had thought he was pushed. Asking for my good wishes to be passed on, I put the phone down carefully.

There was a tap on the door. Melanie appeared, clutching a bunch of flowers.

'Isn't this lovely? It says on the little envelope, *To the best headmistress ever*,' she reported. 'See?' Slightly to my surprise, it wasn't written in a childish hand, but computer printed.

I saw. 'But I've only been here five minutes.'

'You must have made a few fans, anyway.' She laid the bouquet on my desk.

Something didn't feel at all right. Not at all. It wasn't Simon, was it, proving that he knew all about me? Please God, no!

My hands were literally shaking as I opened the envelope. It wasn't from Simon. Nor was it even for me. *For dear Mrs Gough. We all really, really miss you.* Again it was printed.

When I silently showed it to her, Melanie went red, then pale. 'Oh dear. That isn't very kind, is it?'

I said lightly, 'It's a very kind gesture to Mrs Gough.'

'No.' She shook her head firmly. 'Someone knew exactly what they were doing when they had it delivered to the school. They knew she doesn't work here now. They were getting at you.'

I didn't need that sort of sympathy. 'Let's just get it to Mrs Gough.'

'How can I? She moved down to the Algarve when she retired. Everyone in the school knew about it. They even did a project on the different regions of Portugal.'

'Someone must have forgotten. Tell you what, could you get on to the florist that delivered it and get them to contact the person who ordered it? Then it won't be our problem any more.'

She looked at me with embarrassing compassion. 'OK. Then I'll make you a coffee.'

'Thanks. But perhaps in a few minutes.' I pointed. Through the window we could see the contents of the black sack I'd so carefully strung up spilt on to the snow, in so much disarray that clearly more than gravity had been involved. When could that have happened? Before school every child was supervised, the only ones having any access to the cycle shed area being those needing to park their sledges. Since there were only three propped up against the back wall of the shed, it should be easy enough to question the owners. However, unless they'd perched, acrobat fashion, on each other's shoulders, I couldn't see how children had managed to reach it. I suppose they could have treated it like a *piñata*, walloping it with handy sticks till it shed its load, but that would have meant forward planning. Meanwhile, every last shirt had to be gathered up. But I had learnt my lesson. I would peg each one to the washing line I brought over from my house, and get Melanie to text or email every last parent to request them to claim their child's property before the end of the week. Anything left over would be put in the charity bin.

When I eventually got to her office, my hands blue with cold, there was no coffee waiting. Melanie soon sprang into action, but was so busy jabbering almost tearful apologies I put up a hand to stop her.

'I can't understand it. I've looked by the door, where they were left, I've looked everywhere. I think I'm going mad—'

'"They?" What's the problem? Just sit down, I'll make the coffee.'

She took an ostentatiously deep breath, but didn't exhale to relax.

'I know when people tell you to calm down it does the opposite, but do try to relax, Melanie, or you'll do yourself no good at all. Here. Careful. It's hot, remember.'

She pulled a face and put the mug on her desk next to mine. 'It's the flowers. I was going to contact the florist to tell them to collect them – right?'

I leant against the edge of the window sill. 'Right.' The cold pressed in from outside. It was time to stand up again. If I started shivering she'd be more upset.

'But there was no sign of any florist's label or card or anything. And I didn't see the delivery van. There was just this buzz on the entryphone. No one asked to be let in, so I assumed it was just some child being naughty. But then one of the mothers buzzed – she'd brought her son's lunch box – and she produced the flowers. She said they'd been propped up against the door.'

'I'd assumed you'd taken off the cellophane to avoid making a mess in my office – I know you're that sort of woman, Melanie! But now you're saying there never was any wrapper and that the card – well, you can buy a card like that anywhere, I suppose, so long as you've enough computer skills to print it.'

'But why? Who'd do anything like that? An act of unkindness.'

'A fairly expensive act of unkindness, too.'

She shook her head. 'No, they're not that good – I stuck them in a bucket of water in the staff loo, by the way. I thought they might be just Monday-morning flowers, left over after the weekend. After all, a lot of florists don't even bother opening on Mondays, since they've not got fresh stock. But these really are a bit on the tatty side: a couple of bunches of filling-station flowers, you know the sort of thing, just rearranged. If only I'd checked properly I'd have binned them.' She sounded more upset than even I felt. 'Who'd do such a thing?' She gasped, as a confidential penny dropped. 'Your name change and everything: could it be someone from your past?'

'It could. But even I never knew of the existence of Mrs Gough until recently. No one from my past would ever have heard of her. Surely?' I added as much for my benefit as for hers.

There was a miserable silence. I had better break it. 'Those football shirts. Any idea which of the lads might have got it into his testosterone-fuelled head to do that?'

91

She shook her head. 'I should have thought that Tom might be the man to ask. He knows the sporty ones quite well.'

Which reminded me – how might his plans for the stockrooms be going? 'I'll talk to him,' I said. 'Goodness me – all this before it's even break time.' I managed a rueful grin, which didn't begin to approach cheerful.

'All this and the locksmith too,' Melanie added, buzzing him in as he confirmed his ID.

Soon I was the proud possessor of a new set of keys. Melanie and I labelled them all for their new custodians. Even with an extra spare for the office, there was one left over.

'Everyone in the country used to leave a key under a flowerpot,' she said, brandishing them.

'I think I might know the academic equivalent of a flowerpot,' I said. 'Thanks.'

The flower delivery did leave an unpleasant taste in my mouth, not least because Melanie was obviously so upset on my behalf. She even moved them from the women's loo to the men's lest the sight disturbed me. Frankly, I think she was more upset than I was – my main emotion was gratitude that there was nothing to connect them to Simon. But I had other things to busy myself with, including my afternoon's teaching. Clearly the governors had been wrong to write off Mrs Gough's replacement as 'some supply teacher': the children obviously enjoyed learning and exploring ideas, and spoke with ease and fluency. The end of school bell went all too quickly.

The kids heading home, I was about to embark on my

post-school prowl when Helen called me into her classroom. 'You asked me to check on any pupils with problems,' she said, 'so I've spoken to the parents of the two littles with toilet issues – you remember?'

'I do. Have you got time for a coffee?'

'I need to get off after this, thanks. Physio appointment.' The gist of her report was that some of the children had said they'd seen an eye watching them in the loos. Just a twinkly eye. Unblinking. Nothing more. 'I checked. Nothing. I even held their hands and tried to make them go in with me, but Tammy in particular got very distressed.'

'So you didn't go ahead with the experiment – very wise. No toilet problems at home? Nightmares?'

'Just those loos. My guess is that one of the other kids hid in there and jumped them, but they just talked about a gleaming eye.'

'Both of them? Tammy and—?'

'Marmaduke. Where do parents find these names, eh? Yes, both of them. Separately. And no, I couldn't see anything in the boys' loo either. Or maybe someone didn't flush the loo properly and they were upset by . . . by faecal matter?'

'That's a possibility. Any other children I should be alerted to?'

'Prudence apart?'

'Prudence especially. What's she been up to this time?'

My carefully neutral tone didn't fool a fellow-pro for a second. 'You don't like her, do you? Well, it's all right – no one does.'

'Actually, Helen, it's not all right. Teachers can't have playground responses to the pupils. We need to suss out what drives her. What are her parents like?'

'I think she arrived late in their lives. They treat her like glass. Actually, they wanted to send her to Ewen House, the private school in town, but she refused to wear the uniform – screamed herself sick, held her breath till she passed out.'

'Charming. Does she still do that?'

'Not here. It doesn't work here. Mrs Gough saw to that. She couldn't organise a booze-up in a brewery but she was a good teacher.'

'Were any of the children particularly fond of her? Prudence, for example?'

'Adored her. In a strange tale-telling way.'

'About her or to her?'

'As far as I know, just the latter.'

'I'd best watch out, then – she keeps telling tales to me.'

'About staff or pupils? Oh, both, of course. She's a prize snitch. But she's up to something else, now – I know she is. I just don't know what.'

I looked at my watch. 'Let me know the instant you do! Off you go, now. And thanks, Helen – this has been useful.'

'There are a few more names in here.' She passed me a folder.

'Just one thing,' I added, as we left the room. 'I'm a bit of a Girl Guide at heart – I like to be prepared. Where do you keep the balls for tomorrow afternoon's after-school club?'

She turned back and opened one of the big cupboards running the width of the back wall. 'Bottom shelf here – now where on earth might they be? I never put them in the stockroom for obvious reasons. I'd best look.'

'Not till after your physio appointment. Like the man says, tomorrow is another day.'

One on which, I reflected, as I waved her off, I could have been left with egg all over my face. I needed to get some balls now. In the literal, not the metaphorical sense. Texting Davies's nephew that I was running late and couldn't be home till seven-thirty, I set off in search of a sports shop. Just because I was paranoid didn't mean that anyone was going to beat me.

No one was going to beat me. And yet it seemed that someone – something – had.

I had no electricity, and water was cascading down the stairs. It was a good job Davies's nephew Sam, tall, straight and stolid, was beside me, or I might have thrown up.

'Looks like I was too late,' Sam said succinctly. 'Any idea where your stopcock is?'

'I only arrived a week ago.' Which, come to think of it, was hardly an answer.

Perhaps it was. Without so much as a sigh, he went hunting, and came back triumphant. The cascade slowed to a trickle, and finally stopped. 'You'd better contact your insurance,' he said. 'Property and contents.'

If he could be calm, I'd better be calm too. 'The property cover would be the landlord's problem, wouldn't it? Or the letting agent's?'

'If you phone him, I'll explain what happened. Got a torch? You might want to see what clothes and stuff you can salvage. And book yourself a hotel for the night.'

'Can't I stay—?'

His look shut me up as I passed him my phone. He could hear for himself. The letting agent was closed for the day. The emergency number was well-nigh inaudible. Between us we worked it out. I dialled again. Voicemail. Sam grabbed the phone and left a message, his plumbing experience giving him an authority that belied his youth.

I packed an overnight bag, intending to head out to a hotel; there was a very good one, complete with spa and swimming pool, a couple of miles away. But Sam, grabbing the bag in a sweet old-fashioned gesture, stopped abruptly, pointing to my car. 'Won't be going far in that tonight,' he said dryly. 'One puncture I could deal with for you: not two.' He walked round the car. 'Correction – four.'

Fortunately my emergency camping kit was still dry, so I could decamp to the school. Chuntering, Sam helped me reluctantly with other essentials, one of which, I insisted, was the microwave – after all, there were plenty of ready meals busily defrosting in my freezer. I flourished one, and an indulgent dessert. I pressed a selection of other meals into his hands, pointing out that the only place I could keep them cold was in the snow. By the time I remembered I could have stowed them in the freezer in the school kitchen it was too late: there was no way I could change my mind.

'Now, it's high time you headed home. You've been more than kind. I won't starve and I won't freeze,' I said bracingly. As I waved him towards his car, I added, 'And don't forget an invoice for your time.'

'I'd have done that for anyone.'

'I believe you. But you don't have to do it free for my landlord who caused the problem in the first place.'

He grinned. 'I wonder what sort of place they'll find for you. There can't be that many rentals going begging round here.'

CHAPTER TEN

The problem with being a teacher is that if there's any part of your job you can't do, you let someone down. This morning I should have been watching the Open the Book team again, but as I explained to Tamsin, as she signed in, collected visitor passes and picked up key B, I really needed a roof over my head, and to get that I needed to stir the letting agent into action as soon as someone at his office deigned to pick up the phone.

She put her hand on my arm. 'Don't worry, Jane. We've been doing it unsupervised for a term or more with no disasters – we can manage another session. No, don't think of apologising. Go and do what you have to do.'

Unsupervised? Not in my school. I had detailed a startled Tom to take my place, lending him my iPod, on to which I'd downloaded some quiet music to settle the children as they sat down and a stirring march to go out to. The docking station wasn't really up to the job, but it would have to do.

Helen's report on the snow? That was due today,

wasn't it? And there it was in my in-box. Good for her. I'd better forward it to all the governors. On the other hand, I'd rather know what she'd said first. I scanned it quickly: she'd done a good job, evaluating all the activities in relation to the teaching aims they fulfilled, and generally finding them highly satisfactory. A survey of the children showed, as you'd expect, a great deal of satisfaction, though she carefully noted one anonymous child's complaint that her hair had got wet (Prudence, I guessed). Parents? She'd even done a straw poll to find that about seventy-five per cent understood and approved of all the outdoor exercise. Twenty per cent objected to the risks to which their children had been exposed: what if one had fallen? What about their poor offspring getting cold hands and feet?

I could live with the ratio, particularly as a blessed five per cent declared that we were the professionals and should be allowed to do our job as we saw fit. I sent the report on its way to the governors, with a note saying how much I appreciated my young colleague doing such thorough work despite all the other calls on her time. I copied it to Helen.

Now to my own concerns. I believe I actually rolled up my sleeves as I started making phone calls.

'I thought landlords or their agents would have a pool of alternative accommodation to draw on. And my contract says that in the event of the house becoming uninhabitable, then it is your responsibility to rehouse me.' I confronted James Ford, the agent, in the majesty of my office.

The poor man, not long out of uni, I suspected, wrung

his beautifully manicured hands. He might have been Uriah Heep. The upshot was that he had no properties within a twenty-mile radius, let alone ten.

'I find that hard to believe,' I said coolly.

'It's the London influence, you see. People can sell their London properties at enormous profit and move down here – there are a number of villages with a mainline railway station so they can commute. That's why there's an absolute dearth of properties to rent.'

'So my contract is worth?' I snapped my fingers.

'Sadly . . . Perhaps you could stay with a friend? Someone in the village?'

I was fairly certain that even now dear Melanie would be on the phone badgering her friends to find me a place. 'When I have been here only ten days, am I really likely to have a friend with whom I could sofa-surf? Not good enough, Mr Ford. Get on to your insurance company and come back here with a sensible suggestion by five-thirty. I will talk to my insurance about the damage to my property, meanwhile. Till five-thirty, then.' I stood up, and offered him my hand. 'Of course, if you have no ideas I'll have to make a call to my solicitor.'

His was shaking. His palms were wet. He was genuinely scared – but not of me, surely?

Certainly I didn't present a very dignified figure when I returned to my office at the end of school. I don't know who had enjoyed themselves more in the ball skills club, the pupils or me. So, still sweating and panting in my tracksuit and trainers, I had collapsed at my desk with no prospect of a shower when, to my surprise, PC Davies appeared.

'Sam called me,' he said, moving the tubes of tennis balls to one side and sitting down. 'We're just on our way back from an RTA and thought we might cadge a cup of tea.' As he spoke, Taylor came in, looking very young and very wan. I sat her down in my chair and fetched another. Melanie might have had her coat on ready to leave, but she produced three mugs, milk, sugar and a plate of biscuits without being asked.

'That fluff,' Davies said slowly, eschewing sugar and biscuits. 'The stuff you found on your stairs the other night. Have you still got it?'

'Funnily enough I have. You looked interested, Ms Taylor. And when police officers look interested, they usually have a reason.' I unlocked my desk drawers, felt behind a box of assorted rubber bands, and produced the little bag.

Davies nodded. 'We wouldn't have been interested if Sam hadn't phoned to tell me about your flood – and about your car. He's bright, that kid.'

'He is, isn't he – and nice with it,' I added with a smile. 'Do I gather that Sam's got your investigative genes?'

'He's no fool, let's say. He can't understand why anyone should leave a house unlagged in an area known for its cold winds. He couldn't understand four punctures. Then I recalled the shirts and the fluff and I started thinking. I suppose you didn't strip the insulation and puncture your tyres yourself?'

'Why should I? This is my dream job.'

'Perhaps you're finding it too hard and are looking for an excuse to get out?'

'After only a week, Penny? Look, I've been on the

run, changing addresses, changing jobs, for years. Now that my ex-husband, Simon Wilshere, is in jail for persistent stalking, criminal damage, actual bodily harm and a couple of other things, I wanted to find stability. The governors here know I had to change my name, though I spared them all the grimmest details. But you can check him out on Holmes or whatever your database is called these days.' I gulped some tea. It was too hot and scalded as it went down. 'I also received some flowers I certainly didn't send myself.' I told them about Melanie's find.

'If you didn't do all these things – and assuming your story hangs together, I'm tempted to believe you – then who did? And why?' Penny asked.

'As to the first, I haven't a clue. Why? I've even less of a theory. I do know that I'm not very popular round here, and again I don't know why. Genuinely. All I want to do is turn the school around, but ever since I chased off an intruder at the end of my first day—'

'The day before the football shirts got nicked?'

'Right.' What had I said? I've never been one to betray my feelings. I straightened my back. 'Would you mind if I checked the whole of my car over? Just in case?'

'In case of what? I'll do it. Got your keys handy?' Davies was on his feet.

'That was a weird change of subject,' Penny said as he closed the door behind him. Her colour was back and she looked as bright and alert as one could wish. 'There's something you're not telling us, isn't there?'

'It's just that – some places I've lived, and believe me I've been to a lot of places in my efforts to escape Simon,

I've been made really welcome. But not here. Even the pub landlady, whom you'd have expected to be professionally friendly, was stand-offish. I don't like whingeing. That's why I changed the subject.'

Davies was with us again. 'Apart from the flat tyres, I can't open the doors, but that might be just because they've frozen shut. Or because they've been superglued, of course. Can you get me a kettle of hot water and I'll find out?'

Sheltering from the wind, Penny and I watched his experiment. 'Looks more like criminal damage than an act of God,' she observed as in turn we tried and failed to breach the car's defences. From time to time the alarm showed how our efforts were resented.

'OK,' Lloyd said. 'Have it towed away, but make sure you get a detailed list of the damage – and not just for your insurance company. This sort of thing annoys me. Sometimes I can understand people being little urban warriors. There's a commuter village or two round here so beset with appalling car parking – even on complete strangers' drives, would you believe? – that they sometimes get overenthusiastic with the superglue deterrent. You can understand, sort of. But yours wasn't doing any harm to anyone. God, it's cold. Look, you'd best get in; we'll be on our way.'

I walked them to their car. 'There's just one more thing you ought to know. I had an oil delivery the other night, and the driver ended flat on his face. He had an idea he was pushed. I was worried enough to phone the company. Seems he's all right – but it might have been serious.'

Penny jotted, but her blue fingers would hardly hold her biro. Lloyd's advice was good. I waved them off from the shelter of the school and headed indoors like a rabbit dodging a ferret.

'I am authorised by my client's insurance company to offer you a night's stay at a hotel on their approved list so that the property can be assessed. Without prejudice.' James Ford looked even less happy than on his previous visit to the school.

Without speaking, I held out my hand for the list. Nodding him to a chair, I raised an eyebrow the way I did for particularly bright pupils pretending to be obtuse. 'And which of these outposts of civilisation could you recommend? No? Let's see what TripAdvisor has to say, shall we?' Obligingly, I turned the monitor so that he could see each in turn. 'What an interesting collection of two- and one-star reviews from the TripAdvisor reviewers. Tell me, Mr Ford, to which of these would you send your mother or older sister?'

He gobbled like a turkey celebrating the passing of Christmas.

'Very well, then tell me where you *would* send them, and I'll go there. Ah! Excuse me – that sounds like the pickup truck for my car. I'd better see to it.'

'I have to admit that James Ford's female relatives have very good taste in hotels,' I told Pat on the phone much later that evening. I was in a warm chic double room, booked, to my amazement, by Ford himself while my car was being winched onto the flatbed truck. He'd even insisted on giving me a lift, on the grounds that at this time of the evening most local taxis would be collecting people from the commuter stations. I continued, 'A Hotel Mondiale, no less. Complete with spa, gym and swimming pool. Pity I've not brought my leggings and leotard or my swimmies.' And a pity I hadn't moved here last night. I really had got noble self-sacrifice to an art.

'Buy them from the hotel. Claim on your insurance. How long do you reckon you're going to be homeless?'

'Until they find me a new rental property. Pat, this is so frustrating. There aren't enough hours in the day already, and here I am two miles away from the school without a car – until my insurance sorts out a temporary replacement. Which may well get the same treatment, of course.' I managed a laugh. 'I may have to tweak the angle of our new security lights to protect it. When we get them.'

'Have you eaten yet?'

'Not hungry.'

'Well, stuff the marking and all the other things you're going to fob me off with, get yourself into that pool—'

'But—'

'I know you've got scars. No one'll notice. And if they do they'll just think you've been in a car crash – which pretty well describes your relationship with that shit anyway. Not so much a crash as a prolonged pile-up, actually. Now go and swim twenty lengths and work up an appetite. I know you and your not eating when you're stressed. OK? And have a glass or two of wine with your food, too. Just do it. Oh, and by the way, I'm coming down this weekend – it sounds as if you need a spare pair of hands whatever happens.'

As he often did, he ended the call just as I drew breath to protest.

A couple of hours later, I had a text: *How many lengths?*

Fourteen, I replied. *One glass of Merlot. And an excellent steak.*

CHAPTER ELEVEN

Fortunately I had separate insurance cover for vandalism, and the following day a new nicely anonymous silver Fiesta arrived at school during lunchtime. I left it parked with the other staff cars in the little on-site car park, which was the one place in the school with proper security – a really hefty combination padlock. The martyr half of me whispered that I ought to source cheaper accommodation; the other half knew I didn't have time to repack and decamp, and what the hell since the problem wasn't of my causing. I grabbed ten minutes of my lunchtime, which like any teacher's was notional rather than actual, to go over to the house. In daylight it was easier to pick out which of my belongings I had to ditch, which I could revive and which put into store. I suppose there were about equal quantities of each. I ordered a mini-skip – no time for trips to the tip, of course – and tried to get on with my job, which this afternoon involved teaching again. As I went into class, I ran into Tom, laden with folders. Which reminded me: 'Tom, any progress on the working party?

We've had mice in one of the stockrooms, so God knows what lurks in the other.'

'Let's get this straight, Ms Cowan. I don't have time to scratch my own fucking arse, and everyone else is as stretched as they can be. So no, I haven't got any sodding progress to report. What do you propose to do about it? Put me in detention? Have me on litter patrol?'

'Put a note on your file about you using unsuitable language in front of our pupils, Tom. And invite you to express the problems in writing, so I can take the problem to the governors. Your class is waiting.'

So was mine, but it would have to wait until my fury had dropped to manageable levels. My hope was that no one had heard the exchange. But I wasn't surprised when Prudence materialised beside me like an avenging Cheshire Cat. 'Mr Mason shouldn't use words like that, should he, Ms Cowan? It's very unprofessional. Are you going to suspend him? I think you ought.'

I suspected she saw the effort I was making not to lose my temper. 'Thank you for your advice, Prudence,' I said, with absolute calm. 'I shall give it due consideration. Meanwhile you and I are both late for our class, which is very disrespectful to your colleagues, isn't it? In you go.'

By the time the lesson got under way I had so much adrenalin charging through my system I was on fire – I probably gave the best lesson I'd ever taught. Fortunately. It was hard to concentrate on anything when I had the Tom Mason business hanging over me. It was almost as if he wanted to be suspended, but we were too short-staffed and there were too many other calls on my budget to contemplate doing without his services and bringing in a supply teacher to do his work. I'd gathered that Tom didn't have too many fans on the board of governors – I'd been the only one to speak up for him. So I was tempted to phone Brian Dawes and drop the problem in his lap. If I did, Dawes would accuse me of being unable to discipline my staff; if I didn't, and Dawes didn't think my actions were strong enough, I'd be accused of weakness. Damned either way. Maybe a spot of lateral thinking . . .

What had someone once said? *Make 'em laugh; make 'em cry; make 'em wait?*

Tom was clearly disconcerted when, sitting him down in my office, I offered him coffee and asked what time he had to get away. Life couldn't be easy when you had children of such different ages.

'The youngest is in the Music and Movement club on sufferance – much too young, of course. And the others stay at their homework club till I roll up, whatever time that might be.'

'And once you get them all home, it must be—'

'Hell on wheels. If Naomi's got a late surgery, I get Elly-May tea and try to shoehorn her into bed. But sometimes the older ones wind her up for the sheer hell of it, it seems to me.'

'What time of night do you finish your marking and prep?'

'When I've finished. Twelve. Or I get up at five to do a bit more.' He suddenly remembered he was supposed to be truculent. 'Are you about to send me on some time- management course?'

'Can't spare you. And everyone on the staff, including

myself, would have to join you. But I can't have you swearing at me, Tom, or rather I can – but not in front of the children. And in front of Prudence, in particular. I'm bracing myself for a shocked phone call from her horrified parents. I don't know them well enough to know how to deal with them.'

'You'll probably have to give them my head on a plate.'

'Only if they do the dance of the seven veils. Twice. So what would you do in my position?'

'You can't just fob them off or they'll go straight to Dawes, and demand two heads. I'd tell them that you've given me a formal warning for unprofessional conduct, and I've given you a sincere and heartfelt apology.'

'And have you?'

'I suppose I have, haven't I? I'm sorry, Ms Cowan: you've got enough pressure without the Digbys getting on your back. I will try to sort out a working party, but Saturday's the one day I get to see my kids and keep them on the straight and narrow. Bloody hard when the school they go to is awash with pot and legal highs.'

'It must be. We ought to make it a staff and their families day – have a barbecue and some fun on the sports field. Which means, according to the weather forecast, not yet.'

'Quite. Jesus, I've never known snow lie as long as this down here – though someone was telling me that fifteen years ago it was eight feet deep on Church Hill.'

We shared a grimace. 'Imagine a fine warm spring day . . . We could have quick cricket, and rounders. Even some tennis. Now, did you see that there's a nationwide search for music instruments for schools – people are being asked to search their lofts for long-unplayed fiddles. Why don't we use the parish mag to launch an appeal not just for instruments but also for tennis racquets?'

'That's a brilliant idea.' He sounded sincere. Suddenly he produced an impish grin. 'Anything I can do as immediate penance?'

Between us we managed to push and drag the boxes of books that had so offended me to the recycling bin, gasping for breath before we grabbed handfuls of books and consigned them to a more useful future. We must have dumped about fifty when Tom stopped suddenly.

'You said you'd meant to get the kids to help you with this? It's a good job you didn't, Jane – look.' He held up dog-eared copies of very old magazines. Not *Beano* or *Bunty*. Something altogether more adult. 'Nothing compared with what you can get on the Internet, of course, but – well, I wouldn't want my kids getting so much as a glimpse of these.'

'Heavens: imagine if one of these got blown down the street when the bins are emptied! It'd be the Tower of London for the lot of us. I'll shred them. Any more?'

'Here – these look even nastier.'

We worked in silence on the second box, but found nothing else of note. As soon as we could we dived back into the warmth of the school. I switched on the shredder. 'Tom, I want a signed witness statement from you about what we found and what we're doing. One for you, one for me, actually. Because you never know what allegations might start flying if whoever dumped these . . . this . . . I'm sorry, I can't think of a polite word! . . . whoever dumped the mags suspects we might have found them.'

The phone rang. He actually went pale. 'That'll be the Digbys now.'

It was.

He switched off the shredder, grabbed a piece of paper and started writing. Holding the handset from my ear, I watched. The first was the formal apology I really needed. The second was a statement explaining the circumstances of our unpleasant discovery and the action taken.

Eventually I had a chance to interrupt Mrs Digby's impassioned flow. 'I have Mr Mason's letter of apology before me already, Mrs Digby. I appreciate all you say, and will do everything in my power to ensure that the incident is not repeated. No, I shan't, as Prudence recommends, suspend Mr Mason. And I don't think that asking Mr Mason to apologise to a child who should not have been listening to the conversation is appropriate. But I will discuss the matter with the governors at the earliest opportunity. Meanwhile, I am dealing with a matter of the utmost sensitivity, vital to the well-being of all the children.'

It took a little longer to end the call, and I suspected that neither of us had heard the last of the matter, but at least while I was mouthing platitudes I had come to a conclusion.

'I'm not going to shred these, Tom. So you may have to redraft your statement. I'm going to hand them over to the police. For both our sakes. OK?'

He nodded. 'Imagine if those had got into the kids' hands . . .'

'Quite. I know the doors to both stockrooms are always kept locked, but if you're carrying something out someone might be tempted to take a peep. Tell you what, on your way out could you put some cones across that corridor? I'll print off some notices saying that the corridor is out of bounds until further notice, and spell it out in kiddie-friendly language at tomorrow's assembly.'

He managed a smile. 'Good idea. And, you know what, if I were you I'd even text or email the parents to hammer home the point.'

'Excellent idea. I'll do it as soon as I've phoned the police. Heavens, is that the time? Go and collect your kids – you may want to wash your hands first!'

Lloyd, in civvies and nursing a lager, albeit a non-alcoholic one, made the Mondiale bar a whole lot less impersonal. His wife, Jo, a woman petite enough to make me feel like a giant, joined me in a life-enhancing prosecco. It seemed they were keen ballroom dancers, and since they were on their way back from a class in a village hall it made sense for them to break the journey here. They'd practically had individual tuition tonight, she said, since the snow had put off a lot of people.

'It's so hard for us, Lloyd being tall and me not tall at all,' she said. 'But we love it. And it's one wonderful night together away from the children's homework squabbles.'

Lloyd waited till we'd worn out the topic before tapping the porn mags, which he'd shoved back into the large but discreet Jiffy bag I'd brought them in. 'As you say, there's nothing here as bad as the stuff that's swamped the Net. But someone might prefer others not to know it was there.'

'And someone might have stashed other stuff there,' I said. 'Perhaps the stockrooms silted up accidentally with the passing of time. But they may have been deliberately crammed with rubbish to conceal this cache.'

'If it's anything like the schools I've taught in it's just as likely to be the former,' Jo said.

'You're a teacher? Why didn't I realise? There's usually an instant recognition – as if we all bear an otherwise invisible mark of Cain.'

'Not any more. I had enough of teaching maths to the innumerate. So I moved to insurance. Much better paid, less stress, shorter hours – why work myself into a breakdown? Then I got made redundant.'

'You're a trained, qualified, experienced maths teacher? You're a mythical creature! Actually sitting next to me!' I fanned myself in mock shock. 'You wouldn't be looking for work, would you?' Why else would Lloyd have fixed this meeting? I looked quizzically from one to the other. 'Even as a supply teacher, though, you'd have to have an interview – the governors have removed the hire-and-fire option from my contract.'

Lloyd held up a hand. 'Hold on, hold on – yours might not be the happiest school to work in. What if someone took against Jo like they've taken against you?'

I raised my hands, dropping my head in acknowledgement of a killer blow. Then I said, 'But our maths teaching is well below par. Ofsted picked it up as one of our worst weaknesses. I have to try, don't I?'

'I'll think about it,' Jo said. 'Or we could talk about it over a meal?' She jerked her head in the direction of the restaurant.

Lloyd produced an uxorious sigh. 'I suppose it'll save me having to cook.'

I was in school by six the next morning, trying to catch up on the work I should have done last night. The evening with

Lloyd and Jo Davies had been a bitter-sweet experience. On the one hand I had enjoyed myself hugely, free for an hour or so from worries about my safety and with two very affable people who could well become my friends; on the other I was given a tantalising glimpse of what a loving partnership might be – and try how I might, I could never imagine letting another man get within touching distance of me.

Assuming I ever had time to meet a decent man.

First I had to deal with a silly little boy, who'd interpreted the edict I'd delivered during assembly against going down the stockroom corridor as either a challenge or an invitation to hop over Tom's cones and my No Entry signs and go and check if the doors were locked. He wasn't just caught in the act – he was caught in it by me.

Not surprisingly, Robert couldn't quite explain why. His responses to my questions mostly involved the words, 'No, Ms Cowan; not sure, Ms Cowan; sorry, Ms Cowan.'

In other words, I might have put the fear of God into him, and possibly deterred him from trying again, but I still had no idea what had motivated him. What or who. Why did his eyes keep sliding sideways, as if he was afraid that someone was listening? It was something to discuss with Helen when we broke for lunch.

There was some good news, however. It was delivered by James Ford in person just after my encounter with Robert. They had conjured up a holiday let for me just outside the village – though for a short period only, until the existing bookings had to be honoured. With luck, he added, as with very little certainty, the original property should have been repaired and dried out.

As I remained unconvinced, he produced a tablet and showed me a series of photos of delectable interiors.

'When can I move in?'

He grinned as he picked up the ill-suppressed glee in my voice. 'The sooner the better as far as our insurance company is concerned. Tomorrow? I could organise a welcome hamper too?'

Raising an eyebrow, I gestured at my desk. 'I was here this morning before any sensible person had made their first cuppa of the day. I shall leave as they make their cocoa. I shall do the same tomorrow. So Saturday is the earliest I can manage. And I shall still probably need that hamper,' I added. After all, Saturday was the day I had set aside for tackling the mess in the stockroom with Pat. Well, it would be just a different sort of mess we had to deal with – mine.

His voice was pleasantly conspiratorial. 'I'll make sure the hamper is a really good one. And I've told the holiday people you'll be using their towels and linen, too.'

My smile at the thought of what would no doubt be an enormous thread count must have verged on the blissful. 'And their heating? Ah, you don't know about my theft . . .' I explained.

He looked duly appalled and promised to pay for the oil tank security lock.

'You may have to buy a new hob, too. Using more than one red ring fuses the whole house.'

'Really? Everything's supposed to be in good condition. I'll mention the issue to the owner when I can reach him.'

'Who is it, as a matter of interest?' I asked, not quite idly.

He shook his head. 'Some owners are happy for their

tenants to know them; this one isn't. But I assure you that I will raise your concerns as soon as I can.' The way he looked at me was familiar: it was the way I look at children like Robert I suspect of fibbing. 'The loft insulation . . . the lagging: it's all very puzzling . . .'

'It puzzles me too: if the loft and the tank were once properly lagged, I'd like to know what happened myself. I've a nasty feeling that you suspect it was I who stripped everything out. You do, don't you!'

'Actually not me. But there was someone who floated it as a possibility.'

I spread my hands. 'Why on earth should I? And where would I put all the lagging? In my car, which had to be towed away because someone had spiked all the tyres? In a skip? Quite noticeable. And even if I'd had an hour free to remove everything, can you tell me why I should want to? Without oil the house was freezing, and it was in my interests to save every last little therm of heat. It was so bad I spent most of my time working here – one of the governors complained about the number of hours I spent in school.'

He threw his head back and laughed. 'I've never heard of a boss complaining that someone worked too hard!' His smile faded. 'This used to be a good little school, you know. Mrs Gough let it go, sadly – didn't move with the times. And the best teachers left. A great shame. Anyway, I'm glad you're going to take it in hand. Good luck to you. I'll meet you at Dove Cottage at – say ten o'clock on Saturday morning?'

'Aren't we a little far south for Dove Cottage?'

To my delight he grinned. 'So long as you don't expect to lodge with a poet . . .'

* * *

117

'I demand that you suspend the wretched man!' Brian Dawes said, banging his fist on my desk and ruffling not just my temper but also two piles of paperwork and a heap of folders. 'Immediately. As for your telling the parents that it isn't appropriate for the fool to apologise to their daughter, what planet are you on? What if they go to the papers? What if they sue?'

'I assured Mrs Digby that I had taken immediate and appropriate action. Tom has formally apologised. The matter is on his file. I have emailed all you governors. In truth, Mr Dawes, I hope you don't expect me to take further action: staffing here is stretched so tightly that if I suspended him – and it would have to be on full pay, remember – the children's education would suffer: they need solid, regular presences, not a succession of supply teachers. And, for all his faults, Tom is absolutely committed to the school. He has the sort of devotion that you can only expect of a full-time member of staff, not to mention having an enviable talent.' Would Tom stick his neck out like that for me? I rather doubted it.

'Could you tell me why you and he were seen laughing and joking with each other last night?'

Who on earth could have seen us and snitched? 'Yesterday evening we were dealing with some rubbish I couldn't carry by myself. I don't recall any laughing and joking, as it happens – in fact, we had a very serious discussion about a confidential matter. Confidential,' I repeated.

He didn't quite harrumph but would clearly have liked to. 'I hear, by the way, that you have not taken aboard Mrs Tibbs's criticisms about your use of school oil and electricity.'

I looked him straight in the eye: 'Whose criticisms would you rather I acted on, Mr Dawes's, Mrs Tibbs's or Ofsted's? I simply have to work every evening. Ah, perhaps you've not yet heard that I don't currently have a home to work in. No? A burst pipe has rendered the house uninhabitable.'

'I heard you were camping here. Scarcely dignified behaviour, if I may say so.'

'Exactly. So my current base is a hotel. I believe the letting agents are finding me a new base, albeit temporary.' I got to my feet, smiling. 'Thank you very much for your advice, Mr Dawes. You may rest assured that I will do everything in my power to obtain and maintain the highest standards of professionalism in my staff. As a matter of interest, I have copied you the letter I have sent to the Digbys.'

'You've replied without even consulting me!'

I stood. 'Mr Dawes: if you and your colleagues did not think I was capable of running every aspect of this school, why did you appoint me?'

CHAPTER TWELVE

I neither expected nor received an answer to my question, but I was pleased to have asked it because it was one I should have put to last Saturday's governors' meeting. What had turned a group of perfectly decent men and women into a latter-day version of the Spanish Inquisition, and not the comic Monty Python version, either?

It had to remain a rhetorical question. As Dawes swept out, lips zipped, the phone rang: it was Melanie to break the unwelcome news that the security firm installing the CCTV wouldn't be able to get a vital part until late next week at the earliest.

I could spit fire or do something useful. I did something I'd meant to do earlier – I drafted a piece for the parish mag appealing to my fellow villagers for tennis racquets and musical instruments in usable condition. That felt good too: all I needed was the editor's email address, which I could get from Melanie at the end of her break. Riding high, I contacted Chance to Shine: it would be good to have proper cricket coaches in the summer, and their charity achieved the most amazing results.

Ten minutes of lunchtime left? I deserved a reward. Shopping for clothes with a girlfriend would have fitted the bill nicely, but I had neither friend nor time. However, I was still a fairly standard size and could revert to the strategy I'd used when I was on the run: online shopping, delivered to the school itself. I would even go wild, and order next-day delivery. So there.

I'd just filled my first John Lewis basket and was ready to pay when Melanie phoned through. She normally popped her head round the door: this must be serious. The Digbys were in the building.

Should I quit now and lose all those lovely clothes? I saved the basket.

'Tell them I'll see them in ten minutes,' I said coolly. 'Offer them tea and a seat. And I'll come and escort them myself.'

I put some make-up on, not to mention my boots, which had been lurking under my chair. I cleared my desk of anything confidential. I phoned through to the staffroom to warn Tom to go straight to class. I typed with a speed that surprised me and printed off several documents.

Only then did I sally forth.

What Melanie hadn't told me was that the Digbys hadn't come alone. They'd brought a svelte, bone-thin woman in her thirties whom they introduced as their solicitor, Ms Fellows.

At least I had a big desk to reinforce my authority. Or hide behind.

There were only two visitors' chairs.

Suddenly I had another body in the room too. I'd warned Tom to make himself scarce, yet here he was, peering round my door, as penitent as it was possible to look without sackcloth and ashes. A swift look from me sent him back out again: I didn't want him complicating the issue, or, worse still, getting drawn into whatever battle was going on that even I didn't understand.

I phoned through to Melanie asking her to find another chair, acknowledging as I did so that it wasn't part of her job. And when she asked if she should bring more tea, I gave a swift negative response.

Bless her – she brought a child's chair. The svelte solicitor was suddenly reduced to a cartoon character, knees particularly knobbly as she tried to hitch down the sort of pencil skirt I'd seen no one except myself wear in the country. At least mine, with the accompanying stilettos as high as this woman's, had gone into the skip with the other ruined items. Trousers and boots felt altogether more appropriate.

With a smile, I gestured to the three of them: what did they want to say?

Ms Fellows uttered the sort of jargon that might have made sense if written in a letter but that had very little use as an oral utterance. The Digbys frowned and nodded as if they comprehended every last phoneme.

I reached for my pen. 'Since I have to report this conversation to the governors and probably to the council, may I just check that I am summarising accurately? You believe that Prudence Digby has suffered lasting psychological damage as a result of hearing an offensive word? And you believe that this damage can be redressed by punitive monetary damages and the permanent removal of the speaker from his post. Is that a reasonable precis?' I stressed the penultimate word slightly.

Was I mistaken? Surely Fellows flashed a quickly suppressed grin.

'If this is the case, you must see that I can't continue this conversation: it is a matter for the council's legal advisers, so I must wish you good day.' I stood.

They didn't.

So far, so good.

'Perhaps you have not yet received – rural mail is so slow, isn't it? – my formal apology for the incident. The teacher in question has accepted a written warning. The incident is on file. As Ms Fellows can tell you, this is very serious should he seek promotion here or anywhere else. On the other hand, he's getting the school some very favourable publicity as he leads a drive to get sports equipment for us: here's the press release sent to several local papers.' I passed over three copies.

Search for the next Andy Murray

Former tennis star Tom Mason, head of sport at Wrayford Primary School, wants his young charges to follow in his footsteps. But the children of Wrayford don't have any racquets. He's appealing to all tennis players – past and present – in the area, to donate any racquets they no longer use, whatever condition they're in. 'We want to give all youngsters the chance to participate in this most wonderful game,' says Tom, 35. 'It helps their fitness, develops

co-ordination and most of all is great fun.'
Please contact Tom at the school if you can help.

Ms Fellows shot the Digbys a glance. I wouldn't give them time to exchange words, however.

'But now I think we should address the issue of Prudence's persistent lateness in class. It is rude and disruptive to enter a room when everyone else is focusing on their learning experience.' I hated such clichés, but they deserved them for firing legal ones at me. 'Many of her comments to and about staff are completely inappropriate, whether in front of teachers or her peers. She refuses to accept criticism: as I am sure you're aware her handwriting is so poor that it would embarrass a Year Two child, but when offered help to improve it she declined, telling her teacher that no one needed to write by hand when computers were universal.'

'That's perfectly correct,' Mr Digby said. 'Who needs to worry about - what do you call them? Hooks? Loops?'

His wife joined in. 'When could you last read a professional's handwriting? I mean doctors, lawyers, and so on . . . I'm sure you'll agree that with her enormous talents she'll reach the top of her chosen profession. We thought her next school should fast-track her so she can aim for Cambridge when she's sixteen.'

Poor Prudence. When could she simply enjoy her childhood? But this wasn't the time to comment on their parenting skills.

I gave a non-committal nod. 'She has also started to lurk in corners, behind furniture, that sort of thing, apparently the better to . . . I hesitate to use the word *spy*. Let us describe what she does as eavesdropping.

You may wish to see this memorandum, the contents of which her class teacher would normally raise with you on parents' night. There is in fact talk of referring her to an educational psychiatrist to address her behaviour, which is making her very unpopular with her classmates. If it became known that she was responsible for the departure from the school of a well-liked and very talented teacher, whose own daughter is a pupil, I cannot imagine that the children would be very happy – or their parents, for that matter, with the eleven-plus looming over them.'

Mr Digby's nostrils flared. 'Are you trying to blackmail me?'

I gave a dry smile. 'What? In front of witnesses? I wouldn't be so stupid. What Tom did was very wrong, very wrong indeed. There is no excuse. He hasn't tried to make one. Within minutes he came to me to offer his sincere apologies. I'm sure he'll offer them to you, too, for his unprofessional behaviour. But I have a feeling that when we deal with young children least said is soonest mended, if you'll forgive the old saying. I'm not sure it would be in any way beneficial should he have to apologise face to face to a child who will be in his class next year.'

'If he's still teaching here,' Digby growled.

'And if she's still a pupil here!' Mrs Digby added, her voice rising in pitch. 'If he stays, we'll have no option but to take her away. We'll send her to Ewen House.'

I employed my best *I-know-you're-fibbing* expression. But I said nothing. They would know what I knew.

'Unfortunately the first class of the afternoon is still in progress,' I observed, 'but if you would like me to ask Tom to slip out for a minute or two, I could . . . If, however, you

125

feel you need a longer conversation I will have to ask you to wait till the bell goes for break. We are so short-staffed, as I'm sure Mr Dawes will have told you, that I haven't another teacher to spare to sit with the class.' My gamble paid off: they chose the shorter option.

Tom threatened his class with extinction if he could hear a sound when he returned to the room.

I could have stayed on guard, of course, but I wanted to witness his apology and the Digbys' response. He grovelled; they were appeased.

Possibly.

'What I can't understand,' Tom said, at the end of school, 'is why you were prepared to put your head on the block for me.' He was sitting, head in hands, on the chair lately occupied by Mr Digby. He was very close to tears.

I wasn't about to explain the principle of keeping potential enemies inside your tent pointing outwards rather than having them behaving badly on the outside. In any case, what I said was broadly true. 'If a head can't stand by a member of staff, we're living in a poor world. I chose a bad moment to ask you in public what I should have asked in private, so I was at fault too. What we now need to do is work better together. I've emailed the press release – there's a daily and a weekly paper, right? But I think you should contact the parish mag yourself. People in the village will know you and the personal touch will work better. Personally I'd be happy if you fronted the appeal for musical instruments too: we can't have music in the school without hours of practice at home, can we?'

'Right. Of course. Jane, I'm really, really grateful . . . I can't tell you—'

I cut him short with a grin and a wave of the hands: 'Tom, I've got a really urgent issue to deal with. Go home – shoo!'

I meant to give the impression, of course, that it was school work that was about to occupy me. There probably was something I should have been doing. But what I wanted to do was to complete my online order for new clothes. Then I could celebrate with one of Melanie's pikelets, propping up her radiator. She joined me, as I heaped praise on her for her dealings with the Digbys: we roared with laughter at the thought of the solicitor on the tiny chair. She was careful not to comment on the way I'd resolved the situation: I had a suspicion she didn't entirely agree with me. So I changed the subject: 'Can I ask you for a non-school bit of information? I met an elderly lady called Meg at morning service the other day – full of life and spirit. I'd love to invite myself round for the coffee she said she always has to hand, but I don't even know her full name.'

The mention of my churchgoing rounded Melanie's eyes. Then she narrowed them. 'There are several Megs. How old is yours?'

'Seventies? Lives in a very nice cottage near the church.'

'That doesn't narrow it down very far. Able-bodied?'

'Helped me clear a path down Church Hill.'

'Ah! Meg Webster. I'd have thought her place was not so much a cottage, more a candidate for the National Trust.' Melanie's tone had changed. Not for the better.

I went into neutral-but-jolly mode, as if I was praising a child's ugly artwork. 'It is splendid, isn't it? Not that I got beyond the kitchen.' I left the sentence hanging in mid air, fishing for more information.

'New money.' A distinct note of criticism oozed out.

Taken aback – I would have thought Melanie above such feudal distinctions – I asked mildly, 'What was her job, then?'

'No one's quite sure. She doesn't talk about her past.'

That made two of us. Actually, I'd registered how cautious Meg was on my behalf. Perhaps she was a kindred spirit in more ways than one. Suddenly I was too weary to continue what seemed to have become an interrogation.

'It's time you were off, Melanie – you work such long hours we must owe you weeks of time off in lieu.'

She blinked, jerking her head back as if attacked by a midge.

Was this an entirely new concept? I explained how it had worked in my old schools. But I seemed to have offended her.

'We don't all work just for the money, you know.'

'Who does in teaching?' I asked mildly. 'Melanie, are you OK? Has someone done something to annoy you? Have I offended you somehow?'

She took a deep breath. 'Mrs Gough would have sacked Tom, whatever the repercussions.'

'I don't have that power: only the governors do. I'll say to you what I'd say to them and what I've already said to the Digbys and their knobbly-kneed lawyer: with staffing this close to the bone the kids can't afford to lose a good teacher.' I was about to come out with the tent theory again, but I thought better of it. 'In any other school the head could simply stand in and take classes. But tell me where

I'd find the time.' Can you believe it? I choked back a sob!

She looked at me with less condemnation. 'And of course it's your first headship. Never mind, Jane, some things come more easily with experience.' So I was half-forgiven.

'And with having a roof over your head and time to buy a supply of clean clothes,' I said affably. 'OK, it's really time to call it a day. I've got a pile of marking to do and a mountain of prep. If I need to nag other people to have up-to-date lesson plans, I can't get behind with my own. Oh, just to let you know I'm expecting a few private deliveries here: those clothes I just mentioned. If I'm in class, could you stow everything out of sight? I don't want any passing governor to get the impression that either of us is running a mail-order business.'

'I've booked myself into the village pub and that's all there is to it,' Pat declared when he phoned that night, interrupting as I drafted a lesson on the apostrophe. 'You don't know about village life, that's clear. That lot get so much as a whisper that you've got a bloke – they'd probably call me your fancy man – staying over at yours, your name'll be mud. Trust me. Plus, I shall be able to keep my ears and eyes open and see what gossip I can pick up. I'll see you in the bar at one, OK?'

It had to be OK. I had too much work to prepare to argue – but at least I could look forward to my clothes delivery.

Which came, after an all-day wait, when I had sent everyone home, including Melanie, at six twenty-five. Just as I'd given up hope. Tom had dropped by a copy of the letter he'd written to the parish news. He'd got an interview

129

with both of the local papers and a photo shoot due with one for next Tuesday. The kids had behaved and Prudence had slid into class only a minute after the others, though I had a suspicion that she'd been talking to Robert – not a good combination. I'd got a lot of marking done. So I could celebrate my last night at the Mondiale with a good long swim and an excellent meal.

Tomorrow might be just another day but at least it promised hope in the form of Egyptian cotton sheets and a new outfit or two.

But then, on the dot of six-thirty, came one last email, telling me that the governors wished to convene another meeting for ten the next morning.

It's not often I stare in disbelief. But I almost had to push my jaw back into its original place it had dropped so far.

If I had allowed my blind fury to take over, I would have lost my job. Of course I couldn't be there at ten: I would be moving into a temporary sanctuary. Rationally, I accepted that Brian Dawes couldn't have known that. But I also knew that to call a meeting at such short notice, sending through the email (no agenda again) at a time when I could rightfully have left the building, was at very least unreasonable.

I wrote and discarded several drafts. At last I settled on this:

Good evening, Mr Dawes,
Thank you for calling a governors' meeting for tomorrow. I am sure that there is plenty to discuss. In fact, it would be beneficial if we could move it back till 3 p.m., provided that that is acceptable to all those participating.

Perhaps you would be kind enough to forward the agenda so that I may obtain any information you may require to ensure an efficient use of everyone's time.

Having called his bluff, I had, of course, to prepare for a lot of eventualities. It wasn't until after eight that I finished. But just as I was about to sign off the computer one last time, an email arrived from Mark Stephens, Acting Secretary to the Governors. Sadly, so many people had sent in their apologies for a meeting at any time the next day, he said, that the meeting would not be quorate, and he would have to discuss rescheduling it with the Chair. If that didn't merit one last Mondiale Prosecco I didn't know what did.

CHAPTER THIRTEEN

Designer jeans might have felt right in Dove Cottage, but ordinary workaday ones didn't. Sadly that was all I had: to my disproportionate disappointment not all of my order – which in any case didn't run to designer jeans – had arrived. I could do very smart or very shabby: which would better fit Pat's notion of suitable gear for a pub lunch? I settled for some fairly smart culottes, with boots, of course, and a bright cashmere scarf under my parka – the weather was threatening to blow up yet more snow, French or otherwise. Walking poles? I dismissed them as an affectation since Dove Cottage was only a few metres from the main road, where the pavement had been liberally doused with salt spray.

If the wind outside was bitter cold, The Jolly Cricketers was cosy enough, with the same roaring fire and radiators pumping out satisfactory amounts of heat. There was no sign of Pat. I opened a tab, and established myself at the table I'd chosen before, nursing a G&T.

Diane swept in as I read the menu. 'You've been busy,

haven't you?' It didn't sound like a compliment. 'Talk about new brooms.' Neither did that.

I decided to take it as one. 'I'm lucky to have such amazing staff – all so hard-working and committed.'

'All of them?'

'Every last one. Even the visiting teachers. Did you know the music teacher has to bring along his own music stands as well as the children's instruments? In fact,' I said, 'I wonder if your customers could do something about that. We've put an appeal in the parish mag for instruments people don't play any longer but would hate to throw away. But the personal touch would be so much better – if I could put a poster up in here? Even organise a fundraiser?'

'The grass doesn't grow under your feet, does it?' She narrowed her eyes. 'When were you thinking of?'

'When's a slack time of year for you? We'd need to get the PTA involved . . .'

'And – not that it's any of my business –the governors, I'd say. Because I might want to do a bit of a deal. We support your musicians if you support our cricketers. They've lost the field they used to play on – it's all pegged out for that new housing development.'

'And we've got a lovely big playing field that's begging to be used. I'm sure we could find somewhere in the school for them to change. Diane – it's OK to call you that? – I'm sure we could do a deal. Governors permitting, of course.'

She gave a dry grin. 'It might not be as straightforward as that. But drop round one Monday evening – it's usually quiet then, and we'll talk a bit more. In the meantime, yes, you can put up a poster. I'd best get back to work.' She bustled to the bar, all smiles, to serve Pat. 'Room all right, Mr Webber?'

'Excellent, thanks. Hi, Jane!' He waved across to me.

'I've set up a tab,' I said, getting up to give him a social double-kiss.

'In that case, half of whatever beer you recommend, please, Diane. Thanks.'

Diane fluttered in response to his smile as if he were George Clooney.

As he'd done several times in the past, Pat rolled up his sleeves (yes, it was warm enough in Dove Cottage to do that) and helped me settle in. Not that there was much to do once I'd hung up my few remaining old and the sparse new clothes in the vast wardrobe. While I loaded the triple-A washing machine, suddenly realising what a luxury it was, especially as it came with a matching tumble dryer, he simply padded round touching things. What seemed to please him most was the soft-close kitchen drawers: he opened each in turn, cooing over the contents – top-of-the-range pans and china, not just crockery – before tapping them and watching them slide home. But he also appeared to like the bathroom, and who wouldn't? It occupied more space than the entire ground floor of the caretaker's house, and was infinitely warmer. Without invitation he moved into the bedrooms, first the master and its en suite, then the other.

'All very nice,' he said. 'But before you settle down on that sofa, let's stretch our legs. I like walking in the snow. OK,' he continued, almost seamlessly, as we set out across the courtyard, 'how do you feel about the place?'

'Amazed I should have fallen on my feet,' I said. 'But uneasy: why should I get such luck?'

'It's about time you did. But I'm not picking up happy, relieved vibes, Avo.'

'Funnily enough, I'm not picking them up from you, either.'

He looked genuinely disconcerted. 'Eh?'

'Were you looking for something when you were drooling over the fittings and fitments?' I asked bluntly.

'Should I have been?'

'Probably not. Sorry. It's just me who does that: Simon's legacy.'

He nodded. 'Still in therapy?'

'My Blackburn therapist is trying to refer me to a colleague the other side of Canterbury . . . But she's on sabbatical till the end of February. In any case, I simply don't have time to hurtle round the countryside just to talk to someone about my past. I'm so short of time I've had to buy all my replacement clothes online.'

'Come on: you know that it's more than just talking about your past. It's preparing the ground for you to have a future.' He pushed himself gently across a thickly frozen puddle. 'Hey, people pay pounds to do this in Centenary Square in Brum. Mind you,' he conceded, wobbling to an ungainly halt, 'you can pay a few more quid to hire a plastic penguin to skate with and hold you up.'

I couldn't give him a proper conducted tour round the village because I'd barely seen any of it in daylight, let alone walked round it. So we just mooched. We passed

135

the sad empty frontage of the abandoned shop, a former branch library ripe for redevelopment, the Rectory, a magnificent Georgian building, the three Bentleys parked in front of it suggesting that this was not where Mark Stephens lived, and at last, as we approached the school, an undistinguished house admitting under its breath that it was the vicarage.

By now it was almost too dark to read the times of service on the church noticeboard, but the beams from our mobiles penetrated the condensation enough for us to decide that there was a Common Worship (whatever that was) at nine-thirty the next morning. Pat decreed that we would be there, arriving separately.

'What's this all about?' I asked, stung. 'Is there some problem with Dove Cottage? Not literary enough for you?'

'Don't be daft.' He set us in motion down the lane, which was already beginning to freeze over. 'This is a village, Avo. Like I said, I stay at yours and it'll be all over the village. Seems to me you've got enough problems, girl, without carelessly adding to them. Bloody hell,' he added, as he nearly measured his length, 'where's a sodding plastic penguin when you need one?'

This time the congregation was a little larger, twenty or so. Most of the ladies sported wonderful fur hats, not many faux fur either, I suspected. I wish I'd been brave enough to sport a bobble hat: as it was I was grateful for my thick crop of hair. Brian Dawes and Toby Wells took their places in the front pew. Mrs Tibbs scuttled into the one behind them. Sadly there was no sign of Meg Webster.

I wasn't the only one to stare when we stood to sing the

first hymn. All these years that Pat had helped and supported me and to my shame I hadn't even known he sang, let alone that he was a tenor of pretty well professional standard. The choirmaster, if that's the term for an elderly man beating time for three equally elderly wobbly sopranos and a youngish booming alto, didn't have my inhibitions. He turned in mid verse with the most beatific expression on his face. Once the service was over, he positively elbowed his way through the parishioners and shook Pat by the hand, almost embracing him.

I took a step back: let the two men enjoy their musical talk. Mrs Tibbs nodded at me with a social smile, but her words weren't especially kind: 'Still burning the midnight oil, I see?'

'And today it'll be a bit of afternoon oil too,' I said affably. 'Better the day, my mother used to say, better the deed. I've had no responses from parents about those disgusting football shirts and I propose to get rid of them before school tomorrow.'

'I can't argue with that. Such an eyesore on that house. At least no one could have seen the refuse sack.'

'I hope not. They were so rank and smelly after their soaking I couldn't have had them back in the building – a health hazard, I'm sure.'

'And of course Health and Safety is king these days. Poor Mrs Gough got tired of being supposed to do risk assessments for simply everything.'

'I'm sure every head does,' I said diplomatically. But I said it to thin air. She had found someone else to speak to, a woman with a hat that was surely mink.

As the rest of the congregation absorbed her into

their huddle – I was reminded irreverently of emperor penguins – Mark took pity on my isolation and addressed himself to me, his smile, though tired to the point of exhaustion, gently conspiratorial. He eased me towards the font, massive and surely Saxon in origin. 'We governors rotate the role of secretary,' he said quietly. 'I thought it was time to exercise some common sense over these weekend meetings. If we're not careful we shall have one every Saturday, and it happens,' he added dryly, 'to be the day I write my sermon.'

'I wish I could say I was a connoisseur of sermons. But I've never been a churchgoer. Until now,' I conceded, in response to his smile. 'Anyway, it sounded very good to me: concise and beautifully argued. Who could ask for more?'

'Taking a text from *The Guardian* was a bit of a risk,' he said. 'I knew I could get away with it with the usual stalwarts, but I didn't expect such distinguished company.' His eyes slid towards Dawes. You know,' he said, unexpectedly easing us out into the icy porch, considerately closing the heavy door behind us to keep the feeble warmth inside, 'I might like to take up your offer of the church hall for Sunday worship while the weather's this cold. It's not without its risks, but on the quiet I've sounded out some of the governors and many are sympathetic to the idea.'

'But not all? You'd need a clear majority,' I warned. 'Does anyone have power of veto?'

He looked swiftly over my shoulder; the door was opening and Toby Wells shot out so fast he almost knocked Mark over. Over his shoulder he shouted something about swimming lessons.

Mark sighed. 'I know of many parents giving up chunks

of valuable weekends to get their kids to pools. And junior rugby. And cricket nets.'

'I've never been one for getting fit while getting wet myself, but I can't deny the benefits. Even if it does mean sprinting out of church,' I said.

'Is that friend of yours – the good-looking young man with the voice – staying long?'

'Pat? Just for the weekend. Because we had no idea of the accommodation I was going to be offered he's observing the proprieties and staying at The Jolly Cricketers.'

'Oh! You're not—?'

'Not in that sort of relationship, no. Old friends,' I added firmly.

'And an old friend is better than a new lover,' he agreed quaintly. 'It's a pity for the choir's sake he's only a visitor. If he's kidnapped and only appears in church on Sundays, please don't be surprised.'

'I'll try not to be. I just hope for your congregation's sake that it's for Sundays in the school hall.'

Pat insisted on a brisk walk, followed by an early lunch at the pub. I steered the conversation to him this time, in particular, of course, to his previously hidden talent.

'What else is there I don't know about you?' I joked, only to see shutters of a surprising formality come down. 'After all these years,' I added, referring to his strange reluctance as much as the past.

'You only know me as your support officer,' he said.

Slapped verbally in the face, I took moments to respond. 'Of course. We've always talked about my needs, my feelings. But we've had a lot of other conversations,

Pat – about your parents wanting you to be a doctor, about your sister wanting to go into politics but pulling out when your mother got cancer. Your car crash. Your marathon training. A lot of people would say I know you quite well. But I can see now I don't. Is there stuff you can't tell me?' Did he have a wife and children, for instance? And if so, how did they feel about his trotting round the countryside all hours of the night and day, and even at weekends – when there might well be children's swimming lessons? Somehow I couldn't ask outright. And if he had, he wasn't going to admit it freely right now.

'Well, I can tell you this: my gaffer wants to pull me out of what I'm doing now. With all these budget cuts there's a dire shortage of bodies. And he reckons that now Simon's been sent down for so long, I ought to be doing something else. I didn't want to tell you straight out like this. I told him I wanted you to suggest it – to say that you could take your L-plates off and drive on your own now.'

My chin went up. 'I'm sure I can.' It's a good job that working with kids teaches you to lie convincingly.

He touched his water glass to mine. 'Well, I'm damned sure you can't. Not until you've really found your feet in this village. And in the school. You might have that vicar eating out of your hand, but a lot more would rather bite it off. And I can't see for the life of me why. What I'll do is try to nip down at the end of the week – I doubt if it'll be the whole weekend, mind – and I'll sniff around some more.'

It sounded as if he was about to leave now, when I'd somehow persuaded myself that I had his company for the afternoon, at least. My voice as even as I could make it, I asked, 'What has your nose told you so far?'

'Nothing I could put my finger on, if you forgive yet another mixed metaphor. If it's any consolation, I don't think they've anything against you personally. But no small community likes change, and though you're acting on orders from Ofsted, people don't know that. The vicar's not exactly Mr Popular, either: apparently even the sainted Mrs Gough had a row with him, and he only started to take occasional assemblies after she'd retired. Did you know he's not picking up a salary or whatever the C of E calls it? He's a "house for duty" priest – in other words, he lives rent-free in quite a nice house but pays for it by leading services and doing pastoral work.'

'How on earth can he afford that?' I demanded. 'How can anyone work for free? Freeish,' I conceded.

'I gather he joined the church quite late in life – he'd already had another career when he had the call.'

'It must have been a pretty lucrative one to fund – how many years of penury?'

'Ten, fifteen years?'

'A very lucrative one. And why stay, if he's never really fitted in? I tell you, I won't stay that long, unless things improve,' I promised either him or myself. 'Anyone else in their black books?'

'Not by name. The question for you is whether you're going to strike up an alliance with the vicar – safety in numbers – or whether you're going to keep a safe distance from him.'

'And thus avoid adding his enemies to my existing ones? It seems sensible but not very moral. In any case, I've already suggested he applies to the governors for permission to use the school hall while the church boiler is out of commission.'

He rolled his eyes. 'Looks as if you've already nailed your colours to the mast, then.'

'So you're into naval as opposed to nasal metaphors now. Time – cliché alert! – for you to hit the road, isn't it, Pat? The weather forecast's pretty poor, isn't it? Again!'

'And for the next few days. Whatever happened to global warming?'

'They decided to call it climate change – which is what this is, just that it's cold when we've come to expect mildness.'

He rolled his eyes at my teacherliness. 'And what'll you do? Hunker down in your new palace?'

I shook my head. 'I shall be back in school. I want to get rid of those shirts once and for all and attack another couple of boxes – either because they're full of useless rubbish or because it'll provide something else for our nice neighbourhood cop, PC Lloyd Davies, to worry about.'

'More porn? Let's hope you don't find anything worse. And, no messing, call me or this Davies guy if you do. It's not exactly hiding in plain sight, but it's not a bad idea, stashing stuff in an overfull school stockroom. It'd be more sensible to sort it out during school hours, though. Wouldn't it?' he prompted me.

'It would. But there aren't exactly hours of spare time when the kids are there. And wearing gardening clothes isn't entirely compatible with my head teacher image.'

We said an awkward farewell in the pub car park. I wasn't at all sure what had gone wrong, and was as usual inclined to blame myself. I knew from bitter experience that the only way to stop myself going over and over every word of every conversation was to get physical. It was the stockroom for me this afternoon. Or perhaps, I thought, as the snow came down again, I should confine myself to getting rid of the noxious shirts and retreat to what was rapidly becoming a holiday igloo for the rest of the day.

At least, I reflected, as I burnt midnight oil marking, I wouldn't get complaints about burning the school's.

CHAPTER FOURTEEN

'Prudence! What is going on in that child's head?' Helen demanded as she poured cold water into her mid morning tea. From the expression on her face it was still too hot to drink comfortably. 'It's the third time I've chased her out of the staff loos. She says they're nicer than the girls' and we're being authoritarian and elitist to reserve them for our use.'

'What did you say?' asked Tom.

'I asked her whether in the interests of equality we should have gender-free loos too. Mistake. Never do sarcasm with Prudence. She said every school now needed ones for people transitioning. Precocious or what?'

'Or what, I'd say. Except I daren't say anything. Not to or about Prudence. The boss saved my bacon once: I can't gamble on that again.'

'Let's look on the bright side,' I said, making them both jump. 'Sorry – I didn't mean to lurk. We've only got Prudence for another eighteen months: her parents have her for life.'

'If she lives that long,' Helen observed. 'Jane: do you want to deal with her?'

'It looks a bit over the top if I do. Did you get anything more out of young Robert, by the way?'

She shook her head. 'It's strange: he's always been such a docile, biddable kid. But I found him going through the classroom waste bin the other day. And more worrying, by my desk – and I'd left my laptop open on it.'

'Robert? Robert Bowman? But he's such a sweetie he could play a sheep in the Nativity without needing any disguise,' Liz declared. 'Someone's pulling his strings, you mark my words. The only question is who.'

A frantic knocking on the staffroom door prevented any speculation: it was Lucy, one of the tiniest children in year one, with the news that Rosie had fallen in the playground and there was blood. As if to testify to the seriousness of Rosie's injury, she threw up over Tom's shoes. '999, the playground lady said,' she added through her mess.

When I got outside, having got Melanie to make the call and look after Lucy, Rosie was still lying on the playground, presumably where she had fallen. Her head was cradled by Kate Morgan, a solidly reliable woman, who had stripped off her coat to cover the injured child. Rose was crying that her leg hurt, though it was also clear that her arm was badly broken. Liz, who was our first-aider, eased a foil blanket under and round her, but insisted she shouldn't be moved. The other kids were being shooed away by Fearn, with amazing composure and authority. The quiet was disconcerting – it was as if a hundred breaths were being held, any conversations as muted as at a funeral. Then at last we all heard a siren. The sigh of relief was palpable. Tom, now in trainers, ran into the road to flag down the longed for ambulance. Then there was a gasp of disappointment: all we had was a medic on a motorbike. But at least he was an expert. He praised Kate and Liz, comforted Rosie and got to work. The leg injury, it seemed, was no more than a couple of cuts and a bad case of gravel rash. It was the arm that was the real problem. I'm sure I wasn't the only one to pick up the stress on the word *real*.

We marched the children back to their classrooms via the kitchen to prevent further rubber-necking and, of course, the trauma of seeing blood that parents like the Digbys would insist had ruined their kids' psyches for life. Fearn volunteered to take Liz's class as long as she needed to be with Rosie. So far, so good. And even better when a proper ambulance arrived.

No one but me could break to her family the news that Rosie was on her way to hospital. The responsible adult was listed as her grandfather, Richard Morris, the governor who had helped me with the traffic problems. To my relief, he took the news philosophically enough; thanking me for sending Liz in the ambulance with Rosie, he said that it was more important for him to get to A&E than to bother with any questions now. Although I agreed, I offered to involve the police.

'For a playground accident? You're joking.'

'Some schools do. But I prefer the common sense approach. So thank you.' Meanwhile I promised that if possible a written report would be waiting in his in-box when he got back home.

Not that it was going to be easy to write. Or to find out what ought to be in it. Lucy, by now thoroughly hysterical and still throwing up, needed her mother, who was teaching on the far side of the county: it was one thing for Melanie to deal with tears, another to expect her to deal with endless vomit. Kate, who had acted so promptly and calmly, was now in a state of near collapse, blaming herself because she hadn't actually seen the accident. So who had?

If only I had more staff to turn to.

I didn't. Taking the plastic bucket from Melanie, I said the only thing I could think of. 'While I empty this, can you find Mr Dawes's number, please?'

Dawes brought welcome reinforcements with him: Mrs Walker and Mrs Tibbs, who knew Lucy and sat with her in Melanie's office.

'This is what I propose, but this is a serious incident and I felt the governors should be involved from the start,' I said, seating the first two in my office. 'Firstly, although Richard doesn't want to call the police to investigate a playground accident, I feel I must offer you the option anyway.'

Dawes almost spluttered. 'You can't be serious. These are children, not criminals.'

The women nodded.

'Excellent. I'd be very much against it myself, but I'm pleased to have your agreement. An in-house enquiry is best, at this stage at least. Now, I'd like to keep all the children together in the hall – I've got some reasonably educational videos that will keep them in one place and take their minds off things. We have, apparently, three witnesses, two girls and a boy, and I feel it would be better to talk to them separately.' Why was I worried that one of them was Robert?

Mrs Walker nodded sagely. 'We don't want them hysterically imagining details and having their friends corroborate them, do we? Do you need us as childminders or as witnesses?'

'We should question them, surely?'

'No, that would be too intimidating, Brian. I'll sit in with the girls, shall I, Jane? And Brian with the boy?'

'Excellent idea.' But Dawes's smile disappeared as he turned to me. 'What about the playground supervisor? How could she let such a serious accident happen?'

'I gather Kate was speaking to another child – but I want it put on record that she dealt quite admirably with the accident the moment she became aware of it.'

'Good. But I think we should speak to her all the same, don't you?'

Where had I got the idea that the governors were intimidating? Today they were simply helpful professionals.

Suspiciously, questioned in my office, all three children said almost the same thing. Or the same nothing. Yes, they'd been standing near where Rosie fell, but no, they'd not seen her actually fall.

'Could she have tripped?' I asked Robert.

'Suppose so. All these kids running round – it's obvious someone's going to fall on the ice, isn't it?'

Robert, making an adult observation like that?

'How many children have you seen falling on the ice?'

'A few. Before we learnt how to slide. And grown-ups. Because they don't know about sliding.'

I could hear Terry, the oil delivery driver's words: *But you know what they say: 'Did you fall or were you pushed?'*

And I recalled my own headlong tumble. Surely nothing to do with Robert – Robert, who was ideal casting for a gentle sheep. 'Could she have been tripped?'

'I didn't see anyone trip her,' he said flat-voiced, as if he'd been coached. 'Someone should have stopped children running around if it wasn't safe.'

'Didn't someone tell all you children not to run around?' I asked. I might be keen on getting at the truth but I couldn't bargain on Dawes remaining amicable. 'During assembly? Every morning? No?'

A mutter eventually suggested that he might have heard me speak a few words on the subject.

The girls, both in Tom's top-year class, were both inclined to surliness, the sort of thing I usually associate with hormonal adolescents. They shared Robert's inclination to blame people supposedly in charge.

I smelt blood. My own.

Fortunately Felicity Walker didn't buy their theory. She told first one, then the other, that Ms Morgan was an excellent supervisor. And then she asked, firing the question I'd been longing to put, 'If you didn't actually see Rosie fall, why do you say you're a witness?'

The first child, Emma Hamilton, hedged; she was a girl so beautiful and so aware of her gifts that she looked as if later in life she could have a latter-day Nelson at her feet. She was very bright, too; already her teachers were predicting Oxbridge for her. She said she'd just happened to be the first on the spot after Robert. Ten minutes later, in the same scenario, Sophia (never Sophie), who happened to be the daughter of Toby Wells, one of our governors, said much the same.

'In short,' I said, when the last child had returned to the hall, 'no one had actually seen a perpetrator, and all complained that they weren't supervised properly. Moreover, they all came forward as witnesses. Why?'

'Do you think there could actually be a problem with Kate Morgan?' Dawes asked. 'I know you said she did everything she could, but she wasn't actually on hand when the accident happened.'

'This is the first time I've ever heard any sort of complaint against her.' I brought up her confidential file. 'No, there's nothing here on the computer – Mrs Gough wrote her a glowing testimonial when she thought of training to become a classroom assistant.' I turned the screen so they could see it.

Mrs Tibbs – Alison – read it infuriatingly slowly. At last she looked up. 'I've occasionally watched her from my bedroom window.' Was it she who lived in Old School House? Who accidentally or deliberately hijacked my oil delivery? 'It may seem to some like spying –' I suspected her eyes slid in my direction – ' but the governors' duty is to the school.' Including checking on how I was increasing the school's fuel bills, no doubt. 'I've never seen anything to suggest she's not doing her best. Of course, all the children want to talk to her, but she stands tall and looks around even while she's holding their hands.'

I had a sudden vision of Kate as a meerkat. I suppressed it firmly. 'Mr Dawes?'

'All three singing from the same hymn sheet. That's what I thought,' he snorted. 'Robert's a big lad – he could easily have tripped the poor little child.'

'Robert? Do anything unkind? To be honest, I don't

think he's got the brains,' Felicity said. 'Jane – you're keeping very quiet.'

'I don't actually know these children as well you do, of course. But I do know children in general. And like you, Chair, I think those stories, or lack of them, sound rehearsed. Organised.' And I could only think of one child with the brains and personality to organise it. 'But before I say anything more I really think we should see if Kate's able to talk to us.'

She was. She was more green than pale, and still visibly shaking. Tears kept welling into her eyes.

'If I don't blame myself, who can I blame?' she demanded, as Felicity tried to assure her that no one suspected her of any wrongdoing. 'It happened on my watch!'

'But you can't be everywhere and you can't have eyes in the back of your head,' Felicity said. 'And you certainly weren't responsible for the effect of gravity on a falling object.' She pushed the plate of biscuits across. 'Please – sugar's supposed to be good for a shock. Or have they decided it's bad these days? You look as if you need a stiff brandy.'

Dawes looked at me. 'I don't suppose—?'

'Not on school premises,' I assured him. 'But I could organise some coffee – or a cup of tea? Excuse me a moment.'

Lucy's mother had apparently just taken her still ailing daughter away. Despite the cold, Melanie had thrown open all the windows. She'd obviously been liberal with the air-freshener too, but nothing could eradicate the smell of vomit. She looked as if she herself was ready to throw up too.

'Go home and shower and change,' I said. 'Wash your hair, too. Then you'll feel much better.' I held up a hand as she began to argue: 'Use some of that time off in lieu I mentioned. Off you go. And, Melanie, bring us some fresh milk and a supply of biscuits on your way back – that should ease your conscience if nothing else will.'

I got the impression that the governors had used my absence to try to put Kate at ease: her colour was better, and her hand, taking the mug, was steadier.

All three looked at me expectantly.

'I'm not in the blame game where children on the loose are concerned. I know they ignore instructions – they take no notice of No Entry signs, are selectively deaf when instructions are given and often make me think there's something in the doctrine of original sin. All I want to hear – all we all want to hear – is what happened in your area of the playground. Any tantrums? Any tears? Any exciting little secrets whispered in your ear?'

'Tash lost a glove; Ian found it. Connor and Dale started kicking snow; some flew in the direction of Angelica, you know, the Turners' youngest, who set up a howl. All pretty normal. Prudence found a scrunchie, which she handed to me. She speculated whose it might be. I told her I'd look after it and lodge it with Melanie as lost property, but she said she'd go and ask every girl with long hair if she'd lost it.' She stopped, frowning.

'Did she? Go and ask the other girls?'

'No. She didn't. She kept messing with her own hair – I almost thought she wanted me to hand over the scrunchie

152

to her. Then I heard the scream. The rest you know. There was a lot of blood.'

I caught her eye, and mouthed, 'Make sure I have the cleaning bill for your coat. Right?'

Dawes had been writing, and now looked up. 'So you didn't see anything of the accident?'

'I was so distracted by the scrunchie business. But Robert was very close to Rosie, very close indeed. You should ask him.'

'Emma and Sophia?'

'Miles away. OK, yards – except I should call them metres. Looking at something in Sophia's hand.'

'Not at the accident?'

'No. In fact they were probably the only kids in the playground who didn't turn round and start running towards Rosie.'

Felicity and I exchanged glances; we all did.

'As a matter of interest, what do you make of these kids – Robert, for example?' Felicity asked.

'He's never going to win *Mastermind*, is he, poor lad? Generally nice. Always waves to me if we meet in the village.'

'The girls?'

'Ten going on thirty. That's Sophia and Emma. As for Prudence – do you know, I get the feeling that she thinks I'm beneath her. Snooty little madam. But she doesn't mix very well. Doesn't do girly giggles with the others. She's – she's a watcher, not a joiner in.'

'She's wasted in the playground,' Alison declared, as Kate closed the door behind her. 'What a pity she didn't go in for that retraining.'

'I wonder what stopped her. I'll make sure I speak to her about it – try to persuade her to have another shot.' I made a note. If I wasn't careful it would get lost in all the other notes. 'Lord, is that the time! The kids should be breaking for lunch in three minutes. I'm quite sure my colleagues have everything in hand but I would just like to check.' And to see if Melanie was back, of course. And to remind everyone that there had to be a staff meeting this afternoon, albeit one with a different item dominating the agenda.

Alison and Felicity exchanged a glance. 'I'm quite sure that between us we could organise a light lunch,' Alison said. 'There is clearly work still to be done here, and though we could adjourn to my house, I am quite sure that you would rather stay here, Jane. So the picnic will come to you. Brian – is that acceptable to you?'

'I could do with stretching my legs. I'll come and be your native porter.'

Did they want to talk about me behind my back? Just at the moment I hardly cared. I had a school to run, and that meant the speediest possible return to normality.

CHAPTER FIFTEEN

As long as Fearn was prepared to stand in for Liz, with Tom combining his class and mine in the hall, we could have fairly normal afternoon lessons. But nothing else felt normal. A sandwich lunch with the governors, complete with china plates and linen napkins brought in an old-fashioned wicker picnic basket, didn't feel normal. Neither did the offer of wine, which all three of us women declined, leaving Dawes to sip claret on his own. From a crystal glass, of course. The subject that taxed us most was whether we should question Prudence, and if so, how.

'Let me lay my cards on the table,' I said, wondering whether to keep one or two up my sleeve anyway. 'Mr Dawes and I had a measure of disagreement over the way I dealt with a previous issue involving Prudence. You've seen copies of my correspondence with the parents, and my account of our meeting. For obvious reasons, I don't wish to be seen in any way as pursuing a vendetta against the child. We are aware that the parents wouldn't hesitate to involve their legal adviser again if they thought I was.

But she does, on occasion, behave quite inappropriately, challenging teachers' authority. She's now insisting on using the staff loo, for instance.'

'Have you spoken to her parents?' Alison asked.

'I decided that this was a matter for her class teacher to deal with. The lower key the better.' I risked a glance at Dawes. His face was completely impassive.

'Quite right,' Felicity said. 'She's clearly constantly seeking attention, and in other circumstances I would say that her strange conversation with Kate was just another aspect of this. However, its timing . . . One of us really ought to have a good hard talk with her. Not to make any accusations.'

'She'll know if you single her out,' I warned. 'She's a very bright girl indeed. Right at the top of her peer group.'

'So we have to talk to other pupils too – then it looks as if she's just been picked at random. It's all very time-consuming, however,' Alison sighed, looking at her watch.

'Five minutes with each child? Teams of two?' Dawes said, also checking the time. 'Names out of a hat?'

Of course, Dawes's name was plucked out to partner me. And of course we got Prudence to talk to, after the youngest in reception who mercifully hadn't seen anything because she was brushing her teddy bear's fur.

'In my opinion,' Prudence declared, 'this was an accident waiting to happen.' Her adult vocabulary failed her in the next sentence, however. 'The playground lady keeps talking to the children. She doesn't watch all the time.'

'What should she have watched today?' I asked.

'Children running around. Sliding. Building in the snow.'

'What did you watch today?'

'Where to put my feet.'

'And Rosie? Where was she putting her feet?'

'How should I know?'

'Did you actually see her fall?'

'No. I heard the scream. But I shouldn't think she was pushed, would you? Or tripped? A lot of children do stupid things like running round because the playground lady isn't watching properly. Especially boys. One might even have been chasing her. It wouldn't happen if the teachers were outside watching us.' Thus spake the senior Digbys, no doubt.

'It must have been awful to hear that scream,' I said. 'What did you do?'

'What everyone else did, I suppose – turned to have a look.'

'And where were you?' Dawes asked. 'Who were you playing with at the time?'

Prudence's look told Dawes all too clearly that she didn't do playing.

'So what were you doing?' he pursued.

'Wondering what to do with a scrunchie I'd found – looking to see if anyone's hair had come down and I could give it to her. Or to him, of course – the boys are supposed to have their hair tied back these days, aren't they, Ms Cowan? In the interests of equality, I suppose.'

Dawes stared at her flowing locks. 'An edict honoured more in the breach than the observance, I see.'

She was nonplussed for the first time.

My turn. 'You were obviously being very public-spirited. Thank you. So what happened to the lost scrunchie? Have you still got it?'

Her eyes widened. 'Is someone accusing me of stealing it?'

'Not that I know of. All I want to know is what you did with it.'

'So you can announce it at assembly? A scrunchie?' Her contempt was palpable.

I think I stared her down.

Dawes said, 'It was a simple question, Prudence. A simple answer, if you please.'

'I meant to give it to the school secretary. But in the confusion I may have given it to the playground supervisor. Yes, I'm sure I did. Perhaps she forgot to hand it in.' She shook her head in apparent despair.

'Did you talk long?' he persisted.

'With all that panic going on? I don't think so!' Her tone suggested not so much lack of doubt on her part but stupidity on his for asking the question.

'That's pretty well all then, Prudence,' I said. 'Just one thing,' I added, as she stood up. 'If you did think someone might have pushed or tripped poor little Rosie, it wouldn't be telling tales if you told us – it would be whistle-blowing, I'd say.'

Shaking her head, she made her way to the door. 'If only you permitted phones in school we could have taken pictures. If only there were more staff on duty, or CCTV. Is that all? Because that's the bell for change of lesson.' She left without waiting for a reply.

Dawes appeared to be washing his face. 'What a piece of work! To think I thought you were victimising her.'

'She's certainly very unusual,' I said mildly. 'I have to pinch myself sometimes to remind myself that for all her amazing verbal skills, she's a child, and probably a very unhappy one.'

'Unhappy? Isn't Rosie Morris the one who should be unhappy right now?'

'Right now. But in general she's very sunny, full of wonder and delight. I'd say she was very happy – and she has that wonderful relationship with her grandfather. And she didn't deserve to be tripped or pushed today. As young Prudence rightly observed, we really need CCTV. Which should have been fitted today, but for a missing component. Life is full of ifs and maybes, though . . .' I allowed myself to drop the ruminations: 'What do you think we should do about Prudence and her possible role in today's events, Mr Dawes?'

'Oh, I think after today we know each other well enough to use Christian names, don't you, Jane? You're right to worry that the parents will accuse you of pursuing a vendetta. And we have no proof. If they get restive, refer them straight to me. Now, if we put pressure on Robert and the two girls, they'll no doubt go running off to their parents who'll want *their* solicitors involved. We want something both light enough to put off accusers and heavy enough to deter a repetition.'

'My instinct is for me to ask an outsider in to lay down the law. If I invite you into assembly to do it, it'll make your impartiality suspect. So I'm wondering if a policeman acquaintance of mine might pay us a quick visit.'

'The handsome black man with the wonderful singing voice?'

I looked at him quizzically, but the question I put was serious: 'How did you know he was a police officer?'

'Diane at the Cricketers. Very sharp woman. Just a friend, is he?'

I ignored the slight emphasis on *just*. 'He was one of the officers who protected me before my ex-husband was put in jail.' Why the hell had I let that out? 'You'll recall I've had to change my name.'

'Was he some master criminal, this husband of yours? Like on that TV programme about prisoners and their wives?'

'Nothing so glamorous. Just a nasty little scum of a wife-beater.'

There was a tap at the door; Alison and Felicity slipped in. It was time to share our disquiet and more tea with them.

And to share it again at the staff meeting. But chiefly I wanted to congratulate and thank everyone, stressing the need for staff solidarity. Liz staggered in five minutes after we'd started, grey with fatigue, accompanied by Richard Morris, looking ten years older than when I'd last seen him.

'Rosie's fine. She's got to stay in overnight but her mum's with her. Back home ASAP, and back here ASAP too.'

'Did she say anything about how she came to fall?' asked Tom.

'Nope. Says she can't remember. Just up one minute and down the next. But that doesn't mean,' Liz continued, 'that – sorry, Richard – she was telling the whole truth. I've promised to pop in when she gets home, so I'll see if she's remembered anything.'

'What the hell do you mean by not telling the whole truth?' For a moment I was afraid Richard might hit her.

'She might be afraid of dropping someone in it. That's all. Not that she's a compulsive liar or anything.'

'It's my turn to be sorry, Liz. The reason people have children while they're young is because old age does this to you,' he said, groaning as he collapsed into a chair. 'Now, I'm only here because I wanted to tell everyone what a saint Liz has been, an absolute saint. I'm old enough to worry about mothers working when they've got small children, but I tell you this, Liz couldn't have treated her own child better.' I wasn't sure I saw the logic, but it was good to hear her praised. 'Now, Jane, you said you'd let me have a written report—'

'And so I will when I've worked out what to say. The governors and I suspect that Rosie was tripped, but why and by whom we're not able to say yet – and possibly never will be. We have agreed a bullet point summary, which you'll get later this evening. And we've drafted a letter to Rosie's mother.' I passed a copy across. 'Feel free to add anything.'

'Thanks. Is it OK if I just hang around for a few minutes?' He produced a pen from an inner pocket and kept it poised over the paper.

I could hardly say no. I continued, 'We have quite a long agenda, so I'm going to time-constrain each item. Tom: your media encounter tomorrow – anything we can do to facilitate things?'

'It's at lunchtime at the sports centre. I've got permission from Will and Sukie's parents to take them along for the photoshoot. I've signed the car use papers and they're with Melanie. Parish mag article in the parish mag in-box.'

'Thanks and good luck . . .'

We worked our way so briskly through the other items that I added an AOB. 'I've had a request from the village cricket team to use our playing field for weekend games. Since the players may well prove useful role models for our boys and girls, I am minded to open negotiations. Would that be OK?'

'Would they be coaching the kids? Would they need those tedious background checks?' Richard asked, making us all jump.

'As for coaching, I'm in contact with the charity devoted to taking cricket to schools, Chance to Shine. All of their staff and volunteers will have been checked. So no local players should be involved. If they are, yes, they'll need checks.'

'Fine. I'll tell the other governors I'm in favour as and when you report progress to them. By the way, has anyone heard that the church wants to use the hall here until their boiler is repaired?'

Where had he got that from? But on the whole I was glad that it was he who'd brought up the subject.

'No objection, anyone? Excellent. Right, I'll tell the other governors. This is fine,' he continued, passing back the draft letter. 'Thanks for letting me see it. Sorry to gatecrash, all. I must be off.' He put a hand on Liz's shoulder. 'Jesus, Liz, if you're as knackered as I am, I hope this meeting winds up soon. See you soon, one and all.'

'Sleeping with the enemy, I hear,' Diane said, pouring me a glass of Malbec. 'Look at your face! Only joking, Jane. Try this – on the house. It's a new line. I hear you did very well today. It takes some style to rope in someone who's been

162

trying to undermine you ever since you arrived. Cheers!' She touched my glass with hers. We nodded approval of the Malbec.

I should have come back with a jokey response. Instead I sounded pious. 'Wherever did you get that idea from? The governors have a huge amount of responsibility, you know – they can end up in jail if things go wrong.'

'Really? Remind me not to volunteer, then. Now, I've got a nice bit of fillet steak – could you fancy that? Fresh oil in the chip pan?'

I tried to retrieve the situation I'd lost. 'That might be construed as bribery and corruption! But there's no need for anything like that – the governors were so knackered after their day dealing with kids they more or less nodded through the cricket club suggestion. It'll have to be rubber-stamped at the next full meeting, of course, but with Dawes behind it . . . If any of the players wanted to have closer dealings with the children, then they'd have to submit to background checks, but that applies to everyone.'

She looked surprised. 'Even to the governors?'

'I suppose so. Anyone likely to be in contact with individual children.'

'OK. So it's yes to steak and chips? How do you like it? Medium rare? Veggies or salad? Not really salad weather, is it? Now go and sit down before you fall down. And you can tell me all about your gorgeous young man later, after we've settled details of the musical instrument appeal.'

I set her right.

'Not your young man! You ought to remedy that! I gather he could sing the socks off a nightingale too.'

'Oh, he can. You should have seen their faces when he joined in the first hymn. You know they'll be holding services in the school hall till the boiler's repaired? It helps having the vicar doubling as a governor, I suppose. Though given they'll have to use the kids' chairs – unless they bring their own – I suppose it won't be a *big* congregation!'

'Boom, boom! It isn't just the boiler, of course – one of the windows is caving in, so you may have them for longer than you expect. And what about their midweek prayers? Won't they be a bit disruptive? Mind you, I dare say they could always hold them in a phone box . . .'

I would have given anything to be able to phone Pat and regale him with the day's events – maybe even pick his brain about the best way of dealing with Prudence. But I had resolved not to bother him again, except in an emergency. Somehow falling asleep on the soft leather sofa didn't seem to constitute an emergency.

At least, while much later when I was cleaning my teeth, I remembered to call Richard for the latest news of Rosie – she was comfortable and sleeping. He sounded genuinely pleased I'd asked. I ought to start on the report I'd promised him. But just for once something would have to take precedence over school work: the deep bath and the high thread-count Egyptian sheets.

CHAPTER SIXTEEN

Peering from behind Melanie's blinds the next morning, I fancied the school-gate mothers hung around rather longer than usual, with a tendency to give meaningful glances. However, their conversations were shortened by the arrival of the police community support officer, ready to wage war on illegal parkers. His work done, he was giving one last look round when I had an idea – why bother Lloyd, whom I'd thought yesterday might provide a little talk on the importance of telling the truth, when there was a tame person in uniform who had to be at the school anyway? I nipped out and asked. Although clearly taken aback, the young man managed to produce a smile and a nod of tentative agreement. He'd have to clear it with his boss, of course, but would quite like to, actually. How about Thursday? It would give him time to prepare what he wanted to say. Should he contact me to discuss his material in case I saw any problems he didn't?

What a wonderful young man. Ian Cooper. A young

man with a degree in philosophy, no less, acting as little more than a lollipop man. That was today's employment situation for you.

I was so delighted with my little success that I almost forgot it was Open the Book day. Would it be very wrong to take my coffee with me? Actually it would: it would be disrespectful and would give the children entirely the wrong message. And what was the prospect of cold coffee compared with a vigorous performance of the parable of the Good Samaritan?

As the children silently left the hall – the 'Grand March' from *Aida* was today's music – I kept back Robert and Sophia. They were to wait by the front door to open it when Fred the Fiddle, more respectfully known as Mr Heath, arrived with his armful of musical instruments and to help him carry them. The tent principle, again, of course – with the added bonus that should they say anything about yesterday's events, then Melanie would overhear. I'd attached a note to Fred's ID telling him about my musical instrument project, and asking for his comments.

The Open the Book team were in no hurry to be away, so I fell into conversation with Dougie, the man with a now useless key.

'I'm sorry we had to change the locks and to stop you using the kitchen route,' I said. 'But Ofsted were worried about security, and when Ofsted say *Jump*—'

'All you can do is ask how high. Don't worry: I was in local government for years so I'm used to dealing with the whims of them up there. Now, I see you've been trying to tidy up that stockroom – it was about time someone did, if you ask me. It must be a real time capsule. I'm a bit of a local history buff, you know, and I'd be happy to lend you a hand, if you didn't mind me keeping anything of interest, that is.'

'So you *are* the Good Samaritan, in real life as well as in your performance! But it would have to be lending a very careful hand, Dougie, because some of those boxes are very precariously perched, and I'd hate you to be buried underneath them. Like Leonard Bast,' I added.

'Ah! Someone who knows her E. M. Forster!' He grinned. 'Or like that composer Alkan, of course. Right. I'll go with that. They say you've been working all hours here so I gather it'd have to be an after-school project? Tell you what, I'll email Melanie with a list of times I'm free.'

What a good day this was becoming. Perhaps.

Actually it got even better. Fred the Fiddle actually smiled when he popped into my office later.

'A concert at the Cricketers?' he repeated. 'Well, one or two of the children are actually able to play a few notes,' he said, setting down his coffee on my desk. 'In tune, I mean. We couldn't run to a full-scale concert, but we could play a few tunes. The choir's pretty good – they're learning to sing, as opposed to chanting rhythmically. Not my doing, I'm the first to admit, but music's music, isn't it?'

'It is indeed. And we'd only want a short event – Diane needs paying customers, not just enraptured parents. Ideally, and I know this is a big ask, we could do with at least one piece in which all the children could play, however badly,' I added, as he pulled a face. 'Just one. I was always last to be picked for the hockey team,' I lied, 'and I'm sure it scarred me for life. Not to mention my parents.'

'And these days disappointed parents sue, don't they? OK, a scratchy ensemble it is. And a smaller group who can show off their actual talents.' He gathered up his mug, and got to his feet.

'And I'll contact all the musicians' parents to get permission. Just check – is this list up-to-date? It's one I inherited.'

He ran his finger down the list, taking a pencil from my desk tidy to annotate it: 'Dropped out last term; yes, still coming; doing very well; dropped out at Christmas; yes; yes; yes; dropped out at Christmas. Wish this one would drop out. Yes; yes; yes. And this one's very promising.'

We shared a smile at the good news.

Two of the names in front of me were familiar: Robert and Sophia. 'Did they just drop out?'

'Yes. Christmas. Dropped? I'd have loved to have pushed them from a great height.'

I could have sworn the door moved infinitesimally. But by the time I'd got from behind my desk and flung it wide open, there was no one there. My stomach sank. I had a nasty feeling a child had overheard him. He knew he was joking; I knew he was joking. But taken right out of context it might have been construed as a fairly inappropriate comment. Shrugging, I returned to our conversation.

'Did you get a note saying they weren't coming any more? From Mrs Gough or from the parents?'

'No. Not in all the time I've been coming. Neither had ever borrowed an instrument to take home, so that's it, as far as I'm concerned. Problem?'

'It wouldn't have been,' I said, not sure I was telling the truth, 'but Ofsted's obsessed with paperwork. They want everything recorded. Dates and everything,' I said, tapping the vague list. 'Any you can remember, anyway. And next time – to save my bacon – any time a child says they're giving up, say they can't till you've had a letter from their parents and talked to me. What interests me, you see, is what they're up to when they're not with you. Have they gone back to regular classes as they ought, or are they up to something else?'

'You've got a nasty suspicious mind, if I may say so. OK, I take your point. Parents' letters and a sample of DNA – right?'

'Right.'

The first job, then, was to check if the ex-musicians had given up with their parents' permission, and what they were doing when they should have been training to become world-class violinists or whatever. It would be hard to tell unless the teachers had sharp memories. Over the top it might be in a tiny school like this, but in an ideal world children would be registered not just for morning and afternoons as they were here, but for individual sessions. My brain groaned for my poor colleagues even as I pondered the idea. Meanwhile I would email the parents of the dropouts to confirm that they had permission to quit. Next, an email to the remaining children's parents, to explain what we hoped to do and why, and asking permission for their child to be involved. I copied both to all the governors, of course: those I worked with yesterday might have earned haloes, but they could return to normal

169

today. Then I did what I should have done an hour ago: I phoned Richard for news of Rosie.

'She's already talking about coming back to school,' he said, his voice almost breaking with relief. 'But I'm saying she shouldn't while it's so icy.'

'I'll bring some work round for her when you think she's ready,' I said.

'Would you really do that? That's very kind.' He sounded as if he meant it.

I made a note. And remembered, in time for me to wish them well and wave them off, that today Will and Sukie were going to the sports centre with Tom. By the time I got back, actually thinking about lunch, I found Robert's mother waiting in Melanie's office, breathing fire.

'I'm not furious with you, Ms Cowan. Don't think that. This happened when no one was properly in charge. And some of us appreciate how hard you've been working to pull things together. I know Rob's only skived a couple of weeks, but what I want to know is what he's been doing when he should have been in his lesson?'

'Me too, Ms Bowman,' I said, ushering her into my office and closing the door. 'Often we complain about Ofsted demanding all sorts of systems for recording apparently trivial matters, but at times like this we can see why they're important. I've asked Ms Grove to come and see me as soon as she's finished her class; would you care to wait here until I find out what she knows?'

'I'd rather hear it from Helen Grove's own lips,' Ms Bowman declared. 'She always says what a sweet child he is and here she is letting him get away with murder.'

'It's hardly her fault. As far as she's concerned, Robert is still playing the fiddle with Mr Heath. But all the time he's playing hookey. Oh dear. Sorry.'

But Ms Bowman was laughing with me.

Helen was practically in tears, however, when she joined us. 'I've really let you down. And Robert.'

Ms Bowman shook her head. 'It's Robert that's let himself down. Lying little toad. What are you going to do, Ms Cowan?'

'It's more a case of what we all do. There must be some punishment, but only if you agree with it.'

'Agree? I tell you, for the next few weeks he can wave his pocket money goodbye, and his computer time too. That's what'll happen at home: what'll you do to back me up?'

'I'm a great believer in making the punishment fit the crime—'

'Like the Lord High Executioner!' she said with a grin. 'But you can't make him do violin lessons again, surely. It's not Mr Heath you want to punish.'

If only all parents were like this one. 'Shall we all give it some thought?' I suggested. 'Meanwhile, Ms Bowman, there are other slight problems. The first is trivial: although I specifically told the whole school that the corridor with the stockrooms is out of bounds until we've got rid of all the rubbish inside, almost immediately Robert tried to open one of the stockroom doors.'

'Stockrooms? They were changing rooms in my day. They were until Mrs Gough came.'

Why on earth? 'Any idea why she should think it better for the children to change in their classrooms?' I asked Helen.

She shook her head: 'Before my time.'

171

'Anyway, I had to tell Robert off, obviously. In fact, I was quite fierce. Then I thought no more about it. Possibly you shouldn't either – I just want you to have the full picture.'

'There's something else, isn't there? Helen, what's he done now?'

She almost wriggled with embarrassment: 'He's such a lovely boy, normally. But he – the other day I found him rooting through my waste bin. I have an idea he'd been looking at things on my computer too. But it's so uncharacteristic I didn't like to challenge him.'

'All little incidents,' I said. 'Hardly worth raising one's voice for. But there is one other thing: you heard about yesterday's accident? Obviously we have to find out what happened, and—'

'You're not saying he caused it. Please say he didn't!'

'I truly can't say either way,' I answered for her.

'I can't believe it.' She actually went white. 'None of this is like him at all. Some things are just naughtiness. He's a kid: you'd expect it. But breaking a child's arm . . .'

'We don't know that. And even if he did mean to trip her – big if! – he probably didn't expect her to fall as badly as that.' I passed her a tissue. 'Just as a matter of interest, did anything happen at home during the holidays?'

'No. He did the work he'd been set – though he did find it very hard, and I had to sit with him to make sure it was done. He watched a bit of TV, played on his computer – not for very long, not compared with other children, at least. And I made sure he played outside with his mates – he likes his bit of football. His best Christmas present was an Arsenal shirt.'

I looked up quickly. 'I hope I didn't throw away one of

his old shirts when I started clearing out the stockroom.'

She wrinkled her nose: 'I'd put it another way – I hope he wasn't one of the little swine that draped them all over your house. What goes wrong in their heads, Ms Cowan? Unlike some he's got two parents, with no family problems at all. Everyone says they love him. And suddenly something throws a switch in his head and he goes off the rails.'

'Not very far, I'm sure,' Helen said fervently. 'He's done nothing really bad—'

'Yet!'

'We'll all work together to make sure he doesn't. Meanwhile,' I said, 'I'm wondering if he's made a new friend who's exerting a bit of influence. Some of his replies yesterday when I spoke to everyone about Rosie's accident were remarkably like other children's. Kids often do things differently when they've combined with others—'

'Like in *Lord of the Flies*? That's very reassuring, I don't think.'

'No pig-killing yet,' Helen said. 'Do you know what, I wonder if Robert should be given the job of cupboard tidying for the amount of time he's skived. Public and useful. And when he's finished he has an end result. If the weather was better I'd suggest litter-gathering, but I don't want to delay his punishment.'

'Fine by me,' Ms Bowman declared, 'but double it. Tell me,' she added as she got up to go, 'did any other children get up to the same thing?'

'You know I can't name names, Ms Bowman—'

'I didn't ask you to. I just asked you if any others skived like this.'

'I have asked some other parents if they had given

permission for their child to withdraw from music, but no one has yet contacted me,' I said truthfully.

'If it turns out there's a little gang of kids involved, I'd like to know. I'm sure the other parents would too.'

I wasn't so sure.

I was even less sure when a reporter from the local paper rang me to ask if it was true that our resident music teacher had threatened violence against his pupils.

CHAPTER SEVENTEEN

'I said to him I would make due enquiries and phone him back,' I told Brian Dawes, who was looking decidedly less friendly than yesterday.

'You didn't ask him where the hell he'd got hold of the idea?'

'I suspect I know all too well where he got hold of the idea, which is why I said the bare minimum. Look, if we were having a conversation in here and you said, "I could wring your neck," would you expect the press to report that as a threat to kill me?'

I'd actually made him laugh, if grimly. 'I'd want to know how they got hold of the idea.'

'You could probably assume I didn't tell them. Which would mean either that the room was bugged or that someone eavesdropped. I know my role is important, but it hardly deals in state secrets. So I'd be tempted to assume the latter.'

'Of course. And from the speed with which you summoned me, I gather you have a good idea who the eavesdropper might be?' He stared first into his coffee then at me. 'And that you believe a sensitive reaction is called for?'

'Unless you want the Digbys to arrive with a solicitor again. Yes, Prudence. What I suspect she heard was Mr Heath saying he'd like to have dropped some of his pupils from a great height.' I explained our skiving problem. 'Incidentally, two of the kids who have contrived to give up music without telling their class teacher are two we thought might be involved in yesterday's problem – Robert and Sophia. I don't like any of this, and that's the truth.'

'Has Prudence dropped out too?'

'Absolutely not. Heath regards her as very promising – I believe she has her own cello at home and practises regularly.'

'So why should she bear him any malice?'

'Good question.'

'But not as good as your original one. How else would this trivial conversation get out?'

While he sipped the last of his coffee, I brought up Heath's file. A quick check showed that his record was relatively up to date: Mrs Gough rated him very highly, as did the parents of those he taught. But all that was irrelevant – men now in jail for abusing their pupils probably had files full of admiring testimonials. Was violence more or less serious than sexual activity? If the man were suspended it could ruin his career, and perhaps for nothing. Almost certainly for nothing.

At last I said, 'My feeling is that we have to call the editor and say something. Even if it's just that our enquiries are ongoing. And we do, however frail the story, have to talk to Fred Heath. And the other pupils.

Hell, Brian – I hate this. It's giving credence to – to a puff of air!'

'And what do you intend to say?'

'You know, I might just ask them if they can trust their source and remind them of the perils of circulating what could turn out to be libellous allegations. And promise them complete co-operation if the story does have any basis.' I looked at my watch. It was the end of the afternoon already. 'And then I have to see Sophia and Robert and their parents and find out where they were when they weren't with Fred.' And take the ball skills after-school club.

The editor, Julie Freeman, who sounded as if she was about my age, agreed to check the source of the story. She certainly wouldn't run it until she had. But if she thought there really was any basis in fact, she had no option.

'I'd be the first to support you if there is,' I said. 'Meanwhile, when are you going to run the story of our young tennis coach? I'm so proud of him, encouraging young players even though his own career was so cruelly cut short. At least tennis's loss is teaching's gain. I shall have another nice photo opportunity for you soon: The Jolly Cricketers are hosting an evening for us to ask the community for unwanted musical instruments, and to celebrate the fact that the cricketers themselves – I don't know quite how jolly they are! – will be using the school playing field for future matches.' I thought I might be over-egging the pudding if I mentioned that the accused teacher would be organising the concert.

The two children were corralled into their usual classroom, together with their mothers. Ms Bowman kept a cold eye on her son, but Ms Wells's fury seemed directed at me as I arrived two minutes late for our appointment. 'Where have you got hold of the appalling idea that Sophia has given up violin lessons? It's about time the school kept sensible records and didn't rely on the feeble memories of . . . of incompetent staff. Sophia has begged to take her instrument home to practise, but Mr Heath has constantly omitted to lend her one.'

Has he indeed? I made notes but didn't reply. Instead I spoke to Sophia.

'Sophia, did you go to your violin lesson today? No? And last week? Would you like to tell us why not? And why Mr Heath had the idea that you had given up?'

'Don't you mean *dropped*?' she asked. She almost suppressed her smirk but not quite.

'*Dropped*?' I repeated. 'As in eavesdropping?'

She flushed scarlet. Bingo!

'Whether or not you have abandoned your musical studies, you weren't with Mr Heath this morning, nor were you in class. There is no record of your asking permission to leave the school for a medical appointment.'

'Records!' Ms Wells exploded. 'I tell you this school has no notion of record-keeping. Ofsted complained about it. My husband's a governor, you know.'

'Record-keeping was an issue during Mrs Gough's time; things have changed now. I repeat, Sophia, where were you this morning?'

'I had to go to the loo. Miss – Ms – Grove must have forgotten.'

'Forty minutes in the loo. You must have been very poorly. We should have called your mother and asked her to take you home. And what about you, Robert? Were you ill too? This week and last?'

He made no attempt to dissemble: 'I wanted to see in the stockroom.'

'And how did you get in? They're supposed to be kept locked, and even if one was left wide open you know that they're out of bounds. You know that the whole corridor is out of bounds because I told everyone at assembly that it was, and because there are Keep Out signs, and because when I saw you trying to get into the corridor I told you off. I repeat, how did you get in?'

He dropped his eyes and mumbled.

'Louder,' his mother snapped.

'Don't know.' His eyes slid to Sophia's. 'Someone must have left the key in the lock.'

'Really. How careless. Two weeks running, too. I shall have to check. But let me ask you this – if your mother left her front-door key on the desk here and forgot to pick it up, would it make it right for me to use it to get into your house? Robert? Sophia? Now, I am already late for the after-school club – which means that, because of you two, twenty-five other children are being inconvenienced. Ms Bowman, Ms Wells, I can't go any further with this tonight. I would be very grateful if you would talk to your children and consider what punishment is appropriate. I already have Ms Bowman's suggestion, and you might want to co-ordinate yours with hers, Ms Wells. You both have my email address, and should feel free to contact me about this at any time. As for "dropping" things, Sophia, I think you have just "dropped" one of your friends into considerable trouble and managed to prevent injustice being done to a very good teacher. Thank you.'

* * *

I enjoyed the after-school ball-skills session so much I almost hoped that, though I sincerely wanted Helen's leg to recover quickly and completely, the physios might tell her to wait a few weeks before she tested it in the hall. As before, when the session was over my hair was wet with sweat; I was still panting when I called Julie Freeman to tell her I suspected a disgruntled pupil might be at the bottom of the violence story.

'Glad to hear it: I suspected as much when I heard that all we had to go on was an anonymous phone call. The caller's voice was very young, I'd say. I gather the photoshoot and interview with your Tom went very well. You will keep me in the loop about the other developments you were telling me about, won't you?'

Now I could return to my temporary home and have a power shower. I might have a mound of preparation to get through, but that could be done on the elegant dining table that occupied only one corner of a bright kitchen. Throughout it all, I would be warm.

Warm but uneasy. Just because your head is dripping wet it doesn't mean your brain is waterlogged too. What – or who! – could have transformed an easy-going loveable child into a bully capable of breaking a child's arm – assuming Robert had indeed tripped or pushed young Rosie?

And on the subject of transformations, why had Mrs Gough abandoned perfectly useful rooms for the less good practice of sending the boys out of their classrooms while the girls changed, and vice versa? Because she needed storage space, of course. Why else? A lot of storage space? Both rooms were indeed completely full.

Try as I might, however, I could not imagine any

woman, especially the homely looking woman in sensible shoes, finding pleasure in the sort of pornography now in Lloyd's care. But then, I couldn't have imagined a highly respected solicitor taking pleasure in torturing his wife, both mentally and physically, until I had the scars to prove it. I peered at myself in the heated bathroom mirror: did I have the words *Bully me* stamped on my forehead? Or had I, in my paranoia, imagined that Dawes and his colleagues, who had been so supportive yesterday, had once been deeply unpleasant?

Of course I hadn't. Had I?

So what had transformed them? You might have expected them to dance up and down with glee when they saw me in such straits. Yet they couldn't have rallied round more kindly and effectively if I'd been their favourite niece. One thing I did know, however, was that my brain was rapidly becoming mush, and was simply not up to solving the conundrum. But it could at least remember, when I'd finished my evening's work, how to make use of the tin of Prestat chocolate flakes that had come in my welcome pack.

CHAPTER EIGHTEEN

The consensus over Wednesday's mid morning tea and coffee in the staffroom was that evisceration was probably too good for our miscreants, with Tom and Liz sharing a belief that Prudence should be included in the public executions.

'Someone's pulling their strings,' Tom insisted. Ostentatiously he flung open the staffroom door, peering from right to left, before closing it firmly. 'And though we've got some very bright children in the school, they all strike me as being straightforward – not manipulative as I'll swear Prudence is. OK, she and I have form, so I may be biased, but that girl is – please note my technical language – dead creepy.'

'She's Fred's star pupil,' I murmured.

'She's everyone's star pupil. She'll romp through grammar school and take a double-first at Oxford. But none of that will make her less creepy. And I'll swear she set up the Rosie incident, and made sure she was as far from the action as possible – bringing up all that stuff about hair and scrunchies with Kate was just a way of getting an alibi. As for her contacting the press – what exactly do you propose to do, Jane?'

'Good question. I'm almost glad her mother emailed me to say she was off sick this morning – a stress-induced migraine, would you believe? – because I want to consult all of you. You know her so much better than I do, and some of you know that I have a terrible problem I'm embarrassed to confess publicly – I don't like her, and that's very immature of me.'

'We all ought to be in kindergarten, then,' Tom declared. 'Is there any hard proof that she called the press?'

'Julie Freeman – she's the editor – has promised me a recording of the phone call. I'd rather line up all my weapons before I fly into the attack. But apart from Sophia making that clever quip about *dropping* I have no internal evidence that Prudence has done anything wrong. So what do we do about her puppets? I'd say Robert was afraid of Sophia and maybe even of Emma.'

'And probably terrified of Prudence,' Tom added, sotto voce.

'Robert's mother – who seems a pearl amongst parents—!'

'College lecturer before she got made redundant,' Liz put in.

'She's going to stop his pocket money and ban him using the computer. And he's going to clean a lot of classroom cupboards. I'm not sure we can rely on Ms Wells to do the same – and I can't see her backing any punishment we decide to impose. Apparently – and bang go our attendance stats – she's keeping her poor daughter at home today because she's probably got a cold coming on. According to her all this is our fault – and to a degree it is, because we don't have the right recording systems.'

'And don't go thinking, Jane, that you have to take responsibility for it all,' Melanie said, knocking and entering in one movement. 'I was very fond of Mrs Gough, and the kids loved her to bits, but she was losing her grip as she got older. Just thought you'd want to know that Emma's in tears in the playground. It's not Kate on duty today, remember, but Eileen Woolley. I could see her giving Emma a cuddle, but I thought, after Monday, you might be interested.' She darted out again.

'It'd be more low-key if you had a word, wouldn't it, Helen? If she did help hurt Rosie, I want to nail her, but you might get more out of her. And there's the bell . . .'

I had to wait till our already all-too-brief lunchtime to catch up with Helen.

She dug into a plastic box of what looked like a quinoa salad and came up with an aromatic forkful. 'She said that people had called her names. But of course she wouldn't say who. I did ask her who she liked to play with, and she tried to say she didn't really like playing, in the sort of voice that Prudence or Sophia could manage, but not poor Emma.'

'Poor Emma?' I asked through my belated breakfast bar.

'All through the school she's been the sweetest kid. Like Robert only much more academic. Wouldn't say boo. She's always seemed to enjoy being kind and helpful. She's mothered the littlies. But she's trying to join the big girls now – and I really don't think her heart's in it.'

'If she was part of the plot to trip Rosie, she'd still have to be punished, wouldn't she?'

'But guilt by association in a primary school, Jane? It doesn't seem fair.'

'When was life ever fair?' I asked unkindly. 'Has she ever made any attempt to get into the stockrooms, by the way?'

'Not to my knowledge. Jane, why don't we just hire a skip and get someone like Richard to dump everything into it? I know we all thought there might be important stuff in there, but if there was nothing in there there'd be no reason for them to go in.'

'I can't say I'm not tempted. But if you knew the furore I caused just by trying to throw away a few football shirts . . .' For the time being I'd keep quiet about the porn. In fact I might just consult Lloyd about it – and also see if Jo might be persuaded at least to come and look at the school. I wish I didn't keep taking my eye off the metaphorical ball. But then, I reflected, as the bell went, I'd need as many eyes as Argos – the mythical character, not the store – to keep tabs on everything.

Jo and Lloyd happened to be free that evening, and said they'd be happy to join me at the Cricketers for a meal: the only food I had in my space-age kitchen was that from the welcome pack, and even if I had the full range of a supermarket at my disposal it might take till the end of my tenancy to master the controls on the oven and hob. Not even the microwave was straightforward.

'Do all the holidaymakers have PhDs in astrophysics?' I asked as we settled at what I had come to think of as my table. 'No, they probably have even better models of the same equipment in their Notting Hill homes, don't they? I can recommend the Malbec, by the way.'

'So long as you don't get Jo so drunk she'll agree to start teaching tomorrow,' Lloyd said, asking for a jug of tap water. 'I've got a few days' leave and we're heading off to Cape Verde to get warm.'

'One of the main advantages of not teaching,' Jo observed, 'is not having to queue at an airport behind all your pupils. And the prices, of course. Jane, you look quite peaky – are you all right?'

'It's forgetting to eat that's the problem – and this time I'm not blaming my kitchen. We just need more staff to cover when there's a problem – I actually had to draft in some governors when we had a crisis the other day.' Suddenly, against all the laws of hospitality, I found myself telling them about Rosie's accident. At last, raising my hands in apology, I said, 'No, we've not even enough evidence to keep anyone in detention, let alone refer the miscreants to social workers or whatever. It's just that, like the police, we're cut to the bone.'

'Don't you even have classroom assistants?'

'My predecessor didn't believe in them, and I must say I'd rather have properly qualified teachers to hand. Let me bribe you with some more wine, Jo,' I said with a grin.

'Go on, then. Thanks. Tell you what, I will just look at the place. When we've eaten. We've got time. Tell me what I'll find.'

'It's generally clean and tidy, but very institutional. For instance, there's not nearly as much artwork as I'd like. And,' I added as our starters arrived, 'we don't have any photos of staff or governors, and since no one's yet organised a school council, there are no photos of any kids either. If the school's ever won any trophies, they're all locked away so tidily I've not located the cupboard, let alone the key. And there don't seem to be any little silver cups for sports day prizes and so on. It's such a shame. We've got a huge playing field that's somehow escaped disappearing under a hundred houses, but no sports teams. Jo, I dearly want to develop the kids' potential, but it's going to be a long haul.'

Diane herself came to clear the table and top up our glasses. 'Don't let her put herself down: she's doing very well. Did she tell you about what she's doing for the church and the cricket club? Now, who was having the steak?'

I allowed myself one more quick question about the school: would putting all the contents of the stockrooms in a skip be advisable? 'At one level it would be grand just to get rid of the problem,' I said, 'but at another, doing so without warning all the parents might have disastrous results.'

Jo narrowed her eyes. 'What do you think might happen if you did warn them?'

'I think it might provoke quite drastic action from whoever left stuff like the porn in there. And for the time being I'd just like a really quiet life.'

It was Lloyd who noticed it first: the key labelled Stockroom B was on its hook on the little board that Melanie kept within reach, but it was rocking backwards and forwards.

'That's funny,' he said. 'The front door was locked when you let us in, wasn't it?'

'Yes. Just as I'd left it. But there's something even funnier:

187

the brand-new state-of-the-art security light didn't come on as we approached.'

'It would have had a hard job sensing any movement. Didn't you notice? It was covered in snow,' Jo said. 'Someone with an aim as good as that ought to be in your cricket village team. So, Lloyd, you think someone's just hung up that key and scarpered?'

'That's the best scenario,' I said. 'But there's another. What if someone's still lurking?' I tried to sound cool and insouciant – and probably failed.

'Is it possible to isolate different parts of the school? I'm calling this in as an attempted breaking and entering, by the way,' he added, fishing out his mobile.

'There are lockable doors to each section. The stockroom area is furthest from here – in the new section.'

'OK. I'll find it. I want you two locked in the car – now.'

'Uh-uh. This is my problem, too, Lloyd. The key was hung up and the one next to it – to the other stockroom – was quite still. Let's assume either they've finished with the stockroom and scarpered or they've hung up the key and are hiding somewhere near here. We can check each room and lock up behind us.' I fished my keys from my bag and jiggled them. 'But you're right: Jo's safest locked in your car. And if she suspects anything she can call your colleagues – right?'

'Lock it – promise!' he said, almost pushing her out.

We watched her until we saw her thumb go up.

'Let's start with the staffroom, shall we? And then my office.'

'OK. Hey, what are you doing?'

'Taking my boots off. Quieter that way.'

I would have loved to be able to say that I was confident,

188

but if the kids were supposed to tell the truth, so was I.

'What if you have to run?'

I put them back on again.

We searched every inch of the school. We even checked inside the stockrooms. But there was nothing. No one.

'So it looks as though they were returning the key,' Lloyd said. 'But why should anyone want to get their hands on that old junk?'

'Apart from the porn mags, of course,' I reminded him.

'Of course. Can you see if anything's missing?'

I was in mid shrug when I cried out, 'What the hell's that noise? Your car, Lloyd?'

He sprinted off, but lost his footing on the hall floor.

'Don't worry,' I yelled 'I'm on to it!'

Someone had pretty well written off their car. The whole of the driver's side had been scooped as if by a giant fork. The electronics were rightly offended, sounding the alarm unremittingly, and Jo was trapped inside, screaming with a mixture of terror and rage. Amazingly, despite the proximity of houses and cottages, no one else was on the scene.

Lloyd, his whole body an exclamation mark of disbelief, was frantically pressing his key – to no avail.

'Try turning it manually?' I suggested. 'No – shit!' Through the pulses of orange from the hazard lights, I picked out a hooded figure running up the road. I gave chase, but soon lost whoever it was: my boots weren't made for running, especially on the glass that the road surface was rapidly becoming.

At least they fixed the car alarm. The silence was almost palpable.

'It just happened,' Jo was saying. Her voice was inclined to quaver and I could hear the effort she was putting into making it jaunty. 'There I was, sitting listening to Classic FM, and there was a loud rumble and from nowhere – no, no lights, nothing – this huge tractor appears and hits the side with some gigantic piece of equipment it's towing. Doesn't stop, of course. The driver might not even know. No street lights, of course.'

'You may be right. But I almost think – I know I'm paranoid, but they've been out to get me so long I've had a lot of practice – I almost think it was a diversionary tactic to get us out of the building and allow Mr or Ms Hoodie to escape.'

'Come on, we searched high and low!'

'Low, yes – but not high. What if they got into the roof space? I've never checked but there must be hatches or people wouldn't be able to get up there for maintenance.'

'Call myself a cop . . . never thought, did I?'

'Did *we*. And it's my territory. Even the roof space. Tomorrow's job. If only I have time.'

'Or someone elses's if you have any staff to delegate it to. Now, Jane, you're sure you really didn't get a proper look at Hoodie Person?' Lloyd seemed far more concerned with the runner than with his wife, who, released from her dented prison, was dithering with cold, and, I guessed, shock.

'Just enough to know that whoever it was wasn't carrying anything large. Small – who knows? Pocket-size? Jo, we need to get you inside somewhere warm. My cottage is a bit of a step—'

'Bit of a slide, more like,' she said with a game grin.

'Get inside the school – it should be as safe as houses now.'

When I went to open the door, bizarrely I found it locked: neither of us had had time to do that. And when I put my key in, it jammed tight. Wouldn't come out. 'The bastard's only done the superglue trick,' I told Lloyd.

'Can you call your locksmith? He may have a twenty-four-hour service. Where the hell are you off to now?'

'The old bike shed. Country ways. I know it was a risk, but I've hidden a spare key.'

I could hear him call after me, 'Bloody stupid! And what's the point?'

'Go round the side – kitchen entrance,' I yelled.

But at that moment all hell was let loose. Someone's burglar alarm wailed across the street. As if on cue, blues and twos announced the imminent arrival of a police car. And now, at last, curtains started to twitch.

CHAPTER NINETEEN

Unsurprisingly, the colleagues whom Lloyd had summoned were far more interested in dealing with what sounded like a live incident than in commiserating with a mate with a smashed-up car, and never mind our strange invisible intruder, either. Jo, no longer dithering, was keen to see what was going on; Lloyd was too busy haring hazardously in search of the source of the noise to argue.

'Whose house is it?' Jo gasped, as we slithered along in pursuit.

'It could be Alison Tibbs's – it overlooks the school. Ideal for a governor. If only they had street lights in this benighted place! No, it's further up – Brian Dawes's, maybe.'

Our progress was speeded by a little rash of security lights popping on, and anxious or simply nosey neighbours emerging on to their doorsteps. Would they help? My personal dream was to intercept and floor the irritating figure in the hoodie whom I was beginning to blame for everything that had befallen me since I arrived here. I blamed the Malbec and too much running around in the cold for my lack of logic.

We weren't allowed anywhere near what the police had not unnaturally declared a crime scene: Lloyd, who'd already acquired a bright-wear waistcoat, was holding back a little knot of villagers, some of whom I recognised as parents – some in carpet slippers – and others who were complete strangers. I suspected that between us we were generating more heat than light.

Lloyd became gratifyingly authoritative. 'Did any of you ladies and gentlemen actually witness anything? If you'd be kind enough to give me your names and contact details then you can head home – it's no fun being out on a night when it's minus six and dropping.' He caught first Jo's eye and then mine – we were to lead the reluctant exodus.

Were we indeed? I thought of calling out that we'd wait for him at the school, but stopped abruptly. Jo could easily text him with information I suddenly didn't want anyone else to share. I took her arm and we made our ungainly way back.

'I can't believe you've been crazy enough to leave a key for anyone to find.' Jo was tetchy as we picked our way round to the cycle shed.

Grinning, I spread my hands: 'Find it, then!' Obligingly I lit up the area with my phone, watching her face as she took in the random weeds, stones, loose bricks and assorted litter blown in from wherever. Buckets and an upended empty guinea pig pen completed the still life. The frost made it look almost attractive, but confirmed that nothing had been disturbed.

'Give up,' she said.

'The trouble is, if I disturb the snow, I shan't be able to use this hidey-hole again . . . maybe! Sorry. Enough already.'

Under a broken plastic bucket there was a loose brick. Very tempting. And yes, there was a key underneath. But not the school key. Far too small. So I turned to the guinea pig pen, and its covered accommodation – which for some reason was lockable. The little key opened this. Inside, if you twisted your hand round, you found a nail. It protruded enough for me to have hung the school key on. Sadly, our tracks would indeed betray me: in days to come I'd have to be similarly cunning. In fact, I might suggest to the locksmith that we upgrade from keys to a keypad.

We not only got in through the kitchen, we made it to Melanie's office, where we put the heating on override and brewed tea, clinging to her nice friendly radiator. We didn't run out of conversation, but eventually Jo stood up straight. 'Look, I came here to see the school, and see the school I will. All of it. I'll leave my phone on. Lloyd's number's on speed dial. We'll be fine. Won't we?' she prompted me.

I shook my head doubtfully. I was tall and these days pretty fit – all those ball skill sessions! – but she was so tiny. 'I don't think Lloyd would be impressed if you got hurt, Jo. And I can tell you straight, the governors would have my pelt if I let a potential maths teacher be put out of the frame by my foolhardiness.' At last I managed to add the real reason for my cowardice: 'I've been on the receiving end of too much violence to want to expose myself to more. Sorry.' I rolled up my sleeve, and then my trouser leg. 'Stuff like this hurts. For far longer than you'd think. So I don't really do bravery any more.'

'An accident?'

'Quite deliberate. My ex-husband. I don't care to talk about it much. My therapist believes it's better not to keep revisiting unpleasant times.'

'Does burying it make it go away?' she asked, clearly not convinced.

'Picking scabs doesn't always help healing,' I countered. 'However much they itch.'

We set off. Jo clearly agreed with me that the school was too impersonal, though she conceded that I could soon do something about that. So we turned our attention to looking for roof hatches. Although we located two, neither of us was quite ready to be heroic and conduct a further search, news which pleased Lloyd, apparently. He texted back that there was a lot to do before he could join us and he'd be pleased to find us in one piece. Irritatingly he did not respond to Jo's next text: *Where R U? Whose house?*

One place Jo hadn't seen was my office, so we headed back towards it. Outside it I stopped short.

Why was I so cowardly this evening? Until now I'd felt so secure in my territory that I'd even slept here almost dreamlessly, hadn't I? Was some sort of sixth sense operating? Hardly. I didn't believe in intuition, just intelligent observation. Something, somewhere, was amiss. As if on cue, a text from Lloyd arrived. 'He wants us to let him in. Via the kitchen, I suppose?' She tapped away. 'We'll be fine just retracing our steps, won't we?' She sounded so kind and encouraging I could have screamed.

That was the wonderful thing about Pat: he was always bracing, never kind or sympathetic. However, thinking about his apparent defection wasn't going to make things any better. Then we heard a noise. Hardly audible, but a noise. Yes, from my office. Gazing at each other, we both froze. Which was best, to retreat or confront the intruder?

'I'm going to fling open the door,' I mouthed, passing Jo the key. 'Stand back. If there's a problem, just run for it and let Lloyd in!'

'You're sure?'

'Absolutely.' I pulled a face. 'If only there was something we could use as a weapon.'

'I've got this. She dug in her bag and produced a mini hairspray. 'I bet it would make his eyes sting.'

We braced ourselves: 'Now!'

I flung open the door – nothing.

But the noise came again. Definitely from inside the room. If the source wasn't under anything, it had to be in something.

Making my arms as long as I could, I dragged open a desk drawer. And another. And the last.

Out scrambled a large black rat.

Lloyd claimed he heard our screams from halfway down the lane; it was only our violent eruption from the kitchen door that stopped him summoning armed reinforcements.

A quick inspection of the playground soon located the cage that the rat and possibly some companions had travelled in. I passed Lloyd a bin liner, though I couldn't believe that anyone cunning enough to leave me such an interesting gift wouldn't have been wearing gloves.

Probably thick leather gloves, come to think of it.

'How kind people are,' he said ironically, picking up his evidence and returning to the warmth of the building. He checked his phone and nodded: he was happy with the photo he'd taken of it *in situ*. Locking the door behind him, he said, 'Rodent infestation. So I suppose you have to close the school now. After all your efforts to keep going during the snow.'

'I don't think we can blame my hoodie friend for the weather,' I objected. 'That's an act of God. But I do blame him for the rat.'

'God or the hoodie?' Jo put in. 'I've never understood why He created slugs, either.'

Lloyd pointedly ignored her. 'Which way did it go?'

I shrugged helplessly, then rallied. 'When we screamed – and I make no apologies at all! – it turned tail.' They groaned at the inadvertent pun. 'But the good news is that it must be somewhere in the old part of the school. We made damned sure it didn't follow us into the hall. The bad news is that the old part is where everything happens: office, classrooms, my room, cloakrooms for coats and wellies. Oh, and all the electrics: a good bit of concentrated gnawing could put everything, but everything, out of action.' I indulged in a short burst of language that would have had Prudence fainting away. 'What the hell can I do? I have no option but to close, do I? And, however late it is, I'd better notify the governors now.' I had my phone ready. Then I stopped. 'Dawes is the sort of man it's better to have a plan B for.' I was almost literally scratching my head before I noticed Lloyd's dry chuckle.

'I fancy he's got enough on his plate at the moment. It

was his house that was broken into. There's a right mess inside.'

I frowned. 'But surely the alarm would make any potential burglar take to his heels – you wouldn't hang about with that noise around your ears. Unless you were deaf. And your colleagues were there in minutes. Plus, if the burglar was our hoodie he'd only have had seconds to do anything anyway.'

He laughed. 'Ever thought of joining the service, Jane? My thinking exactly. Look, I've got the AA coming out to the car, but you two might be happier making your way back to your cottage, Jane.'

I shook my head firmly. 'I'm not letting that little sod defeat me. Let's make sure my office at least is still unoccupied. We can all sit there while you wait for them, and then you can stay over at mine if it's easier. I'd lend you my car but of course it's a hire one.' The garage had so much snow crash damage to worry about I had a nasty suspicion that because I hadn't been in their ear three times daily my impenetrable vehicle was at the bottom of their list.

'It'd be nice to have a few weapons,' Jo said. 'If not to kill any rats, at least to encourage them to find somewhere else to play.'

'The stockrooms are in such a mess I couldn't lay hands on so much as a rounders bat, I'm afraid.'

In what we were pretty sure was a rat-free room, after I'd made a formal statement about the hooded youth I'd seen running from the school towards Dawes's house, we fell into an uneasy silence. I had to stop apologising for all the chaos, because Jo would chime in with her own grovels for insisting on coming to inspect the place after our meal.

'It's a good job you did,' I countered. 'At least I know my enemy is here – the furry one, at least. Look, I'm going to see if we can get a rat-catcher—'

Lloyd coughed. 'Rodent operative—'

'Who would come out tonight. They have people-proof traps for mice – I assume they do for their big cousins. And if he can't, how about some sort of away-day for the kids tomorrow? It'd mean a marathon effort on the computer and phone, but I might just manage it.'

'A coach trip?' Lloyd offered. 'That sort of thing? It'd be hard to organise at this time of night, however – impossible, more like.

'What about the village hall?' Jo suggested. 'It'll already have had all the health and safety checks going. And any groups already booked in will surely give way graciously.'

In this village? I wouldn't bank on it. But I said nothing.

'And for a walk across the road,' she continued, 'you won't need to go to all the trouble of getting waiver forms signed.'

And as a bonus Adele and her kitchen staff and dinner ladies would surely be able to produce something in even a village hall kitchen. Better than rat pie, anyway.

'Wow: she's not just a rare and endangered species of teacher,' I said, 'but a genius too.'

'That's why I married her.' Lloyd checked his phone. 'Ah! The AA have texted to say they're here . . .'

Having Jo to bounce ideas off – not to mention having her give me good advice – made me realise just how much I needed a trusted deputy head, someone paid and given time out of the classroom to take responsibility. Technically I had one, of course, but one on extended sick leave with stress. But if she was unable to return soon, even on a part-time basis, an acting replacement would be top of my wish list when we got the next budget. Or would such a move make her stress levels rise? Meanwhile, I texted Sandie Hill, the woman responsible for letting the village hall, and implored her to help.

'I can help in two ways,' she said, phoning straight back, incredibly cheerfully for someone disturbed while watching the late news. 'First I can definitely clear tomorrow's diary. Second, if you can nip down here right now – I can't leave my kids on their own – I've got a packet of farm-quality rat poison. It comes in solid cubes, bright pink. So you could leave some on saucers or cups overnight and deal with the evidence in the morning. No? Well, my cousin Wayne works for a pest control firm – I'll get him to give you a bell first thing. Mind you the firm's not cheap. How long have you had the little pests? I always said it was a bad idea people going backwards and forwards through the kitchen. Mind you, I thought it would be food poisoning, not rats – or even theft, of course. Anyway, I'll be there to unlock the hall at nine. Is that OK?'

'Eight forty-five would be better.'

'I'll do my best, but I've got to drop my own kids off first, of course – and it all depends on the state of the traffic, not to mention the roads.'

The AA man not only winched the poor injured car aboard his truck to take it away, but ushered Lloyd and Jo into his cab – all part of the service, he declared. When he saw that I was about to trudge home, he insisted on dropping me off first, thus joining Sandie Hill and Terry the tanker driver in my pantheon of rural gods. They were joined soon after seven the next morning: Jonah, the locksmith, promised to be with me within the hour to replace the glued-up lock.

CHAPTER TWENTY

If Jonah was bright and cheerful, whistling tunefully as he worked, Brian Dawes was decidedly tetchy when I phoned to tell him what I'd arranged for the day and why. 'Rats? That sort of thing has never occurred before, not on my watch at least,' he added, as if holding me personally to blame. What had happened to the almost charming man of three days before?

'The pest controllers assure me it's not unusual for rats to find a nice warm home in this weather, and this building has, of course, the bonus of a working kitchen,' I said mildly. I felt that there was no need to tell him that the intruder had been given a helpful lift to its new quarters, and how its means of transport was now regarded as evidence. I kept quiet about the time I'd discovered it too, though these days he and his colleagues seemed more tolerant of my long working hours. 'I have absolute confidence that the staff will be able to adapt to the unusual circumstances, and Adele, the cook, says that the village hall kitchen is actually better than ours here. In any case, all should be back to normal tomorrow, thank goodness. By the way, I hear on the grapevine we're not the only ones with trouble – I was very sorry to hear of your burglary, Brian.'

He didn't seem grateful for my kind interest. 'Nothing much taken; just an almighty mess,' he growled.

'I'm so sorry to hear it – I know how awful it is to have your precious things damaged.'

'No one can know unless – I'm sorry, you had that problem with the old caretaker's house, didn't you? Nothing antique there, though, surely to goodness.'

'Of course not.' And now wasn't the time to tell him how Simon had once smashed all the china my grandmother had left me, piece by irreplaceable piece. Or how he had fed my family photos into the shredder. 'Well, I hope the police catch the miscreant soon.'

'They were here pretty damned quick, I'll say that for them. Said something about another local call. Any idea what that was about?'

'Some helpful soul superglued the school door: it's being repaired even as we speak. And I saw someone I suspected of doing it running away in your direction, as it happens.'

'What?' he barked.

'Yes, I've made a statement to the police. And then, in, as they say, a separate incident, a parked car was badly damaged by what appears to have been a heavy vehicle.'

'People park anywhere these days – asking for trouble,' he said dismissively. 'So what are these children going to do all day, jammed together like sardines?'

As if the abrupt change of subject didn't surprise me, I said, 'We already had a talk booked from our police community support officer, Ian Cooper—'

'Why?' he asked sharply.

Had he forgotten already?

'He's going to talk about telling the truth, remember, and any other moral issues that even young children should be able to understand. After that? Some group lessons – I trust the staff to improvise. There's a very good weather forecast, so we can have nice long playtimes – of course as long as we ensure that the actual school building is out of bounds, there's no reason why we can't use the playground as usual. And the Open the Book team are going to put on an extra assembly performance after lunch. There's nothing wrong with quiet personal reading times. I'm sure we shall keep all the parents happy and all the children safe.'

'I wish you joy of the former!' This time his laugh sounded entirely genuine. 'Look, if I have a moment I'll come down and see if there's anything I can do, shall I? I'm supposed to stay in for some forensic chappies or chappesses, but I can't see them doing anything useful. So expect me some time after mid morning.'

Chappesses? Was someone due some gender issues training?

Ian Cooper, looking every inch a real policeman, had prepared his material well, and even produced a child-friendly power-point presentation. There was some small group work, with teams of all ages coming up with responses to different moral scenarios he'd set.

'I did some of this stuff when I was an undergraduate,' he said, while all the young heads were bent over their question sheets. 'Slightly different situations, but basically involving the same instincts and reasoned answers.'

'You're doing brilliantly,' I said truthfully. 'You're wasted on our yellow-line patrol.'

'Funnily enough, that was what my boss said this morning. In fact, if I hadn't dug my toes in about giving this talk, then I'd have been the other side of the county. We're very short-staffed, but a promise is a promise, I said.'

'I hope keeping this one doesn't spoil your career.'

'If you're giving a talk about morals, I think you should try to live by them,' he said.

Who could argue?

His plenary session was exemplary: our Ian was not only a born teacher but also a born leader. I just hoped his career path would match his abilities – and that the children, who'd been so engrossed by the problems he'd set, would retain even the tiniest bit of what they'd learnt. To lie? To cheat? To take the easy route? Or to stick to their principles even when it wasn't easy – just as Ian had this morning.

With his permission, I told them about his dilemma when I stepped forward to thank him. The children were genuinely shocked when they heard he'd been told to cancel their session, and even more delighted that he'd kept his promise. Their applause – and that of the teachers – was spontaneous and warm.

And then came a call on his radio, and he was no longer a friendly face, but a cop off to fight crime.

Dawes still hadn't arrived when Melanie, who had made a small meeting room at the front of the hall her temporary office, had a call from the pest control team – would I care to come and see what they'd done and sign their paperwork?

Leaving the more than capable teaching and playground staff to escort the kids across the road to the playground, I did as I was asked. The workmen seemed to have left ajar every door in the building – it was icy cold. I shut a few as I went round on an escorted tour. I couldn't argue about the baited traps they'd left in my office and in the staffroom, but I vetoed the idea of having any where a child might be tempted to investigate.

'In that case,' Wayne told me, 'you'll have to tell the kids not to take any sort of foodstuff into the classroom – no point in luring the rodents into a room and not dealing with them, is there? And rodents can't tell crisps from bait, see?'

I promised an absolute ban. I didn't mention I'd have to impose it on staff too – if you had a pile of marking it was easier to do it at your desk at lunchtime, eating your sandwiches as you went. I'd done it many times myself.

Bidding Wayne and his mates goodbye as they started loading their gear, I automatically went back to my office to print and laminate notices for each door forbidding any sort of food or sweets inside. I was busy texting all the parents to tell them about the classroom food rule and reminding them that their children must strictly observe the Out of Bounds signs, when there was a tap on the door.

'Come in,' I called absently. Foolishly. 'Pat!' I probably squeaked louder than when I'd seen last night's rat. 'What on earth are you doing here? On a Thursday! And how did you get in?'

'Hey, Avo, calm down. Some workman let me in on his way out. I said I'd try and get down, didn't I? And here I am. It's not a fire drill or something, is it? Everyone seems to be outside.'

'Rats,' I said. Possibly ambiguously. 'Coffee? Then when you're sitting comfortably, I'll explain . . .'

'OK,' he said, fifteen minutes later, 'it's clear that someone wants you out of the school.'

'Either me personally or the school as a whole?'

'That's exactly what we need to know. Now, apart from the rat catchers' targets, the school is empty. Right?'

I pointed to an emptying playground. 'They're all traipsing over to the village hall for lunch as we speak.'

'You're looking a bit smart, but I've got police overalls for both of us. Don't ask. Here.' He dug in an anomalous executive briefcase. 'Let's deal with those stockrooms now. With luck, you'll have another present for this guy Lloyd.' It was the same old Pat. Wasn't it?

As we headed for the stockrooms, armed with keys A and B, of course, we attached No Food notices to every door, even the loos, lest someone like Prudence – was there anyone like Prudence? – found a clear loophole to exploit.

The workmen had replaced the cones and Out of Bounds signs at the end of the stockroom corridor. The troublesome loo doors were ajar, however.

'We've had two children reduced to incontinence by the fear of using them,' I told Pat. 'But no one can find anything wrong with them. Can you?'

He peered into the pristine cubicles. 'A quite refreshing lack of graffiti.'

'These are for kids too young to read and write, aren't they?'

'Who knows what talent is in the bud? And these are the famous stockrooms.'

'OK: you choose. Room A or Room B?'

'Let's try the one where you found the porn,' he said.

'Room A – right? I thought you said they were kept locked?' There was a sudden edge to his voice, as if I were a junior officer found wanting.

'The whole building should have been kept locked – but if a workman let you in, I suppose we can blame the same guy for this,' I said as evenly as I could, despite a sudden surge of resentment: who was he to criticise me? If anyone knew how hard I was working to get and keep the school acceptable, it was he.

Switching on the light, he stepped inside. 'Avo, we've got a problem here. Call 999 – now! And we'll need both police and ambulance. Dear God!'

My mobile wouldn't work till I got back into the hall. He was yelling, 'Tell them absolute priority. A child – get it? Crush injuries. And not just a paramedic – it'll have to be an ambulance.'

Perhaps the call-handler heard his voice ride over mine. She promised an instant response. Did I need talking through first aid?

'The man dealing with the patient's a police officer. There's a playing field if we need the air ambulance,' I added.

Pat was administering kiss of life, his body between me and his patient. My pupil. A girl? Although the legs were in trousers, the shoes looked too small and clean for a boy's.

He merely nodded when I told him that help was on its way.

'I've got to call Melanie in the village hall, Pat, to make sure the kids are all kept together. No one must come over here – no excuse whatever. And I'll get the class teachers to register their kids so we know . . .' I could be cool and efficient but not that cool and efficient.

'Good idea. Avo, you don't tell them anything. Anything at all. Let them assume it's to do with the rats. OK?'

'Yes. It'll be shock enough when they know, but I don't want any panic now.'

One thing I couldn't do, of course, was prevent the kids hearing the sound of emergency vehicles. Several. I flagged them down, got them straight to Pat. But I wished they'd turn their lights off: wherever they parked, they'd reflect on the village hall windows and ceiling.

Just as the second paramedic car pulled into the car park, Brian Dawes appeared.

'Been playing ghosts, Jane?' he called with a grin. Then his face straightened: 'Good God, not more trouble at your door? Someone bitten by a rat? Heavens, more of them! God, these emergency people always overreact.'

I didn't dare speak. Running ahead to throw open the kitchen door, I left him standing where he was.

There wasn't much room in the corridor, less in the stockroom itself, of course. I was torn: I mustn't get in the way, but I needed to be at hand.

'Do you have a name?' a paramedic demanded.

'I'm Jane Cowan. The head teacher. I made the call. But I've not seen your patient, so I don't know who it is. I'm trying to find out who's missing. The whole school's in the village hall today. Except—' I didn't need to finish.

'OK. Try and find out.'

I skidded back to the hall.

Melanie intercepted me: 'There's something really bad going on, isn't there?'

'Yes. I'll explain later. Just give me the names of any absentees, Melanie.' Dry-mouthed, I repeated them after her. 'Robert. Emma. Prudence. And they were all registered earlier? You're sure? What about Sophia?'

'Here – but she came back quite late after the session in the playground.'

'Let me know the instant any of them comes back. And if they're not back in five phone or text their parents. And me. OK?'

There was only one child in Stockroom A, wasn't there? Just the one crush victim. So where were the other missing children? Pat and I had actually looked in the loos, hadn't we? For anything that might scare the little ones. So they couldn't be in there. But there was Stockroom B. Could they be in there? And what could they be doing in there?

'Can't I see who it is? I asked a young Asian constable.

She shook her head: 'Not just now. That'd interrupt the medics, ma'am. They're trying to resuscitate her.'

'OK, I'll get you a list of possible names. Would it help to have photos? Give me two minutes to get their files.'

It seemed to take half an hour to make my shaking fingers dig them out of the old-fashioned cabinet, but the constable seemed to think I'd been quite quick.

Crazily they said there was still no question of them letting me see the child. It was a matter of life and death, the constable said simply.

At last Pat, still, like me, clad in white, joined me. 'A girl. Multiple injuries. Didn't dare try chest compression. A kid, Avo. A kid.' He didn't try to hide the tears in his eyes.

'Will she make it?'

'They say they've stabilised her. But they're going to need that field of yours for the chopper.'

'A girl. Long hair?' My mouth wouldn't ask the colour.

'Long. Blonde. Like all the others I saw in the playground.'

Definitely blonde? So it's probably Emma. God, Pat, just let me see her long enough to ID her!'

He shook his head. 'I'm trying to protect you here, Avo. Look, they'll be asking in a minute if you've any idea how this happened. I'm just warning you. It's a good job you've got me to give you an alibi. And in the absence of a nice convenient adult assailant, they'll probably want to know who you'd point the finger of suspicion at, given that playground business you were telling me about.'

I brushed aside the sense he was talking. 'I need to see her. Because someone has to call her parents. Me.'

'They'll have someone to deal with all that. Trained. But it makes sense.' He called softly over his shoulder.

'It'll take ten seconds at most.'

'But it may live with you for the rest of your life.'

It might well. The poor broken doll was Emma.

Pushing past the paramedics, I flung myself into the girls' mini loo, and retched and retched. To my amazement someone held my forehead and kept back my hair. But it wasn't that that had me staggering to my feet and screaming wildly. It was the snake's eye that had so scared the children.

211

CHAPTER TWENTY-ONE

It wasn't a snake, of course. Just the one beady eye of a tiny lens.

'Really, Jane, you're totally overwrought, and why not?' Brian Dawes said. So it was he who'd appeared from nowhere and was now passing me a wad of paper towel to wipe my face. 'What did you see, anyway?' he added less sympathetically, nonetheless helping me to my feet.

Apart from a child so ill she might not survive? And if she did, in what state? Could she ever be bright, vital Emma again?

I took a deep breath, one long enough for me to gather my thoughts. I dropped the towel in the bin, washed my hands, dropped another towel in the bin. 'I thought there was another rat,' I lied. 'They say they come up through sewers, don't they? I had a builder who insisted on keeping loo lids down ever since he'd found one surfacing in his bathroom.' The more I gabbled the more he'd believe me. Maybe. Because one thing was certain: only Pat and his colleagues were going to know what exactly I'd found by getting down to child's eye level. 'I'm sorry to ask you for more help after your kindness – not many people would have done that! And now would you lend me your arm, Brian? I'm not as steady on my feet as I'd like.'

My appeal to his chivalry worked. He eased our way through the paramedics until he found one plainly not doing a lot and handed me over to his care. He clearly meant to retrace his steps along the corridor, but a uniformed policeman stopped him. 'The fewer people round here the better, sir. And can you give my colleague your contact details as you leave? Main door, please. Thank you.' He folded his arms repressively as Brian resumed bluster mode before accepting the inevitable and doing as he was told. I couldn't have intervened. I simply couldn't speak: to me, giving contact details meant questions at the very least and probably eliminating DNA in a crime scene. Pat's. Mine. The children's? I could have thrown up again. Wouldn't . . .

A text came through. The missing kids were back in the village hall. But not Emma.

Not Emma.

Would Emma ever be in the village hall again?

There was a commotion in the corridor: they were moving her now. Somehow I'd not even registered the arrival of the air ambulance, though the sound of its departure would have awakened the dead.

To have used such a term at such a time – I pressed my hands to my face. But now, even as I realised that the use of the chopper meant that Emma must be alive, I found that I was to be on the receiving end of medical attention. It was the last thing I wanted. I wanted to talk to Pat and I wanted to talk to him now.

A young woman at his elbow, he was only a few feet away, stripping off his white overalls, which, ominously, were being stowed in an evidence bag. When I started to peel mine, the same young woman officer headed my way. I gave up on the overalls. Pat was drifting away.

'I really need to speak to Pat,' I said. 'Urgently. Can you bring him over, please?'

She took in the attempts the paramedic was making to check my vital signs and nodded with grim amusement.

Pat didn't seem pleased as he was propelled in my direction.

'Those baby loos,' I said quietly, but leaving him in no doubt that I was serious. 'Get them sealed officially. Just do it, Pat. I'll explain later.'

To say he looked taken aback – he'd always been the one to give peremptory orders – would be a masterpiece of understatement. But he toddled off to find one of his Kent colleagues who was apparently happy to do his bidding.

After the paramedic having found nothing wrong with me that a stiff gin wouldn't cure – or on school property a cup of tea – I decided it was time to exert a modicum of control: I was, after all, on my territory. I asked for, and got, the senior investigating officer, a blonde woman a couple of years older than me who was clearly a gym bunny.

'DCI Mandy Carpenter,' she said, unsmiling, but offering me her hand.

'A DCI attending a simple accident?' I asked unthinkingly. Those I'd met were desk-bound, not leaping around at the first 999 call.

'I literally happened to be passing. But as to it being a simple accident . . . And you are?' she prompted.

'Sorry. I'm Jane Cowan. I'm the head teacher here. What do you need me to do?'

She looked at me with cool amusement. 'I rather got the impression that it was you that wanted us to do things for you.'

'I did. I wanted you to preserve what I suspect is a quite important piece of evidence in a case you don't even know you have yet.' Did that make sense? She nodded slowly, but might have been humouring me. 'But now you have done as I asked, I promise I'll do anything, anything at all, to help you find who hurt one of my children so badly.'

She stared. 'Biologically yours?'

Which of the hundred or so looked like me?

'I'm *in loco parentis* to the lot of them.' My eyes filled – but better that, I suppose, than more nausea. 'I'm sorry.'

'How do you expect to be able to help me?'

'Apart from access to the children's records? I could give you some background information that may well be germane to your enquiry. And I could tell you why I want the loos cordoned off. And locked, please. Because some of our older pupils – like the victim today – seem incapable of obeying direct instructions. Shall we go to my office? I might be more coherent there. And I can organise coffee for you and your team while I fill you in. I can't do either as well as the school secretary who knows far more about the school than I do – I'm new in the post – but I'll do my best. And there are probably pikelets just waiting to be toasted.'

Her face softened and her accent shifted away from clipped received pronunciation. 'Pikelets, our kid? What these soft southerners call crumpets? I didn't think you were really from round here.'

I set us in motion. 'No more than Pat is. Wolverhampton. That's where we met. I've moved around a bit since then. He'll explain more tersely than I can. Unfortunately, one of your colleagues, PC Lloyd Davies, who's dealt with several outbreaks of minor crime here and knows a lot about my past, has just gone on annual leave.' At last, my hands clenched, I asked what I'd needed to ask for the last twenty minutes. 'Emma? That child – that little girl – what's the prognosis?'

'We'll leave that to the medics. What I want to know is how she came to be buried under a pile of cardboard boxes.'

'Did they fall or were they pushed?' If the question was good enough for Terry the oil delivery man, if worded slightly differently, it was good enough for me. But I wished it hadn't sounded so commonplace.

I thought for a moment she was going to fob me off. But at last she said, 'That's what the forensic teams and the medics should be able to sort out between them. And the other children when we bring a team in to talk to them. Tomorrow, I'd say.'

There was no way Melanie's supply of pikelets and butter would stretch to what was rapidly resembling a small army, including men and women sporting white suits like the one I was still unaccountably wearing. DCI Carpenter was obviously treating the incident very seriously. But I did feel that Pat, occupation now gone, deserved to be invited along too. The bonus could be that he and Carpenter might talk shop, which would enable me to glean information I would not otherwise be privy to.

216

It had been easier to get the suit on than it was to peel it off. Eventually, with a dry laugh, Pat gave me a hand. 'I would think we can bin this – Jane never actually entered the stockroom,' he told Carpenter.

'What I'd like to know is why she was wearing it in the first place,' she said reasonably.

'Because I was wearing my best school clothes when Pat turned up, suggesting we try to get rid of some of the boxes in the stockrooms, which had been here since Noah sailed his boat up the cut.' We exchanged a three-way smile at my use of the Black Country idiom. 'At least, ever since my predecessor stopped using them as boys' and girls' changing rooms. For some reason I've not yet fathomed three or four children regularly insisted on trying to get in there, despite endless prohibitions and a row of cones, the ones now stacked in the corner of the hall, which I used to stop – to try to stop! – anyone using the corridor.'

'Haven't you questioned them?'

'Don't think we haven't tried. Sadly schools aren't allowed to use Abu Ghraib interrogation methods any more. Seriously, some parents want to sue if we so much as ask the kids to tie their shoelaces. So no, I've no idea what the fascination was, unless they'd found a further supply of porn mags so filthy I passed the ones we found to your PC Davies.'

Another reasonable question: 'Why not simply bin them? Not in a classroom bin, obviously, but in your big recycling one.'

'They might not have stayed in the bin, however secure you'd think it might be. They might have been scattered to the four winds or pasted all over the school or sent to the media.' Cue the story about the football shirts. 'There were other problems with my house, which Lloyd Davies suspected were part of a campaign, which neither of us could provide a reason for. But now I really think I might be on to something. At one point this morning I had to throw up. As I knelt by the loo my eyes must have been roughly the level a small child's would be. And I found myself looking into a camera lens. That's why I wanted it cordoned off.'

'Bloody hell, Jane. You're joking.'

Mandy stared in open disbelief. 'You're sure?'

'There's an easy way to find out,' I said, getting to my feet.

The outside of the loo was festooned in police Do Not Cross tape, but everyone was simply going about their business and took no notice when we went in.

'You take this cubicle, and I'll take that,' Mandy said. Within seconds she emerged, not amused. 'Nothing. For God's sake, Jane—'

Pat, however, was on his knees as I'd been. 'Fucking hell. She's right, Mandy!'

'Just one thing,' I said, trying not to let my voice betray me, 'now he's seen two adults looking at him, what's whoever is at the other end going to do? Three adults – if you've located the other one, Mandy?'

Her voice came from the other side of the partition. 'Too right I have. But I'm more interested in responding to your question, Jane. The answer is I don't know, but I don't think I'm going to like it. Or rather, you're not going to like it because you can bet your white overall that he'll identify you as his target for a spot of revenge.'

'Or he'll scarper,' Pat said, more hopefully. 'After all, he's made enough effort to make you shift, but you seem to be superglued in place. Or, of course, as Mandy says, he may try even harder. Sorry. Has to be said.'

'All this time I've been wondering whether it was the school or me they were after . . .'

Pat shrugged. 'Could be both.'

'This isn't the best place to talk, is it? And there are policy decisions the police need to be involved in. And the governors, too.'

She motioned – I was to lead the way from the tiny room. I relocked it and returned the tape to something like its original position. The corridor was full of retreating white-clad men and women: it looked as though they'd finished with the stockroom, though the doorway was swathed in tape.

'May I see inside? Apart from Emma, I was probably the last in there. Officially at least,' I added grimly. '

Carpenter shrugged. 'From the threshold, please, and keep your hands in your pockets. Remember they were only looking for the possible cause of the incident at that time. They weren't searching for—'

'For more camera lenses perhaps?' I surveyed the chaos of hurriedly stacked boxes, cheek by jowl with those I'd been afraid would fall on me. I was an adult, with a stronger frame. Even if a box or two had slipped, I surely wouldn't have suffered as badly as the little girl. 'Hell, why didn't I clear this out earlier? I could have done! Should have done!'

'You work, if not 24/7, at least 18/7,' Pat said. 'So which activity would you have cut out? Breathing? Come on, you wanted me to help you last weekend only we got sidetracked.'

And on Sunday afternoon he'd cut and run. 'Not your job anyway,' I said quickly. 'Can we go back to my office?' Behind my desk I'd feel less like a scared little girl. So long as there weren't any rats waiting to jump onto my lap, of course. But even as I set us in motion I realised that there might be worse things than rats there. You could trap them or poison them. But you couldn't do that with hidden cameras.

'OK. I'll get our techies to do a thorough sweep of the whole place,' Mandy said, in response to my stumblingly expressed fears.

'And the cottage she's renting,' Pat added swiftly. 'And actually, why not the caretaker's house – the one that got flooded by burst pipes?'

'What's the point? It's the school that's got the problem.'

'But I may have somehow transferred the problem with me when I started emptying those stockrooms. After all, if the governors can sack me out of hand, it shelves the problem until you have a plan to get rid of the hidden cameras – or you might feel you could risk leaving them in place. The techies will do the stockrooms as well as the loos, won't they?'

'Cameras to watch people nicking paper clips! Come on.'

I shook my head. 'They've only become stockrooms fairly recently. They used to be changing rooms, boys' and girls'. It was my predecessor who turned them into stockrooms.'

'So now you're expecting Kent Police to take over a job

you were too busy to do? Come on, Jane – we're cut to the bone. An electronic scan is all you'll get – we're not shifting all those boxes. No way.'

'Even if what they contain may be of interest? Real interest to you?' I shot back.

'A load of dirty mags? Poof!' She leant forward. 'Do you have any idea how we deal with burglaries these days? By computer. We investigate historic crimes because we can look things up on computer and improve our clear-up rates. We give nice little cautions where ten years ago we'd have made arrests and seen the criminals get five years in jail. So while we're happy to offer specialist resources, we're not dustmen. Sorry,' she added perfunctorily.

I took a deep breath, quite ostentatiously. Then I asked, in my most reasonable tone, 'Do you want us to keep the school building closed while this goes on? I can pen the children into the village hall tomorrow, but they ought to be back here doing proper lessons on Monday.'

'Overtime! Jesus! OK,' she conceded, as Pat, looking as mutinous as I felt, caught her eye. 'The school – it's a priority, I suppose. But your cottage and – what was the other building? The caretaker's house? – will have to wait. Sorry. But feel free to give it an ocular check.'

'Thank you. I'll pass your permission on to the letting agent.' My tone couldn't have been drier. 'I'll call you if I see anything. Meanwhile, I'm assuming that our discovery here will remain confidential? I suspect that having a serious accident on premises will be upsetting enough for some families, but spy cameras would be even worse. And there is another reason. Someone – staff, parent or governor – almost certainly installed them. Maybe they view footage every day. Maybe they got bored when the kids gave up using the loos we've checked. Maybe we'll work out who's guilty before they have another look.'

'I don't see too many airborne pigs,' Pat said. 'By the way, don't forget the school hall will be in use on Sunday morning. You won't want the church congregation and the techies in an unholy mix.'

Looking exasperated, she made a note.

I found myself getting angry. Angrier. 'I take it you'll be focusing your efforts on finding whoever it was who put the cameras there—'

Whatever Mandy had been going to say was cut short by her phone. Her expression told us immediately that the news wasn't good.

'Emma's still in surgery and they say they'll keep her in an induced coma for as long as necessary, but the organ transplant team are talking to her parents. I'd say we're looking down the barrel of an unexplained death enquiry.'

'Murder or manslaughter to you or me,' Pat said helpfully. 'So I don't see it as business as usual tomorrow. There'll be endless formal interviews for you and the staff, for me as I found the poor kid, and, most serious of all, for the kids who were skiving when they should have been in class.'

If I felt pale before, now I could actually feel blood draining from my face. 'They're kids – how can they . . . ?'

'We have specialist officers – though I think we might be using Essex's at the moment. They'll do the interviews with parents or responsible adults present in soft interview rooms . . .'

She didn't explain the last term. She didn't need to. I'd

been in rooms with soft furnishings and soft toys often enough.

'For the adults, it's the sort of thing you see on TV. So I wouldn't advise either of you to leave the district. And you might want to make sure you've got your alibis in order. With reliable witnesses.'

CHAPTER TWENTY-TWO

When I phoned Brian Dawes to pass on the dreadful news about Emma, I told him that the police hadn't finished and that I wanted to confine the children to the village hall the next day. 'And this time even the playground will be out of bounds,' I said firmly.

I hadn't expected him to argue or bluster, but I'd never known him sound so subdued.

'We also have to face up to the fact that the police want to talk to us—'

'*Us?*'

'Staff; the rodent team; me; you, since you were in the area . . .' Perhaps I waited a beat for an apoplectic response. I didn't get one, so I continued as smoothly as I could, 'And of course some of the children, in connection with Emma's . . . injuries.'

'My God. Children!'

'We've never had a satisfactory explanation for their preoccupation with the stockroom – I think the police will want one.' And if Mandy didn't, I did. 'This is not looking good, Brian. And however much we make it clear that the children were disobeying strict instructions – no one wanted any of them messing around when rats were being killed or poison laid down – someone will try and blame us. We did everything we could: even you came down to help. But the media will want someone's scalp.'

'I'll call an emergency meeting of the governors for this evening. A closed meeting. And we will be dealing with the media.' He cut the call.

'He's keeping you out?' Pat slapped the top of my desk. 'The shit!'

'Quite. Something else that worries me more than losing my job, which is clearly on the cards, is that when this reaches the media my cover's going to be blown. No, I know Simon's not going to get me. But he's got friends, Pat, hasn't he? Friends who probably think he's a reasonable guy with a psychotic ex-wife who needs teaching a bit of a lesson.' I took the sort of breath my therapist would have advised. 'Sometimes – those three o'clock in the morning moments – I wonder if Simon has been hounding me from whichever prison he's in. If he has a friend or two who'd enjoy making my life hell for his sake, but also because tormenting helpless people – bullying – is supposed to be quite enjoyable per se.'

'I'd like to tell you you're crazy. But I can't. Give me a complete list of the governors and I'll run a few checks – a lot more willingly than Madam Mandy Carpenter,' he added, with a resentful curl of the lip. 'What is it with that woman? I can't get her at all. Can you?'

I shook my head. At last I managed, 'She doesn't seem very . . . consistent.'

'Consistent? She's bouncing around all over the place. Mind you, she was telling the truth about solving crimes these days. Targets, redundancies, one person doing the job of five.'

'Which is why your boss needs you back?' Hell, my voice cracked. I just hoped he wouldn't be kind to me.

No. He was bracing: 'I know things are bad, Avo, but that doesn't mean you have to give in.'

'I don't do giving in. Do I?' And I wouldn't now. My hand might be trembling so badly it was almost impossible to use the mouse, but at last I found the file I wanted, and printed it off. 'There you are. All the governors' details. Addresses. Phone numbers. Work phone numbers. DBS reference numbers. I'll leave you here, Pat, because I've got to have an emergency meeting of my own – with the staff.'

I slipped through the crowd of parents, most of whom were milling round the school gates, although they knew the kids were elsewhere, as unobtrusively as I could. Watching through a window in the village hall doors, I saw the team working so beautifully with the unsettled kids that had I had it in my power to commend them for awards, I'd have done so on the spot. As it was, all I could do was sail in as if life was a ball and tell everyone that they'd got to come straight back here tomorrow.

'Sorry – it's the rats. I'm just like Cinderella,' I declared, 'waiting for my fairy godmother to turn a few uninvited animals into beautiful horses to pull my coach. She's promised me a ball gown too, and a handsome prince!' Fat chance. 'Will those staying for choir wait here just a few moments, please?'

The others all went off laughing and chatting.

'Let's go to the room Melanie was using,' I said quietly.

She was still there, of course, but in any case she was an integral part of the team, and deserved to share my thanks and gratitude. None of them basked: they all wanted the news about Emma. Helen openly wept. I thought Liz was going to faint; we could see the willpower it took her to say, 'I must pretend there's hope, for the choir's sake. We have to go on, don't we?'

Tom said quietly, 'It's best to say as little as we can. And keeping them occupied will stop them speculating.' He paused as we all nodded agreement. 'Jane, is it right that you found her?'

'No. A policeman friend of mine did. He used to be my liaison officer.' I wouldn't share all the circumstances yet – just in case. 'We keep in touch. He was planning to help me tidy that dratted stockroom.'

He stood stock-still. 'The one I was supposed to draw up a rota to empty and never did. So if she dies, it's my fault.'

'No. It's the fault of whoever pushed the boxes that crushed her. And someone's fault for leaving the room unlocked. And of course we all know – though this stays inside the room for a moment – she should never have been in that room in the first place. Not even in the corridor. So bear that in mind all of you when you want to beat yourselves up.'

'Even so . . .' He was weeping too now.

'Be as kind to each other as you will to the kids. And be kind to yourselves. Tomorrow we'll be here again – there's still the rodent problem to bear in mind. Any child – and any of us! – will be offered counselling if . . . if it becomes necessary.'

'Couldn't we just close the school? I'm sure everyone will understand.'

'There's a governors' meeting this evening – I think they will be making the decision.'

'What will you tell them?' Fearn asked.

'It's a closed meeting.'

I couldn't have asked for a better reaction. 'They're planning to hang you out to dry? Get the union in. Lawyer – you need a lawyer.' All the comments merged. Tom spoke the loudest: 'He wants you as the scapegoat, doesn't he? Get on to your union now – NAHT is it, for heads? You're going to need some legal support, that's obvious.'

'As well as ours,' Liz said firmly. 'We've seen you in action. You can count on us.'

Melanie, calm unflappable Melanie, whose self-control had been iron throughout, tried to speak. 'On all of us,' she said, her voice finally breaking.

How Liz managed to teach her after-school group I would never know. But teachers are a stoic race, often in front of a class when anyone else would have been in bed with a teddy bear and a Lemsip. One woman in my last school had a knife pulled on her but was back teaching the very next day. We were all drifting off when Tom stopped us – heavens, he'd make a good head teacher.

'Jane, I want us teachers to stay behind – OK, we'll need to organise some childcare cover – and put a report together. All the things that have happened recently: the playground "incident", the outbreak of disobedience, Robert's changed behaviour, Prudence dropping me in it. Everything. And also our responses and the action you've taken to prevent accidents, etcetera. Everything. And I'm volunteering to take it to the governors and their secret meeting.'

Helen gave him an odd look. 'We'll take it together, Tom. You and me, or better still all of us, including you, Melanie.' She may have meant to sound positive, but I for one got the feeling that she didn't trust him. 'We'll thrash it out here and now. OK?'

'You must sort that out between you,' I said firmly. 'But I will be grateful for anything you can do to show we're a tough and united staff with the children's well-being always at the front of our minds. Golly, that sounds like an Ofsted report, doesn't it?'

The last person I expected to see waiting outside the school gate was Meg Webster. She had walking poles, but also sported – why wasn't I surprised? – some spiked device on her shoes. Not permanent spikes: some attached by a sort of rubber harness. The only fault I could find was that they clearly weren't electronic.

'My dear girl, you need some support,' she said, 'and I'm here to offer you mine, for what it's worth.'

'Thank you.' Did I sound as nonplussed as I felt?

'Can we go inside or is the place crawling with rats – furry and otherwise?'

'I think it's deserted now, except for my friend Pat. He was on a flying visit when all this kicked off.'

'I've heard of him, haven't I?' she said, slipping off her spikes as I ushered her through the front door. 'He's the young man with the glorious voice. Mark Stephens, poor man, was saying he wanted to kidnap him. But I gather he's not from round here.'

If that was bait I wasn't rising to it. 'No. He's from near Birmingham. I'm back, Pat,' I called helpfully.

He might have been engrossed in something on the screen in front of him but, reaching for the mouse, he killed it and was on his feet shaking hands and wooing the old lady with his wonderful smile. His courtesy was so old-fashioned I almost expected him to kiss her hand. Then – I suppose it's a police skill – although he stayed in the same place he seemed to make himself disappear.

Taking a seat she looked me straight in the eye. 'I run a craft group in the village hall on Monday afternoons. Tuesdays it's gardening club, though that's on its last legs because of lack of support; Wednesday sees me doing Pilates. With the church most weekends, I spend a lot of time with both older and younger villagers, natives and incomers.' I suppressed a gasp at the term. Then I realised she was using it ironically. 'And – forgive the pun – a lot of incomers have a lot of income. Behind the scenes there's some sort of power struggle even I've not worked out yet. But the native faction is led by Brian Dawes and the young bloods by Toby Wells.'

'Sophia's father! I thought from the way he behaved in governors' meetings he was old school – almost a clone of Dawes.'

'He might be, mightn't he? Funnily enough, he's not even an incomer, though his wife shows all the symptoms. Toby was actually a pupil here for a while, though he prefers to refer to his time at public school – I can't recall which one. I believe strings were pulled for some reason. None of this gets you any further, I know, but I wanted you to know that I understand what it's like being an outsider – I've lived here for twenty-odd years but they still regard me as something of an interloper.'

Someone else had said that. About Mrs Gough. After all those years' service she'd been *almost* one of us.

'If you want my advice, my dear, when they sack you – which they assuredly will do, if that child dies – tough it out and get the biggest settlement you can. And then take to your heels and run. Back where you came from.' Nodding home her comment she got to her feet and headed out.

I followed, leaving the door ajar so that Pat would still hear what was being said. 'Mrs Webster—'

'There are some battles you can win,' she said, hand already on the front door, 'and some you can't. And when you're in the middle of a power struggle, I'd say you can't win. Just don't get crushed.' She let go of the door, stooping to reattach her spikes. 'If you need a refuge, come to my cottage. Living in one of Brian's holiday lets can't be pleasant if he's your chief enemy.'

'My enemy!'

'Oh, it's an old-fashioned, even melodramatic term. But he wanted young Tom to take Janet Gough's place, not you. Obvious, I'd have thought.'

Yet Tom seemed to be my number one fan these days. Unwilling to sound naïve enough to suggest that, my mouth asked a question before my brain was even aware of it. 'As a matter of interest, who owns the caretaker's house? Where I started out?'

She frowned. 'It used to be what they called the Education

231

Committee. Then when the cuts started someone bought it. I don't know who – but I could find out. My grandson works for the letting agent.'

'Not James Ford? Nice young man,' I added truthfully. 'He even insisted I stay at a decent hotel.'

She shot me an impish glance. 'We had better not debate who did the insisting, had we? Oh, my dear, how can we joke when a child is dying and you—' She shrugged eloquently. 'Are you sure you have an alibi for when the "accident" happened? You must be their chief suspect.'

Apart from Pat, I must be. I was ready to throw up again. I smiled positively. 'Teachers – just like parents – may talk about murdering their charges but I assure you that I didn't.'

'Of course you didn't. How can I contact you with the information about the caretaker's house?'

Great waves of paranoia surged over me. 'I should imagine I shan't be leaving here till quite late.'

'Excellent. I will phone you here, then.'

CHAPTER TWENTY-THREE

'She said a lot, but I can't say I'm much the wiser,' Pat said, merely glancing up when I returned. 'Except it was good to have my suspicions about the owner of the holiday let confirmed. It's nice to be right.'

'When are you ever not?' I asked ironically. 'Though you might have told me about the cottage . . .' More seriously I added, 'Pat, you look done in. And why not? I've never even asked you how you feel. Finding Emma. Trying to revive her. I can't imagine how you're just managing to sit here as if nothing happened.'

'That's one of the problems of doing this job,' he said. 'They expect you to become inured to all sorts of horrors and, guess what, you do become inured. Same as they expect you to have the stiffest of upper lips and carry on with your job – and guess what, you do.'

I nodded. Then the fear burst out. 'Mrs Webster's just uttered a truth I've been suppressing, despite what Carpenter said: I must be the chief suspect.'

'Nope. That's probably me, since I'm male and not from

round here – and, of course, I found her. Oh, and I'm black. That's only one step up from a wicked illegal immigrant. Let's console ourselves with the knowledge that with one or two glaring exceptions my colleagues usually get the right person in the end. For all the confusion earlier, I'd back Carpenter to sort everything out.' He paused, but I didn't chime in to agree. 'You know, Avo, if it weren't for this Brian Dawes thing I'd go and get the best bottle of booze I could afford and we could go and drink ourselves silly. But I don't somehow fancy doing that in your sort-of boss's place. I'll call the Mondiale for you and the Cricketers for me.'

I gave him my most scathing look. 'Are you imagining that I'm leaving this building with the governors' meeting here planning to sack me?'

'Assuming they meet here. I'd bet it will be in someone's nice big house.'

'You're right. Again. It'll probably be the one next door, Mrs Tibbs's, since Brian Dawes was burgled a couple of days back – you know what, I can't even remember the different days of this week: everything's a blur. But the good news is that the teachers are going to produce a report in support of me and everything I've tried to do. And my union should back me.'

'I thought unions were all pretty toothless these days.'

'They provide support and legal assistance at the very least.'

He didn't look convinced. 'The teachers' move is interesting, though, especially if they go to the media. The trouble is, I suspect it's the parents you need to woo. And if someone's already been prepared to sue, and for such a trivial reason, that doesn't sound terribly likely.'

'And the more fuss is made, the more likely Simon and his mates are to find me.'

'Ah. Simon's mates.' There was a long pause. He broke it with utter banality. 'Hang on, when did you last eat?'

'Eat! Who could eat when all this is going on?'

'Does the pub do takeaways?'

'No idea. In any case—'

He fished out his phone and tapped. I could hear Diane's voice, saying the Cricketers was a pub, not a pizza parlour, but since . . . Very well, she'd organise sandwiches for us.

'And for the teachers still in the village hall,' I reminded him in a stage whisper.

Two lots of sandwiches, it was agreed. And Diane would bring them herself.

'Mrs Webster? She's the widow of some big entrepreneur. Loads of money, but that's not going to help her soon.' Putting down an old-fashioned wicker basket beside her, Diane touched her forehead sadly. 'She's started Alzheimer's, they say. She has good days and ones when she's just a bit off-kilter. And those will start to take over. Yes, it's just gossip, Pat, but it's from a good source, though I certainly wouldn't dream of revealing it. Now, the teachers say they'll be over here in half an hour. Not Melanie – her father's had a nasty turn and she's had to go over and see him. It's not as if he was a halfway decent dad to her, either – left her mum to fend for herself for years. Then he just turned up out of the blue and the silly woman had him back. Would you believe it? And then she dies and poor Melanie's left holding – well, not the baby, of course. But her own children have just had kids, and they're on at her to babysit all hours. They were even trying to persuade her to give up work and be a full-time nanny – unpaid, I'll bet. Just because she's a widow they think she's not entitled to a life! But she dug her toes in. She said she wouldn't as long as Mrs Gough needed her; then as long as the school had no head; then till she'd got you properly run in.'

'She'll be here for a long time, then,' I said.

'You mean she'll be running in your replacement?'

I hope I didn't flinch.

'Do you think that they'll sack her or that she'll resign?' Pat asked, as if I wasn't there.

Perhaps he'd get more out of her if I pretended not to be, much though it went against the grain.

Diane settled down on to the spare chair. 'If it were me I'd cut and run. Letting a child die – not that Emma's dead yet, please God – isn't actually a sacking offence. So she'd be able to sue for wrongful dismissal and make a bundle. And toughing it out isn't exactly an option if the governors are still the same – especially that Toby Wells. Nasty little bugger, pardon my French. I didn't like him when he was a child and I don't like him now. He ran rings round poor Mrs Gough, absolute rings. But he was bright, very bright, and always two steps ahead. I think all the staff heaved a sigh of relief when he passed his eleven-plus and went off to grammar school. But then somehow or other he fetched up at some public school. No idea why. And then he comes back with that miserable cow of a wife and makes a damn nuisance of himself here.'

If I wasn't there, I couldn't observe that other people shared her opinions.

'Little man's disease?' Pat asked, with all the confidence of standing six foot two in his socks.

'You mean behaving like a total bastard to make up for his lack of inches? Well, he was the one who sold the cricket club field, which might prove your theory.' She turned to me as she got to her feet. 'Don't go until you've got this cricket deal cast in stone, will you, Jane?'

When I spoke I surprised myself again. 'It'll take a lot longer than that for them to shift me.'

'Well, good for you.' She seemed genuinely surprised. 'Time I was going. Got a pub to run. No, don't even think of paying,' she said, as I produced my purse. 'This is my treat – mine and the cricket club's.'

'Just one thing, Diane,' Pat said, getting up too, 'you wouldn't have another spare room at the Cricketers, would you? I'm a bit worried about Jane sleeping on her own in that cottage, you know.'

'Not really. I had a couple of late bookings this afternoon – all paid up by credit card, too.' She nudged him. 'I never said you couldn't share. Friends with benefits, you know!'

'I'll be OK, thanks.' I was on my feet too.

'Tell you what, Diane – I'll sleep at hers, and she can have my room with you. The one I had last time, is it? Excellent.' He sounded so authoritative that neither of us argued, not immediately, at least.

'OK. If that's what you want. I lock up about eleven-thirty, Jane.' With a nod, she turned.

I followed her out.

'He's worried about you,' she said. 'But you'll be safe under my roof.'

'Even if someone finds out I'm there? I don't want to bring trouble to your door, Diane.'

She gave a bark of laughter. 'In that case come in through the kitchen. OK?' She disappeared into the dark street; I waited till she was out of sight and locked the door behind her.

'What the hell was that about?' I asked the second I returned to my office. 'Why should you sleep at my place and not me?'

'It was about my wanting to case your joint. After I check out the caretaker's house, that is.'

'You're a suspect in a murder case and you want to add a spot of breaking and entering to your CV?'

'I'll do it very professionally. And I shall wear a mask.'

'A mask!'

'The sort of mask people wear for a bit of DIY sanding. Quite effective. And you can keep obbo if you want. How about that? Come on, Avo, a bit of action will give you a bit of an adrenalin lift and you'll feel much better.'

Funnily enough, it did. Having a real risk to face – my friend being caught breaking the law – trumped the theoretical ones hanging over our heads. In any case, within a very few minutes he was stepping over the inadequate little fence and half-walking, half-sliding across the playground. Although he clearly had something to report, he insisted on going back into the school and locking the door behind us again.

'Very well – tell me what I found,' he said, removing his mask.

'Camera lenses. In the bathroom? Are you expecting some at the cottage too?' I asked, my voice flat with an emotion I couldn't identify. 'In which case, can we assume that Brian Dawes is a very sick voyeur?'

'We can assume that *someone* is. OK, Avo, my Kentish friends haven't the time to search the crime scene thoroughly, and we certainly do not make life worse for ourselves by crossing that official tape. But there's no embargo on emptying the other stockroom, is there? I bet you've still got some black sacks? To hell with our clothes: it'll take your mind off the governors' meeting.'

'The teachers? They should be here in five minutes. Let's wait and have another coffee with them and then start.'

We'd only put the kettle on when the staff deputation appeared, their faces when they found we were on our own the picture of frustration. Giving the impression that they would run the governors to earth wherever they were, they set off purposefully into the night.

Actually Pat was right about the spring-cleaning too: dealing with the years of accumulated stockroom rubbish was almost therapeutic. We quickly fell into a pattern. Pat retrieved a box or sack. I checked the contents. If there was anything worth saving, I labelled it and put it to one side. At the end of half an hour, the black sacks of rubbish outnumbered boxes of possible treasure by eleven to two. Yes, I'd been ruthless: it felt very good. No, I'd found nothing interesting. By now we were both sneezing. Pat actually had to use the asthma inhaler I'd only ever seen him resort to once before.

'Wouldn't wearing your face mask help?'

'I suppose I could give it a try.' He did.

Though he soon started wheezing again, he insisted that we press on until we had half the room clear.

There was still no sign of anything incriminating. Unless there was some reason for a two-litre plastic Wall's Ice Cream box to be stuffed full of old 35 mm cassettes – someone had taken a lot of photos. But until they were developed – and who would have the technology in these digital days? – we wouldn't know if they were simply snaps of long-past sports days. All the same, I locked them in my office safe. He popped some sort of pill, and sprayed his nose. His bloodshot and swimming eyes dared me to comment.

Without speaking, we mounted another attack. Our target was the back wall, even if that meant restacking some boxes without opening them. But our tally slowly rose, in roughly the same proportion as before. Although we found nothing else remotely interesting our progress felt good. But it wasn't good to see Pat gasping at his inhaler again, his ribs and shoulders heaving. I shoved him out into the corridor hoping the air was more breathable there.

'I'll just have a puff of my spray—'

'You stay where you are. I can carry on on my own.'

He didn't argue.

Then my big mouth announced, 'There's something over there – where the plaster has come away. No. Don't come in. I'm just pushing a couple of boxes across as if I don't like signs that the place is falling down. Now I'm going to look really worried about you and shoo you out into the hall.'

Once again he did what he was told. But strangely he did

give me a hug as I emerged into the hall. 'Another camera?' he asked, as if asking tenderly about my health.

'You bet.' I hugged him back. Oscars for us next year.

Back in my office he sneezed his way through half the box of tissues on my desk, but his breathing became easier. 'Always wanted a dog or a cat,' he said, over an apple he'd found in Diane's picnic basket, 'but I'd be like that all the time.'

'You won't get properly better till you've changed your clothes and showered all the dust off your hair and skin. Take yourself off to the Cricketers for half an hour.'

'No, I'll go to your place – I've never tried the bathroom there, have I? It'll be "an experience"! Don't argue.'

'Very well.' I passed him my keys. 'Just to make your journey worthwhile you can bring me some clean clothes. I'm staying here. Just in case. But I shall lock up after you and not open the door till I hear your voice.'

He gave me a grin I can only describe as rueful. 'I thought I was supposed to be the bossy one.'

I scrubbed my hands and got as much dust as possible out of my hair by rubbing it with a damp towel. It didn't do much for the styling, but made me feel better and might reduce the chances of Pat having another allergy attack. Then I tried to settle down at my desk and produce a coherent account of my morning's movements. It took several attempts, but eventually I could prove that – apart from about three minutes between my conversation with Wayne, the rodent man, and Pat's arrival, I had been in full view of other people. But I had to think of it from Mandy Carpenter's point of view: would three minutes have been enough to sneak away on my own, make sure that none of the pest team could see me, enter a room I believed to be locked and kill a child? Surely not.

I ought to have felt better.

Instead, I shivered – the sort of frisson that makes people remark that someone must have walked over their grave. And despite myself, I was very afraid – but not necessarily for my own safety.

Pat had been gone a long time. Far longer than it took to shower and change – and even to run someone else's clothes to earth in a strange house. Where was he? How would he feel if I phoned? As if I was some insecure nagging woman – well, he might not be too far out there. And I couldn't honestly say that I didn't feel safe here, could I? Even when the ring of the school landline set my heart beating so fast I could scarcely lift the handset, let alone speak.

It was the last person on the planet I expected to phone me. Exaggeration. But who would have expected Tamsin Powell, from the Open the Book team, to call me?

'Jane, I hope I'm not interrupting anything. Good. I know you have to work so very hard – and so very late.'

'Any head does,' I pointed out.

'Not necessarily in such challenging circumstances.'

I couldn't disagree with that.

'Now, I wanted you to know that we're all praying for you – all of us Open the Book-ers. Mark – Mark Stephens – popped in to let me know that there was an emergency governors' meeting and that he was afraid that though you've done an exemplary job in the very short time you've been with us that someone wants you gone.

By hook or by crook is what he said. In fact, he went so far as to wonder if this terrible accident to Emma is part of a stunt to humiliate you that went appallingly wrong. I don't know whether he'll carry anyone with him when he defends you. But all of us here – that's Dougie, Belinda and Mary, and me of course – are praying. I never know if our sending God a shopping list makes any difference, but we feel totally impotent and this helps us. And knowing we're doing it might just help you.'

If I'd failed to insert all the usual non-verbal prompts to show I was listening, it was because I was trying to hold back tears. I could deal with insults and viciousness – but not simple kindness.

She must have heard a snuffle. 'Oh, you poor dear. Would you like us – yes, we're on our way.'

I had hardly put down the phone when it rang again.

'Tamsin here, again. By your cottage. You mustn't worry, Jane – that friend of yours – Pat? – is out safely, and the fire brigade is on its way. Ah, here he is!'

'First up, Avo, I'm fine. But my phone's back inside and there's no way I can get back to it.' He gasped – his asthma was back. 'Didn't this friend of yours tell you? The place is on fire.'

'I'm on my way.'

'Nothing you can do here,' he continued between coughs. 'Stay put. D'you hear me? Lock yourself in. Bolt yourself in. Understand?'

I couldn't obey him, not this time. For some reason taking the box of cassettes with me, I flung myself into the hire car – cursing that I had to get out again to scrape off all the ice – and headed for the cottage. Fire crews were already in place, and seemed to have stopped the fire spreading much beyond the kitchen. Clearly they didn't want me popping in to check. At first I couldn't see Pat, but then caught sight of him being transferred from a small Nissan to an ambulance, wearing nothing but a towel, a pashmina and a foil blanket.

I fought my way through the bystanders, including what seemed like half the Open the Book team, to speak to him; he waved away the paramedic administering oxygen long enough to tell me he was fine and ask what the hell I was doing on my own. Oh, and since I was here, could I get his mobile phone, which he fancied was in the bathroom.

The paramedic suggested that since that would take time, I should rendezvous with Pat in Ashford A&E. And why not? I couldn't influence anything at the governors' meeting. I couldn't fight off a siege of the school. I might as well do what I'd always wanted to do – return a tiny favour to someone who, apart from a few moments last weekend, had been unfailingly kind and supportive all the time he'd known me. The miniest of mini favours, true. But it was a start.

CHAPTER TWENTY-FOUR

Accident & Emergency at Ashford Hospital, named after the circulation of the blood man, William Harvey, was busy, and it took me some time to locate Pat. My admission that I wasn't next of kin or a partner meant I had to argue my way in to see him; waving his mobile phone and a bag of clothes seemed to be the clincher, which was fortunate, since the first of the night's drunks were already arriving – soon no one would have a moment to do anything other than deal with crises.

Somewhat less than more covered in a hospital gown, he greeted me with a wave. Something was being pumped into a mask that covered his face: his breathing sounded reassuringly normal, and his ribs heaved far less.

'Got your wheels? Excellent – because I'm out of here.'

My headmistress voice took over. 'Are you sure you're ready to be discharged?' It seemed my opportunity for a martyred night-long wait for him was being denied. On the other hand, what was a bit of martyrdom compared to a safe recovery?

'In my terms, yes. Listen to that lot.' It sounded as if an entire nightclub had arrived. 'And it's not even a weekend boozing night. Makes me feel quite puritanical about the demon drink – though not enough to give it up,' he added with a grin. 'You brought some clothes? Excellent. Now,' he continued as he dressed, 'we walk out as if we own the place. No one'll stop us that way.'

For all his bravado, however, when we passed a harassed nurse en route, he did tell her he was checking out. 'You need the bed space,' he added kindly.

She could not argue.

I was afraid the bitter night air would make him bad again, but he refused to let me bring the car round for him. I suspect it was only the fact he didn't know where I'd parked that stopped him striding out ahead of me to prove how well he was.

'Back to the Cricketers,' he said, checking his texts as I inched on to the main road. 'Diane's heard all about the fire, of course, and says we're both expected there. So we've got a roof over our heads. What about your job, by the way? Have you been sacked or suspended or what?'

I clapped my hand over my mouth. 'You know what, I've not given it a thought since the fire! Dig in my bag, will you, and check my texts? And my voicemail?'

'Nothing,' he said. 'Nothing at all. Now is that good or bad news?'

'Maybe it's just that they've got the old-fashioned courtesy to sack people by formal letter.'

Diane had left a plate of cheese and biscuits in the kitchen for us, and bottles of whisky and brandy. As one we ignored them. But what we couldn't quite ignore was the particularly large elephant in the room – Pat's bedroom to be precise. I suspect that had we had the hottest of hots for each other we were both too exhausted to have done anything about it. I was. But I had all those scars to give me more than my share of prudery and he – maybe he had a wife and Sunday-swimming-lesson kids at home.

I was ready to gabble a suggestion we might sleep head to toe.

But Diane had pre-empted any discussion: she'd split what I presumed had been a king-sized bed into two chaste single ones. And, for good measure, had shoved a cabinet between them.

I set the alarm on my mobile: with luck we might get four hours' sleep.

In fact, Pat got considerably more. Although he'd woken when I did, he rolled over and was snoring again within a minute, somewhat to my relief. Even the noise of the shower didn't disturb him, but I drew the line at trying to use the hairdryer. As for my clothes, they were as filthy as when I'd stripped them off, and stank of smoke.

Diane took one look – or one sniff – and found me a wrap-around skirt, t-shirt and heavy sweater. 'Use my room to dry your hair, for goodness' sake.' She didn't sound kind, just exasperated: she was already running downstairs.

Five minutes later, I discovered that she was indeed fuming, but not at me. The mysterious travellers who'd booked her spare bedrooms had both failed to turn up without explanation. She fulminated as she produced strong coffee and a bacon sandwich. 'Quicker than a full

English,' she observed tersely. 'Clothes? You still look more like a bag lady than a head teacher, you know. And you still smell like a kipper.'

'That'll be my undies. But these are so much better—'

'They'll do till you get to the cottage and can change into your own clothes.'

'You don't suppose they won't let me into the cottage? Hell, Diane, I really don't know how much longer I can do all this.'

'As long as it takes,' she said, the hug she gave me at odds with the apparent heartlessness of her words. 'Now, Jane, I know it's not ideal, but if you need a roof over your head, then there's always one of our rooms. Bugger the pre-existing bookings. If they can't turn up and they don't let me know they can't turn up, then they've forfeited their rights, as far as I'm concerned.' She laughed as I gibbered, mixing gratitude and anxiety in one sentence. 'Off you go: I'll keep an eye on Sleeping Beauty up there.'

Although it was before eight-thirty, when I arrived at Dove Cottage I found an insurance assessor already prowling round inside. I wished the borrowed clothes fitted better. If I'm fighting I like to look like a winner. He removed an elegant but smoke-damaged throw from a sofa and sat down uninvited.

So did I, holding out my hand for his card. Julian Pardew. He wasn't at all like the kindly insurance guy on the TV ads, making sure the child rendered homeless by burst pipes had her toy monkey. And he lacked the address of the Harvey Keitel hard man in another insurance ad.

'Your first rental rendered uninhabitable by a flood, the

second by fire: you are having an interesting time, aren't you, Ms Cowan?'

'I am indeed. But by your tone you think I'm less a victim than a criminal. Am I right?' My tone in turn suggested more sorrow than anger, but in fact he enraged me. There was nothing personal in my dislike. In fact, had I, like him, been a representative of the insurance company responsible for all Brian Dawes's properties, I would have been every bit as suspicious as he was. 'But I certainly wasn't responsible for the cold weather that froze an inadequately insulated set of pipes in a house already cold because someone had stolen one lot of heating oil and someone else had hijacked another delivery. As for the fire, I'd not been in the building since seven-thirty in the morning. How could I have started it?'

'You could have left a tea towel on a toaster.'

'Why on earth would I have done that?'

I think my blank disbelief might have worked. He was shuffling the paperwork he'd spread out beside him.

'People do all sorts of strange things absent-mindedly. You should see the way people with Alzheimer's contrive to cause havoc.'

'Should I, now? Since I only picked up my master's degree last year, I think I can argue a tolerable amount of mental ability. What actually caused the fire, Mr Pardew?'

'I really would like you to tell me that.'

'Give me a clue,' I suggested affably. 'In the building or outside? Accelerant or electrical – and not a toaster, I suspect. Look, I spent half last night in William Harvey A&E with the friend of mine who was caught in the fire. The smoke has done his asthma no good at all, and this little charade is frankly wasting the time I should be spending with my children in the village hall.'

'Ah, yes – another accident on your watch. Oh, more than one! One child with a broken limb, another on life support. Am I right?'

'You are indeed. But you've missed one: an attack by a rat trapped inside a locked drawer.'

'A rat?' It might have been one squeaking.

'Indeed. In a desk drawer. Oh, please sit down again, Mr Pardew. The incident took place at the school, and I promise not to open any drawers here without warning you first. I agree with you absolutely that few if any of these apparent accidents are in fact accidental. I am certainly one common factor in them all, but I suspect that there may be others.'

'Such as?'

'You want me to voice my suspicions and risk being sued for libel? But you might want to accompany me to the school – once I've changed out of these borrowed clothes, that is. The police are due to interview me in half an hour about the terrible event yesterday, and you might find yourself sharing information with DCI Carpenter, the senior investigating officer.' I stood.

He mumbled: apparently he was accepting my invitation.

We travelled in separate cars.

Leaving him to Melanie's ministrations, I started on the morning's batch of texts, emails and phone calls. There was absolutely nothing from the governors: no enquiry about Emma's health, or even about Pat's. There was no mention of my job, and no recommendation about continuing to keep the school open in the village hall. It was of course my decision, and mine alone, but I was surprised no one had tried to influence me. The only thing of interest was a note in Melanie's immaculate script: it was Brian Dawes who owned the former caretaker's house. But there was nothing I could do with the information at the moment. The life of the school was more important than my own interests.

When I phoned him, Mark Stephens sounded strangely reluctant to lead a special assembly to include prayers for Emma – and for the person or persons responsible for her injuries. What was wrong with the man? If Ian, with no formal qualifications, could hold the attention of a hundred youngsters, surely a clergyman, whose training must have included grief counselling, could draw on that and on his years of experience to respond to the crisis? After all, he knew not just the children but also their parents. If anyone could empathise, surely it was he. Finally I extracted a promise from him, not on the grounds of their needing spiritual guidance and comfort but simply because in the absence of proper lessons he would provide some diversion.

At long last came an email from Brian Dawes instructing me not to speak to the media, alongside two from Julie Freeman begging me for information. I forwarded them to Dawes, not meekly, but nonetheless with a certain amount of relief that I could spend my time and energy on other matters.

These included an interview with the police, who had without consultation hijacked the staffroom. What they would have done had the staff needed it I didn't bother to ask – no doubt they would have ejected me from my office. At least DCI Carpenter did me the courtesy of letting me stay there for the time being – and even chose to interview me there, though I did have to instruct Melanie to block any calls.

After brusquely dismissing my enquiry about poor little Emma – apparently she was now stable, whatever that meant – Carpenter homed in on my blank five minutes like a wasp spotting a beer can.

'It doesn't take long to kill someone, Ms Cowan. Or at least to attempt to.'

I rolled up my sleeves to reveal my scars. 'Don't think I'm not aware of that. But there are differences in the circumstances. My former husband knew where I was, had a weapon and even, in his perverted mind, a motive. As far as I knew, Emma was with her classmates under the supervision of my highly professional staff. She certainly shouldn't have been in the stockroom. I didn't know she was in the stockroom. Incidentally, I still don't know why she was in the stockroom.' I paused before responding to her implicit question: 'Are you suggesting that in between Wayne's departure and Pat's arrival I made a speculative dash to the far side of the building to see if I might by some chance find a potential victim?'

'I'm asking the questions, thank you, Ms Cowan.'

'That's a great shame. Otherwise I could have asked you if you wanted to see what Pat and I found last night – before the fire.'

'We'll talk about your foraging later. It's these missing minutes I'm interested in.'

She was. She genuinely was.

And I was at a loss. Until my phone chirruped to announce a text.

'Leave that, please.'

'Of course.' But the silly sound flicked a switch in my brain. I almost felt a physical jolt. At last, I said slowly, unable to suppress a disbelieving smile, 'My alibi . . . You know, I sent a lot of texts in those missing five minutes. Do you want to see the times involved?' I turned the phone to face her.

She might have been pleased. If she was, she went to a great deal of effort not to show it. And not to show any interest in the ice cream box of film cassettes, which I carried round with me like a plastic albatross. At least she was decidedly more interested in the information about the stockroom camera I'd uncovered.

'What did you do when you found it?' She frowned in concern.

'I pretended I'd not noticed it. In fact, I shoved some boxes back in front of it. If I was anxious when we located the cameras in the loos, when there was a school full of police officers to protect me, how do you imagine I felt when all I had was Pat, in the throes of a really bad asthma attack?' When she didn't respond, I continued, 'Incidentally, did you know that my new temporary home has been rendered unusable? A fire caused by an electrical fault, they say. Or, of course, according to the insurance assessor, in a moment of senile amnesia I could have stuffed a tea towel in the toaster. Mandy, the police have a wonderful reputation for supporting their own. If you can't protect *me*, remember that Pat might easily have died last night. The assessor is rightly suspicious—'

'Rightly?'

'I would be in his situation. He's waiting in the school secretary's office to talk to you.' I had a feeling he might be

253

there some time. With Melanie's coffee so good, he might well be so full of caffeine he'd be walking on the ceiling by the time Mandy got round to him. 'But you and I know something else, don't we? That my violent and sadistic ex-husband could be behind a lot of these attacks, just as easily as someone wanting me out of the school.'

'He's still in jail. Up in Durham, as far as I know.' She'd done her homework, then. And she was thawing. 'In fact, it doesn't have to be either/or, does it? Unlikely, as it seems one person could be behind both.' She gave a sudden, warm smile that took me completely aback. 'You know what, Jane, one woman to another? I'm this close to calling in the Major Incident Team. But I really don't want it to look as if I can't handle it.'

'You and me both. We both want the attacker found, and the rest of these kids safe and me in one piece. But neither of us wants to lose face. The trouble from your point of view, Mandy, is that the person who knows even more about my past than I do is another officer, and a man to boot. Pat. So if you didn't mind working with someone from West Midlands Police as opposed to the Essex force you're supposed to be co-operating with, he might share everything and save you a lot of time. There's my ex's huge range of contacts, for instance. We're not talking about the criminal underworld, Mandy – Simon numbered QCs among his nice middle-class friends. People who sit in the best seat at the theatre or concerts. Who go to private views. Who have second homes all over the place.'

'Who are probably highly respected school governors, if not necessarily here in Kent,' she summed up neatly.

I'd leave it to Pat to tell her who he had been illicitly checking up on last night.

She looked at her watch and gasped. 'I've got a meeting five minutes ago. You know we've commandeered your staffroom: is that OK?'

Better late than never. 'Fine by me. But I really would co-opt Pat, if I were you. If he's awake yet.' She copied his details into her phone. 'Not to mention that Pardew guy, who must be completely awash with caffeine by now.'

Her official nod of appreciation was soon replaced by something else. 'How are you really surviving? No sleep, no food by the look of it?'

'The way you manage. Now I must go and see how the kids are faring over the road.'

She had reached for her phone: 'By the way, I'm calling in the techies immediately. I'll also get them to process those cassettes ASAP. And the crime scene team can come and look at both stockrooms. And we'll need school records going back to the year dot.'

'You need Melanie. She's a genius with coffee, remember, and has everything at her fingertips. And if she doesn't, she'll know someone who does.'

'Do you think she'll have bought any more pikelets?'

CHAPTER TWENTY-FIVE

I was glad I had made the decision to keep the school open. It wouldn't have been possible without the support of the staff, of course, and I might not even still have a job without their intervention. It was wonderful to see them going purposefully about their work in the village hall. The kids, in small mixed-age groups, seemed totally absorbed in what they were doing.

At a lift of my eyebrow, Tom left his group and slipped unobtrusively towards me. We edged back out of the front door into the cold sunlight. Suddenly I longed for a thaw.

'Thanks for doing all this – without even being asked. I really appreciate what everyone is doing, you know.' If I continued in that vein my voice would crack. 'I meant to be here well before registration but I got delayed by the insurance assessor and then by the police,' I said dryly.

'Yeah – we were shocked by that fire. Is that mate of yours OK?'

'Sleeping off the smoke down at the Cricketers. How did your encounter with the governors go last night?'

'Surprisingly well. We gave it as our professional opinion that even though some parents might want to keep their children at home, the kids needed familiar routine, and that it was the school's function to provide them with a framework. And we said we thought you were the one to give it ongoing stability and purpose. No one seemed inclined to argue, though there were one or two who thought you were too accident prone. As if that was your fault, somehow. And then we got news of the fire at your cottage, and an ambulance on-site there—'

'But how did anyone know? It's not even in the village.'

'Two of the retained firemen called out to the blaze live near the Cricketers. Anyway, people suddenly grew consciences when they thought it might be you.'

'I'd rather they'd had them before poor Emma's accident. Or whatever it was. She's stable, by the way.' For the time being he and the others didn't need to know the precariousness of her grip on life. Who could have dreamt of such a thing, let alone carry it out? How? Most of all, why? As soon as there was a second's silence, my head was filled with questions I simply couldn't answer. Of course it was the job of the police to find out all the answers – but a child on my premises was my responsibility.

However Tom was speaking. 'Thank God for that.'

He'd expect a snappy response. 'Speaking of God, how did Mark Stephens' special assembly go?'

He rolled his eyes.

'That well?'

'We couldn't understand it, Jane: he deals with these kids all the time. But today he just didn't seem able to hack it. Perhaps he could imagine himself having to take poor

257

Emma's funeral . . . Anyway, we prayed a bit, and sang a couple of really inappropriate hymns. I mean, *My God is a great Big God* is great for kids, with all the actions and such, but not when everyone who could understand was bruised with shock and grief and the littlies were just bemused.' He shook his head. 'He left you this note, by the way.'

It was my turn to be bemused, but I'd open the folded slip of paper later.

Tom continued, 'If it's all right with you, instead of letting them loose in the playground at break, we thought we'd take the kids for a walk. A nice crocodile-type walk. Some of the Open the Book team have agreed to ride herd for us so there's no chance of anyone slipping away.'

'And you've organised all this? Well done, Tom.'

He flushed. 'Not just me. All of us. Fearn, too – bringing in the OTB team was her idea, actually.'

'Well done all of you.' It was time to ask the question I'd been dreading. 'Any notable absentees?'

'Funnily enough,' he said, his voice dripping with irony, 'Sophia and Prudence. Though Robert is here. If ever a parent frogmarched her child it was Mrs Bowman.'

We both laughed grimly. 'Sophia and Prudence?' I prompted him. 'Phone calls from their parents?'

'Zilch. I'm afraid – you know we had no option – we had to tell the police when they asked. They said they'd send special officers to find out where they were and talk to them. I know they'll have a responsible adult alongside, but do you think one of us ought to be there? A familiar face?'

'The way you and I feel about one of them at least, I'd say absolutely not!'

He hung his head, like a shamefaced child.

My phone whistled cheerfully to announce a text. Pat. 'I'm going to have to leave you to it, I'm afraid. Sorry.'

'No problem. Er . . . Jane . . . are you getting on OK with the police? They're . . .'

'They're not going to send me to the Tower of London yet,' I said. 'Look, somehow I'm going to have to bring in a succession of supply teachers to give you good people a break. You can't go on like this.'

He looked me straight in the eye. 'And neither, Jane, can you.'

Tom was right, of course, just as Mandy had been. How much sleep had I had over the last two weeks? How many meals had I skipped? I must tell myself that this nightmare would soon be over, that all I had to do was keep my head down and wait for the experts to deal with everything. Then I would have time to live like a normal human being, or as much like a human as anyone working in a school could hope to live. In the meantime, I would have to text an apology to Mark: unfortunately I wouldn't be able to meet him face to face to discuss the arrangements for Sunday's service in the school hall. In fact, I had no power over the building at the moment, and I suggested he contact DCI Carpenter direct to see when it might be open. I toyed with adding her number, but decided against: she was at least as busy as I was, and must surely have a junior officer briefed to deal with such enquiries.

Texts were more than useful, of course, but sometimes I still preferred to hear a voice, so I responded to the next incoming message with a phone call. It transpired that all

Pat had wanted to know was if I was all right. He was: he'd been invited to go and chafe the fat with Mandy and her mates. At least he wouldn't need a translation of the Black Country idiom to know she wanted a chinwag. He was delighted: he had a lot of information to share with her from his research last night, he said.

'Am I going to be party to it too?' To my own ears I sounded petty. On the other hand, if it was relevant information, I needed to know it, and it might as well be sooner rather than later.

'I thought you'd be too busy headmistressing. Or looking for new accommodation. Or buying new clothes. Yes, you need them. Stuff rescued from a fire always smells kippered. If you've got a spare hour, treat yourself to a trip to Canterbury – outside the village the main roads are OK.' Yes, I'd driven down them fast enough last night. 'Talk later – right?'

'Right.' But a buzz from Melanie told me my shopping spree was over before it was started. I had another visitor.

James Ford, smiling across my desk at me and holding a mug of green tea, had already lined up fresh accommodation. But he was clearly nonplussed by my cautious response.

'Who owns it? Ms Cowan, I really can't tell you that!'

'Very well. I will tell you whose properties I will not move into and you can act accordingly. I have had two very bad experiences in properties owned by Mr Brian Dawes and wish to have another landlord next time. I want a home with no plumbing or electrical problems. Mr Dawes is an excellent governor and a model citizen, but he employs a poor maintenance team. In my opinion,' I added. Until James found what was previously so elusive, I would simply take up Diane's offer to hole up at The Jolly Cricketers.

He thrust back into his bag a bunch of printouts (Dawes must have an extensive portfolio!), producing instead the very latest in smartphones. 'Ah! We do have a vacancy in another holiday let. Honeysuckle Cottage. Yes, I know it's a cliché, but it's what clients like – a pretty name. It's in the village too, not far from where you're based now. I believe it's owned by a young couple. Incomers, I think,' he added dubiously. 'Bear with me.' He sent the details to my own mobile.

The photos and the details were indeed impressive.

'Who would be my landlord?'

'Oh, Ms Cowan, you know I can't tell you that, either. What I will say is that it isn't Mr Dawes. It really is five-star accommodation, you know.'

It certainly looked it. I was just about to agree when I thought of another question, but one I might not ask aloud. How had it just come about that a place was free, when a week ago there was nothing to be had anywhere? Was I really getting paranoid now? I dug deep into the assertiveness training that was part of my original therapy. 'Could you arrange for me to see it before I make any decisions? I'm sure you're free on Saturdays, and I can't imagine that in this weather people are queuing up for a sojourn in rural Kent.' Now Mandy was less inclined to suspect me, with luck she would detail one of her technical officers to check it. 'Meanwhile, I need to retrieve all my belongings from Dove Cottage. Will you clear that with the assessors for me? It's a good job I travel light, isn't it?'

'Actually, it's not just you wanting access to the cottage.

You'll have to wait, I'm afraid, until some guys from the Fire Service have poked round. Goodness knows why – it wasn't all that serious a fire.'

Arson – that would be what they were looking for, surely. Traces of accelerant, like the time Simon tried to set fire to the flat the refuge had found me. I said soberly, 'All fires could be serious. Smoke inhalation apart from anything else. All those nasty fumes . . . I'm sure you're aware that a friend of mine ended up in William Harvey A&E? Has Mr Dawes told you anything about it?'

'Only that it had started in the kitchen. A chip pan, that sort of thing – very common.'

Perhaps a chip pan was one up from a toasted tea towel. But as far as I knew there was no such low-tech thing in the kitchen. I wonder if Dawes just meant to smoke me out or to destroy something. If so, what was he after? Was it something very small that came with a miniature lens? Before that, however, he wanted to offer me his hospitality: a text arrived – from a man I'd expected to be socially punctilious – inviting me to dinner on Saturday. He made no mention of Pat. I'd reply when I felt like it.

To my delight, Mandy Carpenter was one step ahead of me: she had already detailed her technical team to check out Dove Cottage and said she'd be delighted to get them to scan the latest property I'd been offered.

'I couldn't ask another favour, could I?' I asked as she collapsed on to one of my spare chairs. 'They won't tell me who owns this Honeysuckle Cottage, and after two Brian Dawes's properties I'd really like to know.'

She made a note, then looked me straight in the eye.

'What you really want to know is if Dawes installed the cameras in the school, the caretaker's house and Dove Cottage. Right?'

I nodded. 'I had him down as my arch-enemy from the start, but he's been an excellent governor in many, many respects. I don't want him to be a villain.'

'Oh, God, you've not fallen for his old-world charm, have you? Some of the most attractive men I've ever met have committed vile crimes.'

'Tell me about it,' I said ruefully. 'I married Simon.'

A young crime scene investigator popped his head round the door. 'Boss? Something you should see.'

I was on my feet in an instant.

'Sorry, Jane – this means just me. For now,' she conceded.

However important the work I ought to do, I simply couldn't concentrate. Perhaps green tea would be safer than coffee. Melanie shook her head: 'Sorry – young James brought his own. I can get some this weekend.' She jotted.

'Melanie, this is worse for you than it is for me. You know not just the kids but the families, don't you?'

She pointed to a new poster on her wall – one of the Keep Calm series. 'It's all you can do, isn't it? Carry on? Though I did fancy one of the ruder ones.' Her smile segued from brave to sympathetic. 'At least I've got my family around me, Jane. At times – a lot of times, to be honest – they can be a pain. But they've rallied round well – would you believe it, they're cooking me meals instead of expecting to be waited on? But you're on your own, aren't you? And you're quite right, you are drinking far too much coffee.' She looked round conspiratorially, and reached something from her desk. 'I told those gannets of police officers I'd run out.

Pikelets, indeed. Have a good old-fashioned crumpet, Jane.'

'They're called pikelets where I come from too,' I said mildly. 'My grandmother used to make her own. Maybe I ought to learn. When all this is over.'

'It's a bugger, isn't it?' Pat observed. 'All this going down and you can't be part of it. I wonder what they've found. Hey, are you OK?'

'Only half-dead with shock. I didn't hear you come in.'

He perched on the edge of my desk, swinging his feet and wafting imaginary smoke from under his nose. 'Look, there's that huge Outlet at Ashford. I bet it's late night opening on a Friday. We'll go and kit you out. I might get myself a few more socks too. Tell you what, isn't it time they'd sorted out that car of yours? How long can it take to shift a bit of glue?'

As a diversion it worked quite well. Losing my temper with the garage for not telling me my car was likely to be written off – except it turned out it wasn't my car but one belonging to someone called Cohen – felt quite good. The information that it would be another four days before they could even look at mine elicited another therapeutic temper tantrum. Pat always knew what I needed.

He followed it with another suggestion – that we go and check out whatever it was that Mandy hadn't invited us to see. This turned out to be the hall, where she stood arms akimbo in organised chaos. Stacked by the back door was a mound of bagged material – the entire contents of both stockrooms, by the look of it.

'Some spring-clean,' he observed.

'We'll take all the stuff you threw away last night, too,

Pat,' Mandy said, not questioning our arrival, but having a little dig at us to make up for her restraint. 'If only you'd told us the other stockroom was a crime scene.' She spoke as if I were her most junior officer, not someone with whom she's had civilised conversations on equal terms.

Any moment now I'd have another tantrum. 'I think I might have hinted it could be,' I said coldly. How on earth had she forgotten the conversation we'd had about it? Stress, fatigue and overwork, I suppose. But I needed her on my side, so I wouldn't adopt the tone I habitually used when a child had forgotten its homework. And maybe if I empathised a bit more I could understand that she needed a bit of female support. 'Mandy, have you had to bring in the MIT big guns?'

I was rewarded with a brief smile. 'Not yet. There's a lot of work going on with the people we used to call CEOPS, the child protection people trying to stop online exploitation of children. Our technical people are trying to trace the link between active cameras – those in the stockrooms are dead – and whoever is receiving the images. All the children will be interviewed as witnesses sometime soon, when we can round up their parents or carers. Now, thanks to that saint of yours, Melanie, we know who is absent today, and we're trying to locate them and their parents. In their case, specifically parents. I gather from your deputy, Tom whatever his name is, that a couple of them have been . . . difficult this term.'

I ignored Tom's sudden and unpaid promotion: in any case, it would be good to be able to make it official, wouldn't it? Even if it was only a temporary upgrade. 'One or two children have been very difficult. It was partly their behaviour that made me invite PCSO Ian Cooper in to give an assembly talk on the importance of morality.'

Her eyebrows disappeared into her hair. 'A bit heavy for five-year-olds, I'd have thought.'

'Not the way he did it. He's got a rare talent, Mandy – look out for him. It's a requirement that when children establish a pattern of bad behaviour the school has to implement programmes to improve it. My hope was that some unofficial input would improve matters so that we didn't have to go down the official route.' I had to say it before the others could: 'But it certainly didn't have the effect I hoped for, if a child like Emma Hamilton can immediately take herself off into a banned area. If she took herself, of course. If she didn't, Mandy, who took her?'

Suddenly I was praying that it was an adult, not another child. Had I not been all along? Perhaps the police had too: they'd rather it had been me or Pat, wouldn't they? And who could blame them? It was the children themselves, in the Rosie incident, who blamed the problem on lack of proper supervision, including CCTV. They might have been parroting an adult's words, but it had only been my own wish, clearly expressed to the governors.

'It's something we're working on at the moment. Sorry – I have to take this.' She might have raised the phone to her mouth but she spoke to Pat. 'You might be interested too.' And they walked away, leaving me on my own in the empty hall.

My office felt deeply unwelcoming: I felt like a child suddenly abandoned by grown-ups. But I wouldn't howl. I must make myself think. Think like an adult. Where had my thoughts, my logic been during the last twenty-four hours? It was time for me to do what my therapist had recommended – to find a place of calm and silence and centre on myself. Only that way could I start focusing on other people.

But where on earth could I find such a place of refuge? Not in this school, not in this village: that much at least was certain. All I could do was laugh at myself and adjourn to the staff loo with a notepad and pencil – low tech but often effective to help clarify my thoughts. I was literally on my way there when I had a text from Richard Morris. Rosie was home from hospital and would really welcome visits from her friends at the school. Did I recall promising to take her some work? Could I manage it today? She was getting bored already.

Would a walk provide just the period of calm I needed? I was deeply tempted. Then I realised that it might help me, but it would hardly help the staff who would have to interrupt their already chaotic schedule in order to organise the individual assignments Rosie would need. Perhaps I could ask them to do it at the end of school? And perhaps I couldn't! They needed their freedom and whatever relaxation time at home could provide. I texted back: I was sorry to disappoint Rosie but we had problems at the school that required my presence. With luck I would be able to come and see her some time over the weekend. I didn't add that producing work would be my responsibility.

He responded with a glum-face emoticon.

I was tempted to text a cross-face one back. Surely as a governor Richard could imagine the chaos that would have prevailed but for the staff's dedication? Surely even as an ordinary villager he would know how much pressure we were all under? Why had I not made a stand on day one, and every time since when they'd burdened me or my colleagues unreasonably? I had been supine, appeasing. Even the loo mirror showed my posture had collapsed. There I was, round-shouldered and hunched, as if trying to make myself invisible. I reviewed my body, joint by joint. There: I was standing tall literally, and prepared to do so metaphorically. Back at my desk, I sent an email to Dawes, copied to the rest of the governors. Then I headed for the staffroom.

I might have knocked on the door, but I didn't wait for an answer before I entered. You could almost hear the swish as eyebrows shot up – Pat's included.

I sat down uninvited. I used the words I had used in my email to the governors: 'I think it's time I was updated, don't you?'

CHAPTER TWENTY-SIX

My chair, slightly higher than the others, gave me an authority I was determined would not be spurious. 'Ladies and gentlemen, I have responsibilities to my staff and to my pupils. I have responsibility to their parents and to the community at large. I cannot carry out my duties unless I know at least the part of your investigation that is relevant to me and my school. Are we agreed?' In turn I eye-contacted each one, intent on triggering some long-dormant responses to Teacher – some not so long-dormant, too.

'Pat's always been your victim support officer, hasn't he?' Mandy said reasonably, as if that would make me back out of the room in gratitude.

'Yes, he has. And no one will ever know how grateful I am to him. He's saved my sanity and indeed saved my life.' I hoped my smile conveyed everything except love. 'However, if you people see me as just a victim, you will feel sorry for me and that may cloud your judgement. On the other hand, if you think my life is really in jeopardy, I would like to know what you are offering in the way of actual protection.' Experience had long taught me that showing controlled anger was better than getting shrill-voiced with hysteria. 'However, although much of what has been going on has been directed at me, the real victims are surely Rosie and Emma. And maybe – if children turn out to be the perpetrators – they will turn out to be victims themselves.'

More eye contact.

'What's your gut feeling?' Mandy countered. It looked as if it was going to be just the two of us in the conversation.

Very well. 'It wasn't a child that installed those cameras throughout the school and in other locations, was it? And let's not forget that the first probably arrived some years ago – something certainly happened to make Mrs Gough stop using what were then changing rooms and turn them into stockrooms. And most but not all of my troubles began when I changed the stockroom locks and started to clear them out. Ask PC Lloyd Davies.'

She made a note. 'But there's nothing in the staff meeting minutes – your Melanie's a gem, isn't she? – to explain why Mrs Gough took the action she did. Nothing. Did she challenge someone about them? Or simply keep quiet? Could she have challenged someone and been told to say nothing? I'd really like to talk to her, you know. Only it wouldn't half stretch our budget to send someone out to talk to her.'

'Skype?' I ventured.

Her smile verged on the patronising. 'The techies are on to that.'

A pale-faced young woman nodded.

270

I found myself telling them about the bunch of flowers meant ostensibly for Mrs Gough that I'd somehow forgotten about – the sort of amnesia I use to deal with unacceptable memories.

Mandy's face registered a range of emotions I'd not expected. 'Shit! What a nasty, malicious thing to do! Flowers are such a personal gift,' she added, as if needing to apologise, or perhaps excuse her emotions to her team. 'One of your disgruntled staff? Not that they don't all speak highly of you. You know how animals gather round an injured herd member to protect it? That's how they seem to be with you. Seem,' she added more reflectively. In the same breath she added, 'Prudence? Could the flowers be one of her tricks? Don't look so gobsmacked. I've heard all about Prudence, remember. She seems a remarkably unusual child.'

'Who, as you know, is not in school today,' I admitted. 'Look, she is an odd child, probably because she is amazingly gifted and has no equal amongst her peers to cut her down to size. And her parents do all they can to build her ego, not always to her benefit. They never let her simply be a child.'

One of the officers chipped in, 'One of the lads I spoke to said she never read the books the school provided – always "grown-up" ones. Personally I wouldn't have wanted my kids to be reading *We Need to Talk About Kevin*.'

I must have looked as disconcerted as I felt. 'My God! Even so, I can't see her killing one of her cronies. No and no and no.'

She and the team exchanged a look. I didn't dare ask why. But they were going to tell me anyway.

'It's not just that Prudence isn't in school today. She and her family are not at home. None of them. They're not responding to calls or texts. So I've put out a call for her. You know I have to. Because it's a short step from the playground – much shorter than from your office – into that stockroom. And I find it inconceivable that she doesn't know something about what went on. As a witness, at this stage, Jane, as a witness.' She got up and put a hand on my arm. 'We have to, you know. And we have to talk to Robert, too – we've already contacted his mother. She'll be present.' She sat down again.

I found myself setting my lip like a sulky teenager, and tried to make my expression look like a professional's frown. 'I still think it's an adult pulling their strings. Blackmailing them, if you like, into doing appalling things.'

'I hope so. I really hope so. And I'd like your thoughts on who that might be too.'

'Someone with easy access to the school until I changed the locks. Which meant a larger number of people than you could imagine. And even after I upped security someone who still managed to get in. It ought to narrow the field. So possibly a governor, possibly one of the Open the Book team. Or possibly even a contact of our cleaner. Melanie will have all their details.'

'Including the cleaner's?'

'Val. To my shame I don't even know her surname.' I'd never needed to.

A young man slipped out of the room.

Mandy glanced at Pat. 'Pat actually did some highly illicit research last night, which we've managed to make official.'

'About the governors. I didn't have time to tell you, Avo, what with one thing and another. Sorry.'

'Hard to talk with asthma.' We exchanged a grin.

'Before we share our information – Pat's information – tell us about your dealings with them, Jane,' Mandy said.

'As you've all probably gathered, I've not had the best of relationships with the governing body as a whole, once they'd appointed me. There's been both collective and individual hostility. So all I could offer is possibly prejudiced opinions. I'd like to hear what you found, Pat. Especially as one of them wants me to have dinner with him tomorrow and another wants me to visit his grandchild this very day. Oh, and a third wants a face-to-face talk about hiring the village hall. I told him to talk to your team, Mandy.'

'Give you dinner? That'd be?'

'Brian Dawes.'

'Jesus! You've not accepted!'

'As if. And the guy with the granddaughter is Richard Morris. Rosie is the one who had her arm injured in the playground accident.'

'Or possibly playground assault,' she corrected me. 'Interesting. The third governor? The one wanting a face-to-face talk?'

'The vicar. Mark Stephens. He's been fairly supportive.'

'Thank goodness someone has!' She smiled briefly. 'What about contact with other governors, male or female?'

'What I must say is that when there was the major crisis with Rosie, all the governors behaved impeccably. Several, including Brian Dawes, remember, came into school to help interview possible witnesses.'

'So where the school is concerned, they behave professionally; it's only you they seem to be targeting. Do you find that reassuring? I thought not. Now, the witnesses to Rosie's fall would include Robert, Prudence, Sophia and Emma.' Mandy didn't need to check her notes. 'And who helped you, apart from Dawes? Mrs Tibbs and Mrs Walker? Yes? And have you had less than happy contact with any other governor?'

'One nearly knocked Mark over,' I said lightly. 'Running out of church. Had to take his child swimming. Toby Wells.'

'So the child would be Sophia. Hmm.'

Pat looked at me quizzically. 'A slight, whippy-looking guy – might have been into athletics at one time? I remember him bolting while I was talking to someone else. About my police commitments in Brum. Off like a rocket, he went. But then a lot of people don't want to stand next to policemen.'

'I should imagine,' I said, 'that you all already know he's not Mr Popular in the village. He's an ex-pupil, but wasn't apparently liked while he was here. Fetched up at a public school and came back here. He sold the cricket field for housing. Capital offence. He's regarded more as an incomer than a native.'

'Pretty much the mark of Cain, that,' Mandy observed dryly. 'Is there a Mrs Wells?'

'Oh, yes. She accused the school of dereliction of duty when her daughter dropped out of music without telling us or her. And Sophia continued to leave the classroom at the times the teacher assumed she was having a violin lesson. Robert Bowman, too. But his mother supported us all the way.'

'Prudence?'

'No. Wouldn't you know it? She's a talented musician who practises regularly. But we think it was she who tried to ruin the music teacher's reputation by making a vile accusation to the local press.' I couldn't stop myself asking again, 'What is it that's driving those children? Who is it?'

'Ah,' Mandy said, as another young woman slipped into the room, followed by an older man, 'we may have an answer. Perdie and Don, two of our techies. Well, guys?'

Their faces answered. 'Whoever installed the devices has disabled them. None of them is transmitting any more. Not here, not in the caretaker's house, not in Dove Cottage. There's nothing at all to enable us to trace them back. Sorry.'

Pat was the one who responded. 'No problem: it's back to good old-fashioned police work, isn't it?'

Mandy responded to his cheerful irony with a straight face. 'That's fine when you've got the officers to do it. Excuse me: I have to take this.' She didn't move away from us, simply frowning and snapping, 'OK.' Ending the call she said, 'I've got to go. Now. To Maidstone to fight for a budget. Bloody cuts!' She stood. 'Sorry, Jane, I've no choice. We'll get search warrants for all the governors' properties. Males and those females whom Jane has specifically mentioned. Team: you'll all report to DS Thomas when he gets back from the dentist.' She overrode audible groans. 'Needs must when the devil drives. Meanwhile, Pat is officially on secondment to us. Because although we think we're on to some paedophile ring, I've still got this feeling in my water that some of this is personally directed at Jane. As for these invitations coming out of the blue, Jane, I for one wouldn't advise you to accept any of them. Or any others.' She was halfway out of the door when she turned to me: 'That guy Tom. Is everything OK between you? Only he was up for your job, wasn't he? And not everyone takes defeat graciously.'

'Like bloody DS Thomas,' someone muttered.

'This is crazy. We have a whole meeting supposed to be about the governors and I still have no idea what you dug up,' I told Pat as we stood in the middle of the playground drinking yet more coffee. Safely back in the village hall. the children, having had yet another cold lunch – I dreaded what Ofsted would have to say about that! – were now writing about or drawing things they'd seen on their crocodile walk.

'That's because you gatecrashed – quite superbly! – a meeting about something else. You can't really blame Mandy for not being totally prepared when you tore up her agenda.'

I couldn't, could I?

'I wouldn't want to be leading a major enquiry with her resources, I can tell you. If you're this far from cracking up, she's only this far.' His fingers moved from a few millimetres apart to about a centimetre. 'And she's got the media on to her, of course.'

'At least the governors are dealing with that side of things.'

He gawped. 'And you're saying that's a good thing?

Just don't read the papers, girl. Or check your phone. If it's not all over the national media it's only because someone with bird flu-like symptoms has landed at Heathrow, and politicians are scared, very scared. Now, I will spill every single bean about the governors, promise, but it should be somewhere no one can overhear – and no one can interrupt, either,' he added, as I gestured ironically at the empty expanse. Even as I did so, of course, as if to prove his point, not mine, Dougie and Tamsin of the Open the Book team waved from the other side of the playground wall. There was no question of asking them to risk their limbs on the sheet of ice, so we teetered over to them. I was ready to perform formal introductions, but they greeted each other with the relaxed flap of hands that suggested they'd been talking before I turned up last night.

'Now I realise that you're the man with the wonderful singing voice!' Dougie said. 'As it happens, I'm part of the Invicta Operatic Society: we're desperately in need of someone capable of taking the male lead in our next G and S. I don't suppose . . . ?'

'I'm sorry. My secondment here is only temporary,' Pat said, with no hint of the sarcasm that amateur operatics, and Gilbert and Sullivan in particular, often elicit.

'How did your walk go?' I asked quickly, not because I was afraid Pat would react badly if he was pestered but because I really wanted to know.

'I think we all enjoyed it. The grown-ups more than the kids, perhaps. No one does disciplined walking these days, do they?'

'They will soon if I have anything to do with it. And daily running. Meanwhile, I can't tell you how grateful I am for all you've done. And for your kindness last night.'

'No ill effects from the smoke or the cold?' Tamsin was asking Pat. 'Or for you, Jane? If there's anything worse than being ill it's seeing a friend suffering. Look, why don't you pop round for supper this evening? Just a buffet for the OTB team – we always make too much, and you'd be doing us a real favour.'

My stomach froze inside. Another unexpected invitation. I was ready to panic. Paranoia or what? But I heard my voice saying calmly enough, 'I'm so sorry. I can't manage early this evening: there's something I really have to do.' Then it dawned on me that they might mean to include us both. 'What if we could drop round later?'

'Excellent. Of course, I know you have asthma, Pat – do you have food allergies? Can you share a room with a peanut?'

'I can indeed. And will do with pleasure. I don't see us being with you before nine-thirty if at all – and I'm afraid that that would be too late?'

Despite the hospitable denials, it was obvious from the tight smiles that it would.

'Another time, perhaps?'

'Next time I'm down, I hope.'

I didn't object till we were well out of earshot that it wouldn't take me till that hour to pick out a few outfits, especially if we left soon after the end of school.

'I don't care if you could magic them out of thin air by the end of afternoon school: I want you to be in a place bristling with CCTV during the evening. Think about it, Avo: by now everyone in the village will know you're staying at Diane's. What's the betting something nasty happens to the Cricketers, for which you will be blamed? Mandy and her team agree: they're installing cameras there as we speak. But I want a belt and braces approach. Not only will you not show up on their cameras – you'll be well and truly captured on security twenty miles away.'

'What if I'm spotted by the media? *Tragedy School head shops while pupils die?*'

'First up we get dark glasses. And one of those big fur hats. You'll look like Jackie Onassis.'

CHAPTER TWENTY-SEVEN

I was pretty well shopped-out by the time we reached the Outlet. Pat had already propelled us round Canterbury's full-price shops, both of us shopping for England, though I'd easily have won if medals had been involved. Fenwicks, Next, Marks and Spencer – all proved conclusively I'd dropped a dress size since I'd arrived in Kent. But, he insisted, it wasn't just clothing I needed – and some very good shoes too, he conceded – but that vital technological alibi. It wasn't just receipts, either – he wanted CCTV coverage. He made me drop money by the Outlet parking ticket machine, stumble by a crossing, appear to lose my purse by a coffee shop. Little Miss Ditzy, that was me. What did we talk about? The governors? Not a chance. Relative prices and sizes. Was he trying to hide something? Tiredness and hunger apart, I was getting tetchy.

At last he allowed me to collapse in the food area, a huge space crammed with families taking advantage of a vast range of food suppliers. My guess was that the majority of the kids had consumed so much sugar they wouldn't sleep for hours – though most of them should, in my book, have been in bed hours ago.

Although Pat picked a table for four, his body language clearly warned anyone against intruding. He despatched me to buy green tea for both of us, using my credit card, as I had had to do throughout our excursion, for all my purchases, no matter how trivial. Once we were settled, he produced his smartphone.

'Reason two for us to need our space,' he said quietly. 'The low-down I promised on your governors.'

'About bloody time,' I said, mopping tea from my coat where a three-year-old had cannoned into me. 'Pat, I'm tired and hungry and—'

'I daresay. But I'd like you to smile a lot, and gesticulate, as if I was showing you family photos. Right?'

'Right.' I prepared to look amused and excited.

'Let's start with the women, shall we? And—'

'Must we? I can't imagine any woman could do such harm.'

'Myra Hindley? Rosemary West?'

'We're talking about decent middle-class women,' I countered. 'Felicity Walker. Alison Tibbs. We have a decent working relationship these days, but I don't think we'll ever actually like each other. Are you going to cast Alison as a wicked woman?'

'She's a very rich one. She owns half of Canterbury – just think, a couple of hours ago you were prancing around on her territory.'

'I'd have kicked my heels higher, then. Despite my socialist upbringing, however, I can't say that being rich is necessarily a hanging offence.'

'Just a guillotining offence. OK, she came from a wealthy family and then she married money. There's a lot of it about in your village. And although you clearly don't know it, a lot of the villagers are related by blood or by marriage.'

'I suppose that could explain why they don't like people who aren't part of their tribe – incomers . . . But who in particular is related to whom? Alison Tibbs, for a start?'

I sensed rather than heard his chuckle. 'Now why should you pick on her? I thought you decided she wasn't wicked.'

'Wicked or not, she can see into the school grounds and she spies on the playground staff. And she complained about my working late at night, remember, using school fuel not my own. It was probably Mrs Tibbs who told the police I was a burglar, though I've no way of proving that, or that she deliberately hijacked my oil delivery. But she's fiercely loyal to the school itself. On the other hand, I acquit her of crawling into the caretaker's house loft and making off with the insulation.'

'Do you? Why? You're not being ageist, are you? Because my mum was seventy when she lagged her loft herself. Yeah, it was supposed to be me, but I was called out urgently, wasn't I?'

'I suppose Alison's house would be conveniently close to dump the rubbish. And I can't imagine any sensible police officer knocking on her door and asking her if she knew anything about it.'

The staff began a concerted clearing up operation.

'They're thinking about closing, aren't they?' Pat checked his watch. 'We'll go back via the M20 – lots of cameras on that. And we can keep on talking.'

'Keep on? Pat, so far we've spoken about one governor.

This was supposed to give you the chance to tell me everything you've found out. You even had Mandy's blessing. OK, I've shopped till I dropped – but what are clothes when my next pad is likely to explode or be spirited by aliens into outer space?'

He laughed as if I was being genuinely funny. 'Mrs Tibbs has a nephew,' he said. 'It turns out . . . you're not even listening, are you?' he added sharply.

'Prudence. I'm sure I've just seen Prudence. Don't look. Not just yet. She's over by that cookie place. Looks a weird mixture of sixteen and seven. Purple coat. Black leggings. Pixie boots.'

'The pale kid with dark red hair? Now what are you doing?'

It ought to have been obvious. I was going to speak to her. Kindly. Because if ever a kid looked waif-like and lost, it was Prudence. There was no sign of her parents. A couple of youths lounged nearby. She was drifting close to a table where someone had apparently abandoned a pack of sandwiches. Next moment, she was drifting away again, and there was no food on the table. If ever she had financial problems later in life, she'd clearly make an excellent shoplifter. However, she'd picked the wrong table. The people sitting there had merely gone back to the counter to get more food. There was an almost comic moment that I could only see as a mime as the man and woman in their twenties realised they had lost their sandwich. Clearly they were not pleased.

A male security guard reached her before I did. She took flight. I was in her way: I don't even think she recognised me as she kicked my shin and elbowed me in the stomach.

Then she did a stupid thing. She ran into one place she could easily be trapped: the ladies' loo.

I turned to face her pursuers – two other security staff, both women, had joined their colleague. All were jabbering into radios.

Holding up my hands for silence, I eye-contacted the loudest. 'I know the girl. I'm the head teacher at her school. I'll deal with this, if you can ask the other users to leave.'

'It's our job, if you don't mind.'

'Of course it is, and you're trained. But I know the child and I know what problems she's having at the moment. Just let me talk her out.'

'We have procedures.'

'She can't just get away with stuff like that.'

The women were more hostile; their male colleague temporised: 'If you can get her out quietly you can stay with her while we talk to her. OK?'

It was the best I could hope for.

I rejected the idea of using my authority as being one thing to guarantee that Prudence would not co-operate. Neither would I wheedle. I spoke firmly to the bolted door. 'Prudence, I'd like you to come out now because if you don't you'll have the humiliating experience of having the cubicle door unlocked and you'll be hauled out kicking and screaming if necessary. There'll be nothing that either of us can do about it. If you walk out of your own accord and offer a dignified apology, then I'll see what I can do to help.'

There was no response at all. Not so much as a sniffle – but then, I didn't have Prudence down as one who would weep unseen. She'd consider it a waste of effort.

'What on earth brought you out here? It's not the milieu

I'd have expected you to enjoy.' Nor was it. Whatever the attractions of heavily discounted designer goods for adults, she'd consider herself worldly and sophisticated, she'd not go for the shops targeting pocket money-laden teenagers. I'd see her as a retro-shop girl. In her eyes she was certainly too old for the children's play area.

There was still no response. By now I was getting anxious. How much damage could a child do to herself in the course of three minutes? Then I remembered her capacity for holding her breath until she got her own way.

'Very well, if you won't do the mature thing and emerge of your own free will, I shall have to let the security men do what they're supposed to do.' I added coldly, 'Do make sure you've flushed the loo and pulled your knickers up, won't you? And wash your hands before they take you away. I'll see you in school on Monday.' Hardening my heart, because this time I did think I heard a sob – though it might simply have been a gasp as she breathed again – I walked out.

It wasn't just security staff waiting outside, however – it was the police. Pat was standing alongside two women officers. He raised an apologetic hand. 'Don't look at me like that. I had to call it in, didn't I? And at least they're trained to deal with children. And they've asked for you to go along too.'

'Why should I need a responsible adult?' Prudence demanded. 'All I did was pick up a sandwich that someone had walked away from. Probably not a very good sandwich. If instead of chasing me halfway round the Outlet, they'd asked me to return it or to pay I would of course have done so.'

Her self-assurance was not going down well with PC Toni Lowe, the jeans-clad woman waiting for her at Canterbury police station, where we'd been taken, separately, despite my protests. Someone she knew should have been with her even for the comparatively short journey, surely. But perhaps the two PCSOs didn't feel they had the authority to make that sort of decision. If only one of them had been Ian Cooper things wold have been different. At least I was in a soft interview room with her now. I was seated, trying to look calm; she was on her feet, legs braced like a terrier's.

'Am I under arrest?' Prudence pursued. 'For the so-called theft of a sandwich? This sounds like something from Dickens! What will you do with me? Have me transported to the colonies?'

It was impossible to fault the liberal education she was getting at home, but her social skills didn't include realising the effect she was having on someone who'd probably been hoping for a quiet evening with a drink and a pizza at the end of it. Actually I did fault her education: what on earth had her parents been doing to let her speak to people like this?

She turned to me – turned on, would perhaps be a more accurate way of putting it. 'And her! What is she supposed to be doing?'

My mother would have demanded who *she* was – the cat's grandmother? Toni's might have done too: she flushed angrily on my behalf. 'Any young person being questioned by the police needs someone *in loco parentis* – in the place of their parent. We call them a responsible adult.'

Prudence shrugged grandly. 'I suppose she could be a responsible adult, since she's here.' As if making a concession, she sat down.

The room seemed strangely familiar, though I'd never been in it before. Perhaps there was a countrywide model for soft interview rooms, complete with standard-issue soft toys. Absent-mindedly I pulled the nearest, a plump brown bear, on to my lap. The last one in my life, very similar to this, had ended up sliced apart and stuffed into the dustbin. Better that than a living dog or cat, I supposed.

'You never answered my original question, Prudence,' I said quietly, since Toni Lowe seemed to be hanging back. 'What on earth were you doing in the Outlet? And – something I should have asked earlier, perhaps – where are your parents?'

She looked at her watch. 'In Paris. They had tickets for the opera.'

I tried not to look too taken aback, though I could see Lowe's eyes widen.

'So where and with whom are you supposed to be this evening?'

'With Jinty. She used to be my nanny.'

'But you're not with her.'

'She's got this foul husband. Dwayne. He sits and watches football on the TV and drinks lager. At least he goes outside to smoke, but the smell sticks to his clothes. Like you smell of smoke,' she said. 'Tonight, at least.'

Pat had been right: I should have changed into some of the clothes I'd bought earlier. But I wasn't the one supposed to explain herself.

'I can understand why you don't like his company. But won't Jinty be worried you're not there?'

She regarded me scornfully. 'I used my mother's phone

to text her that I didn't need to go after all. And then deleted the message.'

Of course. Though the police would still be able to check if they cared to. 'So you planned to spend the night at home on your own. But you fetched up in a food hall.'

For the first time, I thought her composure cracked. 'There was a problem.'

'Which was?'

'The usual thing.' Her voice dripped with adult ennui. 'Money. I got to Ashford and then the hospital all right, and asked to see Emma, but they kept me waiting for ages so I had to buy some food and it cost more than I'd bargained for. And then they wouldn't let me see her anyway! And she's my best friend!' The last two words made her a little girl again.

Toni spoke for the first time. I feared she knew something I didn't. 'Sometimes they only let family see patients, you know. But you must have been very . . . very frustrated.' Good for her: she'd got Prudence's measure.

'I was. All that effort. Anyway, I had to come away. But I got on the wrong bus. And then I missed my train. And I was terribly hungry. But there will be enough money at home to pay for the sandwich if you care to take me there, PC Lowe. I'm not a thief really.' Her lower lip trembled.

I wasn't entirely convinced. I was fairly sure if she could hold her breath to order she'd be able to weep at will.

Lowe, however, was very kind. 'Of course you're not. And I'll make sure we pass the money on to the people concerned.'

I fished in my purse. 'I can lend Prudence the money. You can pay me back on Monday, can't you?' My smile suggested that I had no doubt whatever of her being in school. 'But I should imagine you're still pretty hungry. I am.'

Lowe went to the door and spoke quietly into her phone. If I registered that she didn't leave the room I was sure Prudence would.

'There: food will be on its way shortly. Then we'll have a proper talk, if you're still happy to have Ms Cowan as your responsible adult. Otherwise we can bring in someone from Social Services.'

'What do you want to talk about? I've offered to pay.' Her chin went up.

Toni Lowe's voice was very calm. 'What I really need to talk about is not why you went to William Harvey but why Emma had to.'

'At this time of night?' I interjected. 'Prudence is a child and ought to be in bed. And surely she ought to have legal representation?'

Prudence raised a scathing eyebrow. 'We pupils understand that there was a tragic accident in school. We've heard precious little since, Miss Cowan. Sorry, Ms Cowan.' Her apologetic smile openly admitted that it was not sincere.

If that was how she wanted to play it . . . But I was an adult, and supposed to be responsible. So I tried once more. 'Prudence has had a shocking day, by the sound of it. I do feel it would be more appropriate to wait till the morning to question her.'

'I am quite sure I can deal with a few questions. This accident, Ms Cowan? To Emma?'

'Had you been in assembly this morning, you could

have prayed for her recovery,' I said as mildly as I could. 'However, as I'm sure you know, accidents rarely just happen. They are usually caused by something.'

She turned to me superbly. 'I was under the impression that you were here to support me, not interrogate me.'

Fortunately for me, a tap on the door announced the arrival of our supper. 'Burgers and chips for two,' announced what I suspected was another plain-clothes officer; she came and sat beside Toni.

'I don't eat junk food. Especially MacDonald's.'

'No problem. We'll just leave the chips there in case the rest of us get hungry. I'm Barbara, by the way.' And, I'd bet a year's salary, the capable mother of at least one toddler.

I tucked in, hoping Prudence would forget my gaffe. I was no more a burger and chips fan than Prudence, but these came with the best sauce: hunger.

'So you've heard no hard facts about poor Emma's accidents,' Toni observed. 'But you might have heard rumours.'

'That would be hearsay.'

'We're not putting anyone on trial, here, Prudence: we just want to clear up any misinformation you might have. So what have you heard?'

I wanted to tell her to beware of Greeks bearing gifts, and of police bringing food. But I didn't. And then I discovered I didn't want to, after all. I wanted some truth, no matter how it was extracted.

'We heard that once again there was a lack of supervision at the school. There was an accident last week caused by the fact that no teachers supervise the children. On Thursday, although the building was supposed to be closed because it had been invaded by rats, someone left all the doors open.'

The only way to stop myself screaming with rage was to help myself to another chip.

Barbara had the measure of her, however. 'So why do people say Emma went inside if she knew she wasn't supposed to? You were all in the village hall for the day, I understand.'

'All I know is that she was involved in an accident. Perhaps she fell on the ice and managed to crawl inside looking for help. Is that what happened?'

She looked at me. In turn I sought the officers' eyes. Could that plausible scenario really be an explanation?

'The trouble is,' Barbara said, 'if that happened, Emma would have certain types of injury. She doesn't. She has injuries that make the doctors think that something happened inside. Inside a room that was out of bounds. That no one was allowed into.'

'I know what out of bounds means, thank you. If it was out of bounds, why wasn't it locked? You know, I really think I'd prefer another responsible adult. All this one does is sit and eat.'

'It's very late anyway, isn't it?' Toni said, at last coming round to my opinion. 'We've arranged emergency accommodation for you, Prudence.'

'I want to go home.'

'Sadly that isn't possible. We have to find somewhere where an adult will take responsibility for you. There's a foster home waiting.'

'But I could go home if, say, Ms Cowan was staying there.'

Toni caught my eye. In other circumstances I'd swear

she winked. 'I'm afraid that we've already asked enough of Ms Cowan. We'll take you to the foster home now.'

We all got to our feet. Except for Prudence. She suddenly launched herself at me, grabbing me round the knees. Tears poured down her face. 'Please, Ms Cowan, please. The policewoman says you're *in loco parentis*! Look after me! I beg you! Please!'

CHAPTER TWENTY-EIGHT

Would I have succumbed even then if a uniformed officer hadn't knocked on the door and asked to speak to me? I don't know. As it was, I was glad to be outside in the impersonal and slightly shabby corridor, where Pat was leaning against the wall, not even pretending to read the notices on the board.

He straightened. 'There's been a development at the Cricketers. Someone was caught messing with the mains electricity supply to plunge the place into darkness. So we won't be staying there. We're going to a safe house instead. Just for the night, I hope.'

I didn't have the strength to take everything in, let alone ask questions. 'So long as we can do two things: get some food and talk as we go?'

He laughed. 'Didn't I see a couple of burgers go into the interview room? You must have hollow legs. OK, food it is. All the gear you bought is still in my car, so at least you'll have a change of clothing with you. Me too,' he conceded with a grin as he propelled me briskly into the secured car park. He waited till he'd manoeuvred out and we were on the move before saying, 'We'll go the long way round, just in case.'

'In case of what?'

'In case the guy my colleagues picked up tonight isn't the only one of your dear ex-husband's mates trying to mess with your head – and indeed your general safety. What do you fancy? Curry or Chinese or—'

'For God's sake, just tell me who it is! I know you're trying to be funny, but please!' I couldn't stop my voice breaking.

He flipped me a tissue from a box in the driver's door. 'Sorry. I thought you'd have guessed by now. Mr Hoodie. Mr Outsize Hoodie with a small wiry body. Mr Churchgoing Hoodie who bolted as soon as he realised I was a cop so he could take his kid to swimming lessons. Allegedly. He doesn't go swimming on Sunday mornings, as it happens.'

'Toby Wells. Why Toby Wells?' I didn't have enough breath to do more than gasp.

'Which school did Simon go to? Malvern? And which public school did young Toby mysteriously fetch up in? Malvern. Their education did them proud in every aspect but one, which probably no school on earth could have dealt with: Simon's profound misogyny, and Toby's general desire to copy Simon. Apart from in one thing, sadly – his sporting ability.'

'Which Simon had in spades. He always claimed to have been approached by Worcestershire to play for the Colts, you know. But Toby's a family man – surely by doing Simon's dirty work he'd be putting his career and the security of his family in jeopardy?' But I added more slowly, 'He's the one that sold the village cricket field despite huge opposition. I thought that might be why everyone says he's a bad lot. On the other hand, perhaps he just enjoys being unpleasant for its own sake. Making people homeless is the grown-up equivalent of pulling wings off flies . . .'

'It'll come out at the trial.'

I shuddered. Of course, there had to be a trial. 'How will his family cope with that? You know his daughter's very close to Prudence.'

He nodded. 'Sophia: yes?'

'Yes. One of those who skived off music. He's not involved with the cameras, is he? He's a father, for goodness' sake. Please say no.'

'There's no evidence yet – and the technical team gave his house a pretty thorough going over. He won't be seeing his computer for a bit, however.' Whatever he'd meant to say next was interrupted by a terrible growl from his stomach. He pulled up behind a lot of other cars outside a run of takeaways. 'Like I said, Indian, Chinese, Thai?'

'Thai.'

'That sounds a bit decisive for you, Avo! I'll get a feast for two. No, you're staying in the car. And for good measure I'm locking you in. But you press that button if you really need to get out.'

'I'd rather come in with you.' I sounded horribly like Prudence demanding kindness.

At least I got my way, and also persuaded him to nip into the nearby late-night convenience store to pick up some overpriced bubbly. 'I know this is premature,' I added, stowing it between my feet so it wouldn't be thrown round too much as he accelerated and headed for the M20.

'I know we ought to wait for the arrest of the camera man. But . . .'

'But, indeed. It'll go well with the Thai, anyway.'

'True. Pat – the other children were questioned today, weren't they? What did they say about Emma's accident? I meant to ask the police at Canterbury but didn't get the chance.'

'They couldn't have told you anything. Any more than I can, not if you're going to be involved with young Prudence tomorrow. Please don't ask me any more. Though I will say this: I think you ought to be supporting the interviewing team, not holding her hand – metaphorically, of course.'

'For a start, I very much doubt if she'd want me to hold her hand. And I do find it terribly hard to have to support her, not join in the cross-questioning. Only in my case the questioning could be very cross indeed.'

'Ho, ho!' He laughed ironically. 'I can't say I'd blame you. Or blame Prudence for opting for someone else, come to think of it. What I'll suggest to Mandy, then, is that you watch the questioning with the pros the other side of the two-way mirror and prompt them every time you see something the interviewers don't register. Mandy will be there, but I'll more likely be watching Toby Wells get the same treatment. It won't be a pretty experience, Avo, but I can't imagine your wanting to sit in ignorance while other people mess up.'

Safe houses were not, in my considerable experience, five-star residences, but this one, in a suburb of Maidstone, was more than acceptable. Someone had already turned on the central heating, there was plenty of hot water, the kitchen was clean – and what looked like Venetian blinds turned out to be made of steel. We perched on spindly bar stools at a strangely chic high table and tucked in.

'So will Wells get bail?' I ventured, asking a question that had been nagging me ever since Pat had told me the news, but which I'd been too scared to ask. Now I was full I felt braver, but Pat no doubt clocked my hand shaking as I topped up our glasses – ordinary tumblers, but who cared?

'If he's got a good lawyer he will. Look how many times Simon was let out when he should have been locked up pending his trial. What my colleagues will be doing now – or more probably, given the cuts, over the weekend or even on Monday – is trying to find if Simon's got any other best mates dancing to his tune. I'm pretty sure Wells won't have been able to alert any of them, but he summoned his own solicitor, not the duty one, who might have done his dirty work for him. Hence this place.' His expansive gesture threatened to overbalance him. 'Too much fizz,' he explained unapologetically. 'Now, for twelve hours or so, before you have to go back and listen to more of young Prudence's lies and evasions, you're safe. On the other hand, Prudence is Prudence.'

At some point after this profound utterance I found I had my forehead in a dish of sticky rice.

The champagne stopped me sleeping as deeply as I'd expected, but the shower and chance to dress in pristine clothes made me feel I was ready for anything, especially the breakfast we bought at some chic country hotel. The excuse for this extravagance was that neither of us fancied elderly cornflakes served with UHT milk, which was all that the safe house could provide.

Pat insisted there was no need to hurry. 'They're probably hoping Prudence's parents will get back from France in time to sit in on the interview. With luck, they'll be reunited already.'

'Will they come with a solicitor? The bony-kneed woman who was supposed to sue the school?'

'I'd have thought it would all be very low-key at this stage.'

'I'm not sure the Digbys do low-key.'

While I tidied myself up in the upmarket loos, Pat called Mandy, greeting me, as I returned, with the news that I had toothpaste on my nose and that the second round in the battle with Prudence would start at eleven.

'*Battle?* She's a kid, Pat: please remember that. With absent parents.'

'I know. I'm sorry. But she's a kid it's hard to take to.'

'Intellectually I suspect she's out of all our leagues. Perhaps that's the problem.'

'So what would be the solution?'

All I could do was shrug helplessly. I changed the subject to more prosaic matters. 'Since we've got a little time to spare, would you mind if when we get to Canterbury I nipped into that nice big Boots? My make-up's back in my case.'

'No problem. I've got to get a couple of birthday cards too.'

A nice domesticated errand. He didn't say who they were for – why should he? And I didn't ask.

I dived into Boots while he set off in search of a WH Smith. He took longer to choose than I did; huddling into my new down-filled hooded jacket I braved the cutting wind and started what was meant to be a quick exploration of the city. But I was stopped outside the second charity shop.

Not by a chugger, asking me to sign away my soul to a charity via monthly direct debits. By a teddy bear in a dump bin. He reached out his paws in the way my late and deeply lamented bear Bob used to do. He wouldn't be another Bob, not even Bob Two. No doubt he would tell me his name as we got better acquainted. He was reluctant to be stowed in a carrier back, insisting on sticking his head out to see what was going on.

'For Prudence?'

'For me.'

Pat clearly wanted to say a lot of things, but swallowed them all. 'Nosey old thing, isn't he?' he observed.

Nosey. Not a bad name at all.

I ought to have been embarrassed to let anyone see my purchase, but braved it out, even waving cheerily at Mark Stephens, scurrying along the other side of the road. He looked straight through me. Did he not recognise me? Why should he, come to think of it? I was in my new plumage in a town where he wouldn't expect me. There was no time for speculation: it was time to return to the police station.

Mandy greeted me with a brief hug, and the news that Emma Hamilton was still stable. She responded to my question about the other truanting children in much the same way as Pat had done. I didn't find it reassuring.

There was no sign yet of Prudence's parents. In their position I would have left Paris in the middle of the opera to get back to her. As it was, it seemed they had spent the night in Paris, and caught an early – but not the earliest – train. Was it because they wanted one with the best connection to Ashford? In fact, it was clear that even the police team felt they were heartless. In a waiting area, two long-faced sadly dressed women were waiting; my money was on their being social service representatives, ready to pounce on the Digbys to discuss their parenting skills.

I sat with Mandy and other members of her team watching through the two-way mirror. Ignoring her overnight foster-mother, Prudence sat forlorn, chewing her hair from time to time. I was almost tempted to give her Nosey. Almost. But not quite. She would no doubt have regarded him with disdain and me with supercilious disbelief. Or vice versa.

Poor child. Poor little girl. And what a dreadful future she might have ahead of her.

At this point she looked at her watch, quite pointedly. 'Surely the police can't keep us waiting much longer?'

The foster-mother whispered something.

'I don't see why we shouldn't start without them,' she responded with a toss of her mane. 'They weren't there when Emma had her fall so why should they need to be here? For goodness' sake!' She tapped her foot as she must have seen her mother tap hers when enraged by someone's lack of co-operation.

'How hard will your colleagues be pressing her?' I asked Mandy, my voice low as if in church, despite the soundproofing.

'Sadly, as hard and as long as it takes. We need hard evidence, Jane, don't we? We have a child who may not survive. Someone attacked her. Or she had a tragic accident, which was nonetheless caused by something or someone. Furthermore, someone was up to no good with those cameras. Someone very sick. God knows what else he was doing. So far our house searches have come up with nothing. If we had the officers, we'd take very damned house in the village to pieces, brick by brick. But we can't, not on my budget. Even if officers work for nothing, which all too often they do.'

'She's a child, remember, despite her sophisticated vocabulary and apparently adult attitudes. A child.'

'So were the boys who killed James Bulger.'

'You're surely not – no, surely . . . I can't . . .'

Mandy was matter-of-fact. 'Something bad happened at your school. Maybe downright evil. We have to root it out. All of us, including you, Jane. And if Prudence is the key to it – I'm not saying she's party to it, mind – we have to harden our hearts. She'll get support and therapy afterwards, of course. As will all those involved.'

'Budget permitting,' I said dryly.

'Any budget ought to stretch to that.' Someone knocked on the door and spoke briefly. With a shrug, Mandy left the room.

Prudence continued to play with her hair, tapping her foot occasionally. At last she said, 'Surely I have some rights? I don't want to wait here any longer.'

The woman with her spoke firmly this time. 'We're here because the police want us here. They're in charge, Prudence, not us. You just have to be patient.' She reached for a magazine, passing Prudence one too. She cast it aside disparagingly. I felt I should have dashed in with *The Guardian* Pat had treated me to, though he was now reading it in a rest area that used to be the staff canteen.

Or maybe with the teddy bear. No, not the bear. Definitely. Until I could have a dog or cat, he would keep me company.

'The Digbys' train – the local connection, not Eurostar – is delayed by an incident on the line. Someone topping himself, that means, usually. Imagine being the driver and knowing that . . . Anyway, they're apparently happy for their daughter – their only daughter, Jane – to go ahead without them. She's only giving us information, they say. As if!'

'You're talking to her as much as a suspect as a witness, then?' I asked sharply.

'And possibly as a victim.' She was as near to being distraught as I was. 'OK. Let's get the trained professionals to get on with it. Dear God, there are times I wish I smoked.'

CHAPTER TWENTY-NINE

'The whole school had a talk on Thursday from a police community support officer. Ian Cooper. Were you there for the talk?' PC Toni Lowe was obviously well briefed. There was an underlying steel about her I'd not noticed the previous evening.

'Of course I was. The whole school was. We were stuck in the village hall. All day.'

It was Barbara's turn. 'Do you recall what Mr Cooper spoke about?'

'Oh, stuff about keeping promises and how he had to stand up to a superior officer who wanted him to work somewhere else. Like we all believed that.'

Prudence's memory was pretty selective. Or had she merely anticipated being asked why she did not stick to telling the truth, as Ian had advocated?

'Anything about telling the truth?' Toni asked.

'You were there, were you?'

'Ian is a colleague of mine.' Toni did not smile. 'Tell me what you did during break.'

'Despite Rosie's accident, the playground is a sheet of ice. It's simply not safe. That's why I'm sure Emma must have fallen over.'

'Or you could try telling the truth – the whole truth, including why you didn't return to the village hall after break.'

'Of course I did. I might have been late . . . Well, I was late, because I'd lost my scrunchie in the playground, but I certainly went back. They gave us disgusting white pasta for lunch.'

'Did Robert go back? And Sophie?'

'Sophia. When they'd helped me look for my scrunchie. Ms Cowan likes us to keep our hair tied back at all times. For safety, or so she says.'

'How sensible. Now, if three of you were trailing backwards and forwards across the playground, looking for something as small as a scrunchie, then surely you'd have noticed something bigger – like a friend so badly hurt she had to crawl.' Toni infused the same scornful doubt into her voice as Prudence employed so irritatingly. Then she paused. 'Tell me what really happened, Prudence. We know three of you skived off after break. We know you weren't in the school building because our colleagues searched it when Emma was found. We also know that Emma was injured in the school itself, not in the playground. Don't we? What would you like to tell me?'

The foster-mother spoke for the first time. 'Let me remind you that Prudence is only ten, officers – this is very forceful questioning considering she's only a witness.'

'I'm nearly eleven.' Which made her sound even more like a child.

I put my hand on Mandy's arm. 'Ms Pearson is right. Surely they should ease up a bit?'

Mandy shrugged. But she spoke into the mike. 'Leave that line of questioning for a moment. Go back to the skiving, maybe?'

Toni, touching her earpiece, nodded briefly. 'There isn't a village shop any more, so where on earth could you go until you returned to the village hall? It was a bit cold for just hanging out outside. Do you have a den? Or use an outbuilding?'

'I thought we were talking about Emma. Do you think they'll let me see her today? I might not be family but I am her best friend.'

'If you could, what would you say?' Barbara asked quietly.

Prudence looked her straight in the eye and opened her mouth. There was absolute silence. Then she said, 'But they won't let me, will they?'

Mandy tore at her hair. 'What'll she be like when she's eighteen?'

'A pompous but brilliant undergraduate. Could you ask her if anything has happened at school to upset her?'

When Barbara relayed the question Prudence frowned. 'Apart from being treated like a child? And being told which lavatories I may and may not use?'

Yes! I caught Mandy's eyes. She responded into the mike, 'Talk about the loos.'

'Which weren't you allowed to use?'

'The ones nearest our classroom.'

'Why not?' Barbara sounded genuinely surprised.

'Because the teachers want to keep them for themselves.'

305

'That's not unusual in my experience. What's wrong with the other loos?'

'There's always a queue.'

'Because?'

'No one likes using the ones at the far end of the hall.' She licked her lips. 'What time did you say that my parents would be here? I might like to wait till then, after all.'

Barbara said, her voice bracing and perhaps too jolly, 'Come on, Prudence, we're only talking about toilets. We all have to poo or pee at some time or other.'

Mistake. 'In fact I'd like to use a loo now.'

Barbara spoke into her phone. 'Of course. While we wait for someone to escort you perhaps you'll just explain why people don't like the loos by the stockrooms? Graffiti? Do they smell?'

'Some of the babies think they see snakes.' She tried to be dismissive.

'And do they? Or do they see something else?'

'I really need the loo, you know. Now. You don't want me to wet myself, do you?'

'You'd be very uncomfortable if you had to sit all day in wet knickers. What do they see in the babies' loos, Prudence, that looks like a snake?'

Her eyes widened, but she seemed to shrink physically. She was spared having to answer by a knock on the door, which announced the arrival of a uniformed woman constable. She escorted Prudence out much as if she was a prison officer with a particularly awkward inmate.

'Surely there's a loo off the interview room?' I asked Mandy.

'Of course. But I just want to unsettle Prudence a little more.'

'Isn't she rattled enough? We all keep forgetting, Mandy, that whatever she might have done, she is a victim too. She reminds me of when I was interviewed after Simon had hurt me – I was as prickly and arrogant as she is because I was too afraid to let in other emotions. The man behind the cameras is surely her version of Simon. Even if she killed Emma herself, I'd swear she did it to please, to appease, Mr Camera.'

'You liberals! There's always something to excuse bad behaviour, isn't there?'

'I didn't say that and I don't think it. What I do think is that we've got a case of grooming here, like the idea or not. So please bear that in mind when you authorise heavy questioning.'

She opened her mouth to argue but shut it again as there was a rap on the door. 'Yes?' she demanded roughly; the door opened. One of the civilian reception staff plunged in.

'Ma'am, there's someone in reception says he's got to talk to you. I said you were busy but he said it's a matter of life and death. He's desperate, you can see that.'

'Tell them to hang fire till I get back,' she said, to her colleagues in general. Perhaps even me.

The police officers talked amongst themselves, black humour much in evidence. One went out for coffee and brought me a cup too. Barbara left the interview room; soon Toni followed. Prudence was returned to the room, but seemed disinclined to talk to Ms Pearson. We waited for the coffee to cool and drank it. There was a great deal of speculation about what could be keeping the boss. At last one of the older ones, Paul, turned to me. 'You were the one who got Ian to talk to your school, weren't you?'

'I was. He was great. He'd be the first to say his appeal to tell the truth didn't make much impression on Prudence, though. What is going on in her head?' I asked rhetorically, though I'd answered the question myself only a few minutes ago.

'If you ask me, I'd agree with you that she's a victim, not a perpetrator. I'd say someone's told her to say nothing, on pain of death. And I might not be exaggerating . . . But it's good they've nailed the guy who was after you. The word is he's not got bail, by the way.'

'Excellent. Thanks.' Why hadn't Mandy told me? Because she was too busy on something more important, that's why.

We waited. Five more minutes passed.

The uniformed constable reappeared. 'The boss says to stand down for a bit. Something's come up. And Ms Cowan is to come with me.'

Mandy was sitting in her goldfish bowl of an office, staring at some invisible point on her desk. 'A long time ago,' she said slowly, 'a young man with a flourishing career – he had his own extremely profitable firm – realised he was addicted to a particularly nasty form of porn. Child porn. Child on child porn, to be precise. He fought the problem – tried to get his kicks from ordinary hard-core adult porn. But it didn't do the trick. He sought and obtained psychiatric help. The problem was at least controlled. He was so grateful he vowed to serve the person who had dealt with it. Not person, actually. That makes it sound as if it was his shrink. He credited God with it. And he left his company with a highly astute management team in charge – it's on the verge of being in the FTSE 100, so they were good – while he went off to train at a theological college. I'm sorry, Jane – I know you got on well with Mark Stephens. He was a gift to the Church because, with the not inconsiderable income from his company, he didn't ask for a stipend. Of course, he never quite got round to confessing his problem.'

'Mark! I saw him this morning,' I said foolishly. 'Waved. I don't think he saw me.'

Mandy gave a sad smile. 'I think he might have had something else on his mind. Something to do with the death of a little girl. Yes, they lost her. They declared her brain dead, and I believe other children will benefit from her organs. Even so, a young life lost. No, he didn't kill her. Not directly. I'm quite sure of that. But it was because of him – his bribery and his coercion – that the kids started going into that stockroom. At first what they did was harmless enough. Then it got less harmless. Sometimes the kids went to his house – what could be more innocent than a trip to the vicarage? Except it wasn't innocent at all. Eventually some of the antics in the stockroom resulted in boxes toppling on poor Emma. The other kids dressed quickly and – as if they were child detectives – ran round to the vicarage to ask him what to do. He denied any responsibility, told them off for coming to his home, told them to lie to any inquisitive adults.'

Mysteriously I found a glass of whisky in my hand. 'Did he pick the children because they were arrogant or assured or did they rebel in some twisted reaction to the evil they were enduring?'

'It's too early to tell. The psychiatrists will have their

hands full for a bit, won't they? And yes, they will get plenty of support. I've an idea they'll be split up and sent to different schools in different areas of the country so they don't feed off each other as I think they did here. You know the idea – if Fred and Rosemary West had been with other people they might have been quite harmless souls.'

I nodded. 'Will the children be named in his trial?'

She shook her head. 'There won't be a trial.'

Something in the tone of her voice told me not to leap up and down in protest. 'Because . . .?'

'That train that was delayed because of an incident? The man who killed himself under its wheels was Mark Stephens. He actually walked into the police station with a full confession both on a memory stick and on paper before he took himself off to Canterbury West and . . .' She spread her hands. 'I'm very sorry. If only we'd searched his house first. It was scheduled for this morning.'

I wasn't capable of rational thought, but questions fired themselves at random. 'Those cassettes – was there anything in them?'

'A lot of sports day photos; school plays, nativities, trips to the zoo and the seaside. Sorry.'

'The porn mags?'

'They'd be about the right era, but why should he leave them there?'

'And why should he have a disagreement with Mrs Gough so bad that he hardly visited the school while she was head? Can you ask her?'

She shook her head. 'Poor thing had a stroke about five weeks ago. You teachers are like us cops – you don't live long enough to enjoy your retirement.' She poured more whisky.

'It's only twelve-thirty!' I drank it anyway. 'Why did Toby start rooting round in the stockrooms? Did he suspect something?'

'We've yet to ask him. But he admits to having messed with your football shirts. And he also admits putting pressure on Brian Dawes to test your mettle, as he puts it. Like getting his aunt the extra fuel oil, though he's adamant he didn't steal the original delivery. Like stripping the lagging out of your loft and off the tanks. And when he broke into Brian Dawes's house he didn't steal anything except the key to Dove Cottage. So you can blame him for the electrical fire. And the problem with the pub electrical supply. The trouble is, he's bright. Like Prudence. Who may or may not be the one who pushed the boxes on top of Emma. It's what the other kids say, anyway. By the way, I can't have you witnessing any more of the questioning – sorry.'

'I'm very relieved. Very.'

'Meanwhile Brian Dawes is in a room off reception. He wanted to talk to you. I wasn't at all sure you'd want to talk to him. He looks very apologetic, mind – what I could see of him behind the biggest bunch of flowers I've ever seen.'

CHAPTER THIRTY

Pat was more than happy to accompany me to confront Dawes, and probably happy to shove the flowers in a painful place if necessary. As it was, it was an excruciatingly polite encounter, but one which I later conceded we had to have. I had to endure an embarrassing, self-justifying and decidedly self-serving apology, of which the flowers were part. But he made one useful offer, probably, however, courtesy of his insurance company: to pay my hotel expenses while I looked for alternative accommodation – if, that is, I was prepared to remain as head of the school. He very much hoped I was. Before I could even raise the issue, he assured me that there would be no more interrogations by the governors for which I had no time to plan, no more unprofessional unpleasantness.

Since I couldn't imagine leaving the children in the lurch while they were confused and traumatised by all that had passed, I agreed to stay, provided he and his fellow governors found ways of easing the staffing budget. I needed extra teachers. He made another suggestion, that surprisingly didn't go down too well when I broached it to the person who would benefit.

'Things are going to be very difficult,' I told my colleagues on Monday morning. 'And I truly need a deputy head – acting till the existing post-holder returns, if she ever does. I'd like anyone interested to see me and then apply. You know how highly I rate you all. But we will follow equal opportunities guidelines.'

The women dropped into my office after lunch to say that they weren't interested in even a temporary upgrading: I had an idea that they were graciously standing aside so that Tom could go for it. It made life easier, but I can't say I really approved.

I was just off to see Rosie, a folder full of appropriate work, when Tom himself appeared at the end of the day. 'I can't apply,' he said baldly.

'No? Have you applied for something somewhere else?'

'No. But I messed up when you started. Seems weeks ago now. And I wouldn't do it now. It was me that left the flowers, Jane, and I'm truly sorry. But I can't possibly be your deputy and get paid for it.'

'We all make mistakes, Tom. And doing the job will stand you in good stead when you go for an outside promotion, or even a headship.'

'You're definitely staying, then?'

'I told you all as much. And I meant it.'

'You know what, I'm really pleased. I've got another idea I want to float, by the way. You remember that Scottish primary school where the kids all run a mile each day? Staff too, by the way. A lot of schools are adopting the idea. In the spring, when the field's dried out, I'd love to introduce it here. Would you agree?'

He was so eager to please I couldn't tell him I'd already thought of it. 'Agree? I'd join in. Right, Tom, I'll expect your formal application by this time tomorrow. By the way, I'm trying to woo a former primary maths specialist – she's on holiday at the moment but as soon as she gets back I shall go on a charm offensive.' Surely she'd consider the offer, now I could guarantee a rodent-free environment.

And soon we had – at last – a snow-free environment. The long-overdue thaw was messy and dreary, but it brought out Mrs Tibbs. She'd been reading about the advantages of school vegetable gardens, she told me. She was a keen gardener: might she offer her services as a volunteer? Watching seeds grow and taking responsibility for the seedlings and plants might take the children's minds off things, she said.

It was the nearest I'd get to an apology. I accepted immediately. I needed all the support I could get.

But not from Pat. Not professional support, at least. Not any longer.

The papers were full of a story of an undercover police officer who'd had a relationship with one of the group he'd infiltrated and had a child with her. Pat had been very quiet, almost distant, since he'd read it, though he didn't mention it. It was clear he couldn't wait to return to the Midlands.

It remained a particularly large elephant in the Cricketers as we picked over a late lunch on Sunday, neither quite meeting the other's eye, as if we were teenagers each waiting for the other to make a move. For some reason something Mark Stephens said to me, when I still regarded him as a decent man whose words were worth listening to:

314

an old friend was better than a new lover. He was right, of course. And I found I couldn't bear what I sensed might be the withdrawal of Mark's friendship. I also found quite painfully that I wanted to move our friendship forward – but did I love him simply because I was grateful and dependent? And if Pat cared for me, which I was fairly sure he did, was it just because he was sorry for me?

We'd got to the car park, under Diane's interested eyes, I suspected, before he said, 'I cannot, cannot be one of those cops who take advantage of a professional relationship . . . It's wrong. On all counts. But . . .'

'Of course. But I really don't need an official minder. Not now I've got Nosey. But I do need friends. Good friends.' I put my hand on his.

Mistake.

He shook it off as if it was a bunch of nettles.

Then he took both of mine and gripped them. 'So you do understand . . . I have to go and tell my boss we can save a bit of money for his budget.' At last he smiled. 'But – shit, Jane . . .'

Possibly if we'd not both been staying under Diane's roof, we'd have resolved the situation without recourse to further conversation. But we were. And he had to be on the M20 any moment now.

'You'll come and see my new place when I get one?' I prompted, my throat tight. 'Kent might be quite nice in the spring.'

'Yes! Yes, of course. And I can see how Nosey's getting on with his new job. But Jane, you will be all right, won't you?'

'Of course.' It was usually the other way round,

315

him assuring me I'd be fine. 'Tell you what, I'll get some samphire when you come and try to cook that salmon dish we had last night.'

'Sounds like a really good plan.'

We didn't kiss. But we clung to each other fiercely.

At last he got in his car, opening the driver's window. 'See you soon, then, our kid – your marking permitting!'

'I'll make bloody sure it does permit.' And I waved him off.

ACKNOWLEDGEMENTS

I am grateful to all the primary teachers and heads, past and present, who have given me invaluable help, and to the Open the Book team I have the pleasure and honour of working with. Kent Police's Jon Green, East Division Press Office (Ashford, Shepway & Dover), took time off from much more pressing matters to respond quickly and efficiently when I needed advice. Thank you, all of you.